THE ISLAND COTTAGE

JANE LOVERING

Boldwood

A CIP catalogue record for this book is available from the British Library.

Paperback ISBN 978-1-80415-262-1

Large Print ISBN 978-1-80415-263-8

Hardback ISBN 978-1-80415-261-4

Ebook ISBN 978-1-80415-264-5

Kindle ISBN 978-1-80415-265-2

Audio CD ISBN 978-1-80415-256-0

MP3 CD ISBN 978-1-80415-257-7

Digital audio download ISBN 978-1-80415-259-1

Boldwood Books Ltd
23 Bowerdean Street
London SW6 3TN
www.boldwoodbooks.com

This book is dedicated to just about the only person in my family who has not yet received a 'book to themselves'. I have no idea how this oversight came about, since she is very much a person of whom I am very fond – I presume all the others were just noisier and bought me more drinks. So, without any blackmail or bribery involved, this book is for my cousin, Theresa, who I very much hope will enjoy reading it and thereafter be inclined to buy me drinks. And dinner. And – look, I'll draw up a list.

Theresa, this one is for you!

1

I had always thought seasickness could be overcome by powering through and keeping one's eye on the horizon. After all, the sensations were only caused by eyes and brain being out of sync – a state of mind, not as though one was actually ill. But as the low cliffs of the unpicturesquely-named Scrabster began to fade into the blue-grey of the sea and the boat rocked, dipped and twisted underneath my feet to make simply standing still feel like trying to climb stairs whilst drunk in high heels, I realised what everyone had meant by the advice, 'Stay on deck if the crossing is rough.'

The sea wasn't even that rough apparently, relatively speaking. A crowd of chatting local women who had, involuntary eavesdropping told me, been on a trip down to Edinburgh were gossiping about how lucky we were that the early May weather was so fine and the sea so good for the journey home. I, meanwhile, held on to the rail and my breakfast on the bucking bronco of a boat and tried not to listen in on their conversation. All this time, the islands grew on the horizon like flat grey mushrooms forming out of the surrounding cloud.

Orkney. A place that had existed in family tales and wildlife programmes featuring well-scrubbed men in large coats. A place I had never thought about and had certainly never intended to visit. A place I was now bound for, with a car full of cleaning equipment and a feeling of impatience that almost forced the seasickness into second place. Orkney. I mean, *why*? Obviously, I knew why *I* was here, to clear out my great-aunt's cottage, put it on the market and leave, but the whole thing – the ship reared again under my feet, dropped one corner into an oncoming wave and nearly toppled me over the rail – was so ridiculous that I was in two minds about not disembarking and simply staying for the return trip.

I didn't have the time for this. My mother, who had guilted me into the journey, didn't realise that I had work. *Clients.* People relying on me to sort out their accounting problems resulting from the April tax year end, and to argue with HMRC about allowable expenses. The phrase 'but you haven't had a holiday for three years and you're starting to look a bit peaky' had worn me down eventually, plus she'd bribed me with the promise of the money from the sale of Great-Aunt Jennet's house if I went over and cleared it out, and I'd been saving for my own place for so long that I'd almost forgotten what it felt like not to share a bathroom with two other people.

The ship bucked again. People around me were pointing and exclaiming about cliffs and that we were passing Hoy, but I couldn't see anything to get worked up about, other than the fact that our destination was now in sight. Land, a flat green scab in the ominously grey sea, looking windswept and deserted.

Oh, bugger.

I pulled my coat closer around me as the persistent wind tried to throw me overboard. Maybe I should have taken up my housemate's offer to borrow her full weatherproof walking gear and long johns, because my sensible black jacket wasn't doing anything to keep out the draught, and everyone around me was dressed as though they were off on an Arctic trekking experience; even the more obvious tourists, who were exhausting themselves taking photographs of every rock and stone we thrummed past, were well wrapped up.

Orkney. Oh, *bugger.*

2

'You take the road to Evie – it's more of a district than an actual *place...*' My mother's instructions echoed in my head as I steered my way up the hill and away from Stromness, the hodge-podge of buildings that clustered around the ferry port, all of them seemingly gazing anxiously out to sea in search of escape. 'I mean, I would have gone myself, but there's your father—' She'd broken off here as though my father was my fault. 'We'd never manage his chair in those places.'

I drove down a narrow lane with passing places and thought that, damn her, she'd been right. Because of my father's wheelchair, they had to drive about in a van so wide you could have used it to transport Shire horses. Hence sending me on this errand, that had meant taking a couple of weeks off work, unpaid because I hadn't been able to get holiday leave at such short notice, to tidy up and market a house that had been empty and deserted for fifty years. But sale of said house would mean money to buy myself somewhere. Somewhere convenient for helping them out, of course, as they relied on me so much. A nice flat, maybe, in the old converted chocolate works – I'd seen a four-page spread in the paper; glossy photographs of wonderful views, bifold doors onto balconies, double-height ceilings and colour-matched bathroom fittings. Overlooking the city walls and only a short walk from the centre...

Was that it?

I'd whipped past a turning, but half caught sight of a name plate attached to a wobbly-looking gate. 'Midness'. It was a large and impressive house just off the road, with a wide gravelled drive leading to it, and I felt my spirits start to rise a little. Aunt Jennet's house didn't look at all as though fifty years of neglect had affected it. All the windows had curtains hanging neatly, not tattered or mostly cobweb, the place seemed clean and cared for, standing on the slight rise of slope with the glint of sunlight shining on a stretch of water behind it.

Wow. Maybe we owned a loch? Mum hadn't mentioned a loch. But then, by her own admission she hadn't been here since she was small, when my grandmother had parcelled her, Uncle James and the cat, William, into a car and driven off to Glasgow to raise her family 'somewhere you could stand upright during the winter', as Grandma had always said, grimly.

None of them had ever come back for more than casual visits. Leaving Great-Aunt Jennet and a handful of miscellaneous great-uncles, second cousins and other assorted relatives to carry on farming, fishing and doing whatever people did to scratch a living on Orkney in the late sixties.

From the looks of the place, that had been making wax effigies and burning incomers, I thought, turning in through the gate and bumping the car over a cattle grid that had weeds poking up through it, as though it formed a prison for monstrous greenery.

Close to, the house proved to be a long, low building, but with a double-storey extension to the side nearest the road, all white-painted as though to try to bring some light to the area. Beyond it, the grassland sloped down towards the shores of a small loch, where a tumble-down boathouse stood, almost in the water and covered in ivy. Above everything, the sky stretched like a taut white hospital sheet, unbroken to the horizon. There were no trees, which gave the whole place an exposed look, but it seemed unashamed. It was the exposure of the life model posing for a painting rather than that of a bather who's had their towel ripped away mid-change.

I parked beside the house and got out. Immediately the front door whipped open. A woman leaped out as though she'd been leaning against the door and it had popped open, precipitating her sharply onto the shingly patch which seemed to stand in for garden.

'And you must be Brid!' The way she said it, as though we were in the middle of a conversation, disconcerted me. I had no idea who she was, how she knew my name, or even if I was in the right place. She pronounced my name properly, with the long 'ee' sound rather than the short 'i', which made it sound as though people wanted to say Bridget but had swallowed the last syllable. Of course, being called 'Breed' hadn't done me any favours at school, but then neither had being taller than every other girl in the year, good at maths and wearing sensible shoes, so my name had really been the least of it.

'Is this Midness?' I asked, although from here I could see the sign on the gate quite clearly. It wobbled in the wind, a waggled certainty of locality. 'And, yes, I'm Brid Harcus.'

The woman was tugged closer by the wind. She was about my age, or slightly older, I thought, maybe edging into her mid-thirties, but the very fair skin that accompanied her red hair looked dry and the wrinkles may have been premature, so she could have been as young as twenty-five. 'I'm Innis. Och, come in, do, the wind would have the skin off your back out here.'

From inside the house came the sound of ferocious arguing,

ending in a rising wail, and a small toddler of indeterminate sex bundled out through the door and clasped the woman around the lower legs, hiding its face against her knees. Without acknowledging the new arrival, Innis turned and began to lead me into the house, having to drag one leg with the child attached, but doing so as though this were such a common occurrence that she was slightly surprised that I did not have an infant connected to my own lower limb.

'Should I put the car somewhere?' I called, wavering hesitatingly between not wanting the car to be in the way, but also not wanting to stand out here in this horizontal wind while Innis shut the door in my face.

She paused, heaving her child-bearing leg over the doorstep. 'It'll be fine,' she said, over her shoulder. 'Nobody'll touch it there.' A pause, and she added, darkly, 'They know what's good for them around here.'

As 'around here' was so deserted as to be practically barren, I took her word for it. But, as she continued inside, I wondered how I was going to break the news that this place, which seemed from the noise to be home not just to her but half the population of the Orcadian archipelago, was about to be sold.

I tried to think how I was going to frame the sentence as I followed Innis on down a narrow corridor to the back of the house, but couldn't come up with anything that didn't make me sound like the world's most rapacious landlord. Why hadn't my mother mentioned tenants? She'd made it sound as though Jennet's house had been deserted for years; I was here to clear out anything vaguely worth keeping and sell up, not bring down eviction on the head of this young woman and her three... four... five children.

'Sorry it's a bit of a state.' Innis shook off the attendant toddler as she passed the small plastic table that contained the others, all crayoning determinedly, and led me into a kitchen that was secured behind a child gate. 'I've not had much time to clean today.'

She knocked her flopping hair away from her face with the back of a wrist. Against her pale skin, her hair looked even more auburn in here, where the small window let in not a lot of light but an even clearer view of the loch.

'It's fine,' I felt compelled to reassure her, whilst still working on the way to tell her she was homeless. 'Really. You must be busy, with all those children.'

Innis bustled over to the kettle and switched it on. I was mildly reassured that it was electric and she didn't have to lay a peat fire or something. I hadn't really done a lot of research into Orkney before I came, and I'd had a vague image of cast-iron ranges and a lack of mains power. The fitted kitchen with microwave, large cooker and recessed lighting made me feel stupid and unprepared. As did the presence of Innis herself, and I was inwardly cursing my mother's, 'You'll only need to be there a few days, a week or so at most. Put the place up for sale and then you can be back.' The rest of her sentence went unspoken, but it ran mostly along the lines of, 'Besides, you need a holiday, you never get away from your job and, yes, I know accountancy is important and you're busy, but you do need to stop working sometimes and not just to run me to the supermarket.' It would then be followed by observations on my being too thin or too pale or not having a nice boyfriend and an old rectory in the countryside, which was my mother's life plan for me.

'Och, the kids aren't all mine!' Innis turned back from the kettle and caught me looking at the kitchen. She smiled. 'Only that one there.' She pointed to the throng of toddlers, but I couldn't see which one she was indicating. 'The grubbiest one.' Innis grinned, and it was a friendly, open smile that made me feel guilty for assuming that all islanders lived like medieval peasants.

'Are you running a kidnapping racket?' I asked, slightly unsettled by her smile. She seemed to know that I was suffering from culture shock.

Now she laughed. 'I'm a childminder! But when the parents don't turn up on time for collection, I'm fairly tempted to start ransoming the buggers, let me tell you.'

'Ah.' Okay, so not only was I going to have to break it to her that she was going to lose her home, she was also going to lose her business. *Mother, I am going to kill you...*

'You'll have come to sort out Jennet's place.' Innis set out two mugs and fetched down a biscuit tin. The rattle of the lid coming off drew the assorted toddlers to the child gate, where they thronged with arms reaching through the metal like a junior episode of *The Walking Dead*.

'Jennet's place?' I asked. It seemed an odd way to speak about her home.

'Aye.' Innis looked at my face and smiled again. 'Oh! You were thinking that *this* was the house?' She poured water into the mugs, put a few biscuits onto a plate then took the tin over and handed out the remains to the starving horde, like a Victorian lady distributing largesse.

'Well, I... No. I was just wondering where it was,' I lied. I already felt displaced and unsettled and it made me feel a little as though Innis was mocking me for my misunderstanding. I doubted that this was intentional, her tone was gentle, and I gave myself a stern talking to. My cultural misapprehensions were not her fault. 'My mother didn't really prepare me very well, it's a short-notice trip.' I felt safe confessing this much.

'We thought it might be.' She pushed a steaming mug towards me. 'Here. Cup of tea and a biscuit. We've moved on a bit past the spring water and oatcakes era now.'

So, she knew exactly what I'd been thinking about Orkney. That was embarrassing too. I was so clearly at a disadvantage here,

when I'd been assuming that I was going to ride in like a technolog-
ically advanced being to the poverty and backwardness of an
isolated society. A bit like finding an undiscovered tribe in the
Amazon and realising they'd invented time travel.

'I'm sorry,' I said humbly. 'I should have done more research,
but Mum has decided that there's no point in keeping Jennet's
place. My dad has MS and can't travel so they're never going to
come here and I... well, my work keeps me in York. And what with
property prices going up and everything...' I tailed off.

Innis turned away to look out of the little window. 'So you're
going to be selling it, then?' she asked. 'Definitely?'

'Well, yes.' Her tone of almost suppressed eagerness surprised
me. 'By the way, these biscuits are good.'

From behind me, the sound of toddlers fighting over crayons
broke out, accompanied by more wailing. 'You might be in for a bit
of a shock.' Innis put her cup down. 'It's not exactly Buckingham
Palace down there.' She climbed over the child gate with the air of
one going over the top at the Somme. 'Not going to make you
millions.'

'We're not after millions.' I raised my voice to carry to her over
the sound of squabbling being sorted out. 'It's more about getting
rid of it. Mum says it's been a thorn in her side since Grandma left
it to her, and she never really understood why Grandma didn't sell
it ages ago.'

'Freya, let Archie have the blue one. No, that's a red one. Give
him the blue one. Finn, you give the biscuit back to Ava. That's a
good boy.' Innis was monologuing to the infants, and I wasn't
entirely sure she'd heard me, until she waded back, bearing a packet
of confiscated crayons. 'So you just want a quick sale and away?'

'Basically, yes.'

'It may take a wee bit longer, y'know. It's in a bit of a state.'

It began to dawn on me that I hadn't booked anywhere to stay on Orkney; I'd been assuming that Jennet's cottage would be habitable and I'd be staying there while I tidied up and put it on sale. Innis, however, was beginning to make it sound as though I should have brought camping equipment. And, possibly, a flame thrower. From the portentous nature of her tone, a sturdy pair of wellingtons and a working knowledge of damp courses might not go amiss either.

'But I'm sure you know what you're about.' Was that a smile, half seen as she turned away? It was quite obvious that I had absolutely no idea what I was 'about', Innis could see my floundering unpreparedness, but at least she was being kind about it. 'Och. That'll be the men back,' she said, jerking her head up at the sound of a vehicle. 'My husband Torstein and his brother.' She refilled the kettle. 'Back from weaving fishing nets out of seaweed and slaughtering herring with their teeth.' This time, the grin she gave me was pure mischief. 'And if you believe that, you're more southerner than I took you for.'

I laughed. 'What do they really do?'

Another tin was taken out of the cupboard. I noticed the LED lights inside the doors, and the carousel that doubled the effective storage space. This kitchen was better than mine.

'Mixed farming. We've got thirty acres, spread over the land here, we're dairy and there's a few sheep, bit of hay and a few acres to oats. Magnus helps out and he makes jewellery over in Kirkwall. They're back from evening milking just now, a bit early because we've only got the ten cows in milk at the moment.'

A couple of thick china mugs joined Innis' and mine on the table, and the boiling water hit the teabags at exactly the same time as the kitchen door opened and two men walked in. It was so beautifully timed that I could only imagine that this was how it went every day. Another biscuit tin was fetched from a high shelf and the lid levered off in an almost choreographed way.

'Whose is the wee car outside?' The biggest of the men, all shoulders and hat, immediately turned to the sink and began to wash his hands. 'We've never got another lost tourist?'

'No, it's Mary-Ellen's girl. Come to sort out Jennet's place and sell up.'

'Oh!'

Both men turned to face me now. Torstein was, presumably, the big-shouldered one, which left Magnus as the taller but slighter of the two. Torstein had hair as red as his wife's, Magnus was dark, although his fair skin and hazel eyes showed that he was probably just a more concentrated shade of auburn. The entire family looked as though they could be annihilated by the sun, like vampires.

Magnus smiled first. 'You'll be finding all this a bit strange then.' He came over and pulled out a chair to sit opposite me at the little table. 'As you've not been before.' His accent wasn't as strong as his brother's, more a sing-song intonation around the vowels, as though his voice had been ironed by another influence.

'How do you know I've not been here before?' I bridled slightly at his words, even though they were mild and not as insulting as I was assuming.

'We'd have seen you.' His brother came in now, seizing a biscuit in each hand and going to the gate to greet the small girl Innis had called Freya with an absent-minded kiss on the head. 'Why would you come, if not to see to Jennet's place, and it's away down the loons there.' He pointed with one of the biscuits. 'Unless you crouched down, and that would just be strange.'

'Aye, but she could have gone round the loch, come at it from the other side,' said Magnus, reasonably. 'After dark.'

'True, true.' Torstein seemed to give this consideration. 'But still creepy.'

'Oh, yes, very creepy.'

They stared at me again.

'Well, I didn't,' I said, with rising confusion. 'I haven't ever been here before, let alone sneaking around after dark.'

Innis laughed suddenly. 'They're teasing you, Brid. We knew you were coming, you see.'

'Aye. It Was Written.' Magnus looked at me over his cup of tea. 'Your coming was foretold.'

'Shut up, you wee bastard.' Innis slapped his arm. 'You're upsetting the lass.'

I must have looked completely out of my depth, because I felt it. Confused, tired, wrong-footed and now they were making my arrival sound almost biblical. The babble of toddler-chat, over which we had to raise our voices, and the local accent, soft though it was, meant that I was struggling to comprehend what was happening here, which wasn't fair. This was supposed to be a three, four-day 'clear out old house and put it on the market' drive-by. I cursed my mother again.

'Sorry.' Magnus pushed the biscuit tin across the table towards me. 'Innis is right, I am only teasing. But I'm right too, it was written that you'd come. Your mother sent an email a couple of days ago.'

Well, that explained how Innis knew who I was and why I was here.

'Why don't you take Brid down to Jennet's place now?' Innis grabbed a damp cloth and sortied her way back into the toddler corral, where she began laying about her, wiping sticky faces and hands and gathering crayoned pictures into a pile. 'This lot will be up for collection in a minute, and Brid doesn't need to have to be introduced to half of Mainland when she's only just arrived.'

'Oh, yes, please.' I put my mug down. After all, the sooner I got this started, the sooner I could be back on that ferry and home. Hopefully with an idea of how soon and for how much we could get the place sold. One step nearer that new-build flat with the designer kitchen and view over the Minster.

'Aye. When I've finished my tea,' Magnus said, equably, scooting his chair back on the tiled floor to make room for his brother to sit alongside him, both of them dipping their hands in the biscuit tin again.

The yells of small children, the bright, modern kitchen and the low burr of Torstein and Magnus as they talked about 'coos' blurred behind a foreground daydream of home. Well, not home, because that was currently a small rented house near the river in York which I shared with two dental students, but the home I wanted. The home that I knew I could make. That magazine-supplement picture of the converted chocolate factory floated before my eyes again, overlaid a touch by my own choice in interior decoration; plushly comfortable furniture, pale carpets and a farm-house-style pine table taking pride of place in an open-plan kitchen, polished daily by a diligent cleaner who would also hoover the stairs and bring fresh flowers once a week.

Or, if Jennet's place was nice enough, and I could sell it to a holiday rental company, maybe I could buy a historic cottage in town? The image changed to me greeting visitors on the doorstep of a charmingly aged house with a view of the river, leading them through into a beamed-ceilinged room full of tasteful sofas and copies of *Country Life* magazine. Then I saw myself bending over an Aga as I created taste-explosion dishes whilst my visitors drank coffee from a bean-to-cup machine on an exquisite sideboard.

'Right. You ready?' Magnus was on his feet now. 'We'll go on down the brae to the house. Have you got any boots, lass?'

'Boots,' I repeated, still half in my fantasy white-furnished world. 'I might have a pair in the car.'

I'd been thinking of my leather boots, which went perfectly with the floaty calf-length skirt and silky-knit cardigan that I had brought for evening visits to any local pubs that might arise.

'Aye. It's a wee bit wet down there. Boggy, y'know? And you can't drive down, so we'll have to carry your luggage. Innis, can Brid borrow your spare wellies?'

I wasn't sure I liked Magnus' half-raised eyebrow and slight smile. It looked – yes, it looked as though he knew perfectly well that I wouldn't have packed wellingtons; that I didn't even *own* wellingtons, and he was grinning to himself at the thought.

Innis called back an affirmative and Torstein went to help her sort out the toddler tangle, so Magnus and I went out of the back door, where the wind began to have another go at my head.

'Is it always this windy?' I asked, stepping into the pair of remarkably robust boots that he indicated, lying by the step. They had little ducks on the ankles. He, I noticed, was wearing a pair of leather boots that looked as though he'd had them fitted by a farrier when he was fourteen and hadn't taken them off since. He'd also got on a pair of overalls with a torn front pocket and an ornamentation of green stains that looked as though milking had also featured more of the rear product of cows than just milk.

'Och, no.' Magnus waited for me, leaning his long frame against the house wall. 'Sometimes we have storms.' He grinned again.

I slithered my feet into the boots, which, by the feel of it, were at least two sizes too big, and squeezed my lips together. This man seemed to be deriving no end of pleasure from my lack of preparation for Orkney and my absence of any prior knowledge. Well, I thought, as we began to walk away from the house and down towards the reeded glitter of the loch, I'd like to see how he got by in York, with the traffic and the vagaries of the ring road and parking, and people constantly needing either reassurance or to be chased for essential paperwork.

I bet he'd struggle with having to drive over to visit parents at the end of a long working day, with having to sit in an overheated living room listening to Mum talking about the soaps. I bet Magnus didn't know what it was like to spend ages in the garden pulling weeds while Dad sat in his chair and tried to teach me to tell vervain from verbena.

Magnus looked as though he hadn't even had parents, he looked like someone grown in the black local soil. Like a person who had farmed forever, whose life had always been this bleak, treeless place and who took for granted striding along in big boots over mud that bubbled.

I felt very alone. Why was I even *here*? Mum and Dad needed me, which was why I went around every evening. Work needed me – well, I needed work too, so that was fair enough, but...

Oh, bugger.

3

We didn't speak on the way. Magnus trod confidently over tussocks of grass that caught at my feet and made me trip in the oversized boots, which held a trace of someone else's sweaty damp socks. Between the tufts, the ground was suspiciously bright green and the wind bent anything longer than a few centimetres into a supplicated curve.

After a minute or two, Magnus stopped. 'This is where Jennet's property starts,' he said, although there was no visible border. Except... looking down at my feet to stop the renegade wellies from catching in another clump and tripping me forward yet again, there was something lying on the ground. A little twist of stalks bound together with more of the same. Grey ears of barley, long eroded by weather into damp husks and weighted down by a large rock. They could almost have been carried in by the wind, except that even my rudimentary agricultural knowledge told me that it was May, all the barley would still be not much more than green sprouts this far north, and the way the bundle was tied together looked deliberate. As did the placing, in the lee of the large tuft that had caught my boots and with the stems under the rock.

'What on earth is that?' I bent down to pick up the soggy bundle, but Magnus put out a sudden hand.

'I wouldn't touch it,' he said. 'Not yet.'

I looked sideways at him, to see if he was joking or deliberately trying to scare me by imbuing a simple local custom with *Blair Witch* vibes, but he looked serious enough. The wind was pulling his dark hair back and making his face seem bleak and exposed.

'Why not? It's just a bit of old corn.'

A hesitation. Because I was watching his face, I could see the small frown that crossed it and then the way he raised his eyes from the ground to look over at the overgrown heap of stones that lay between us and the eye-watering brightness of the loch. 'Better that you don't,' he said, and his words sounded careful. 'Not just now.' Then he turned towards me and there was an expression that I couldn't read somewhere between the brown eyes and the straight mouth. It almost looked as though he felt sorry for me, but not in a 'townie, clearly unprepared for the countryside' way that he had when he'd mentioned borrowing Innis' boots. This was more of the sadness of the guard marching the prisoner to their execution.

'Right,' I said firmly. 'I am not having this. I've come to sell Jennet's house, not take part in some amateur Lovecraftian reconstruction.' And I bent down and picked up the soggy clump of straw.

Magnus breathed in with an audible hiss, but didn't try to stop me this time, as I shredded the barley into the wind, letting the wet husks float away. 'There. Now, if you're going to tell me that I've just brought bad luck on the entire family, you're probably about twenty years too late.' I ostentatiously wiped my hands free of the detritus down the legs of my jeans. 'And I'm not having anything to do with superstitious rubbish.'

The wind cried, caught in a corner of wall, and pummelled the ivy-covered stones in front of us, so the growth undulated and billowed as though the concealed building exhaled.

'So there,' I added, slightly less stridently, because Magnus' silence was beginning to lead me to believe there was an asteroid on its way towards my head, at twenty miles and closing.

After a moment or two of his watching me whilst wearing an unreadable expression, but one from which any trace of pity had vanished, he shrugged. 'Ah, well,' he said. 'It was probably just one of the children playing out here and sticking some rubbish under a stone anyway.'

'Do you do this on purpose?' Needled, I set off again in his foot-steps as we continued our trudge across the wet field. 'Or is it because it's me? Like psychological warfare?'

He stuck both hands in the pockets of the dungaree overalls. 'The tourists expect a bit of the old woo,' he said mildly. 'We have to be a bit unearthly out here, otherwise they all up and head back to Edinburgh or Stirling where there's Marriott hotels and pipers and people say "och, aye" on purpose.'

'Well, I am not a tourist,' I said, tartly. 'I'm a landowner. *And* both my mum and my dad were born here on Orkney, so I'm not exactly some incomer either.'

'Ah. I wondered about that.' Magnus led the way to a stone-flagged path that crossed the remainder of the bog as far as the cottage. Actually, path was putting it strongly, it was a series of paving stones laid end to end, but there its resemblance to anything that could be found anywhere other than this bleak field stopped. 'Your first name is – what, Irish? But Harcus is a good Orcadian name.' He looked at me over his shoulder. 'You're a bit of a crossbreed.'

'I'm named after Dad's mum,' I said stiffly. 'She was from Limerick.'

'So you're a Gaelic lass, through and through then.' Magnus seemed to find this amusing for some reason.

'I suppose so.'

'But you're an accountant? In Yorkshire?'

I pursed my lips at him. 'All the sword dancing and leprechaun-wrangling jobs were taken. It was accountancy or the bra department in Marks and Spencer.'

Now he laughed. It made him look a bit less brooding and less of the lean, well-worn farmer, although it didn't make those dungarees any more palatable. 'Aye, well. We'll see what you think to the cottage, then.' I might have imagined his follow-up words, because the wind was in my ears and I'd just stepped off the path and nearly lost a boot to the sucking mud, but it definitely sounded like, 'And what the cottage thinks of you.'

He's trying to frighten me off, I thought. Weird things woven from straw left lying around, dark hints about the area, the whole Poe impersonation – I wondered why. What they could possibly stand to gain from me running screaming back to the mainland, throwing my hands in the air and swearing never to set foot on this haunted land again?

Oh, apart from the fact that their house was about a quarter of a mile away on the same stretch of land and if I had to make a quick sale, they might just score a few acres of farmland for a very cheap price.

'Right. This is it.' Magnus held out a hand and indicated the creeper-covered stretch of wall. 'Are you ready?'

'Do you say the magic word and the undergrowth parts, or something?' I still sounded sharp.

'No, I unlock the padlock and we open the door,' Magnus replied, his voice level and showing no sign of taking offence. 'Like civilised folk.' He dug in the front pocket of his overalls and pulled out a key. 'We've kept the place up for you, so the roof's intact, and

Innis and Torstein put in electricity and connected the place to the septic tank when they built the house.' He fumbled in the under-growth for a moment and revealed a silver padlock, shiny and obviously well maintained. 'So it ought to be habitable, if nothing else.'

Nothing else. What else was there? It was a house, habitable was practically its only job. 'I wasn't expecting it to produce a Broadway show.' I was now bordering on rude, I realised. 'Sorry. I'm tired and this is...' I waved a hand, although I wasn't sure what this was meant to indicate, other than more plant life. 'Odd,' I finished.

'Is it now?' Magnus fiddled a bit with the padlock. 'It's just a house, Brid.' A bit more fiddling and then he held back an armful of finger-like woody tendrils of growth to reveal a door hidden deep among them. 'And probably earwigs. Do you mind earwigs?' He gave a hearty shove with his shoulder and the door moved inwards reluctantly with the squealing sound of wood over stone. The gap was dark and what little light got between Magnus, the ivy and the door showed me nothing but a wooden bucket just inside. 'After you.'

I hung back. 'Er. Is there likely to be anything big in there?'

Magnus stood patiently, the padlock now bulging his top pocket. 'Like what? We've no leopards here in Orkney.'

'Spiders?'

'Och, we have those. But Innis will have been in this last day or so to put things right and she's a devil for the spiders. You'll be fine. Nothing wrong with a few spiders, anyway,' he added. 'Now, get on in, it's dreich out here and I need to show you where everything is so I can get off home.'

'Home?' For some reason, I'd assumed that he lived around here, near Innis and Torstein, and felt that dislocation again. I was struggling badly, seeing this group as a cross between *The Waltons*

and banjo-strumming swamp dwellers, rather than people with
actual real lives.

As though he knew this, Magnus smiled and waved me inside.

As I passed him, I noticed that he smelled of something else,
underneath the cow dung. A fresh, attractive scent that took him
out of the 'unwashed labourer' league and made me think of the
slender, well-dressed men who stalked the city streets and prowled
the bars; the kind of men I was more used to. The small-business
owners and the self-employed IT lads, carefully shaved and with
their voices modulated out of their native Yorkshire accents, who
emailed me sheaves of paper and panicked about allowable
expenses. Why on earth should Magnus remind me of them? And
why would a milking assistant on a farm even *need* to smell nice?

My footsteps hesitated and I half stopped in the doorway. Magnus
stood beside me, pushing the door open against the resistant thrust of
the creeper which seemed to be trying to drag it closed again, and,
when I looked at him, he was watching me with an expression which
seemed part way between amused and pitying, so I decided not to ask
whether the cows appreciated the aftershave. Anyway, that brief
nose-pleasing smell of spice and citrus was gone now, and all I could
smell was the rank bitterness of torn ivy. I could only assume that
Innis, on her rumoured cleaning visits, opened the door just wide
enough to slide in sideways. The black doorway, ripped from the
leafy wall, was slightly forbidding and I wouldn't have blamed her at
all if she'd gone in with a crucifix and a flaming torch.

'Well, then.' Magnus waited for me to step over the threshold
before he spoke. 'What do you think to the place?'

'I don't know, I can't see it. Do you not believe in windows up
here?' The darkness inside the building was total, the only illumination was the tiny square of daylight from the doorway, and that
was behind me. The blackness smelled of old beds.

'We might not believe in windows – they let the weather in. But we have a firm and abiding faith in electricity.' There was a click and an overhead light went on, illuminating a dim circle of room, cluttered with furniture and junk. 'Is that better?'

There was a great sense of relief in being out of the wind, even if that did mean being in what looked more like a stable for an upper-class horse than a house. 'Are you going to give me a tour?' I asked, when Magnus carried on standing in the doorway.

'No point. This is it.' He waved a hand. 'Och, no, there's a wee kitchenette through that doorway there.' He pointed into the gloom. 'And the toilet is off the kitchen.' His hand waved again, a little more generally. 'As I said, the place got connected to the tank when we built the house, so you'll not have to worry about emptying the bucket.'

'This is *it*?' I swivelled round to find Magnus leaning against the inside wall now, almost as though his body was too tired to support his head without outside help. He was grinning. 'I thought this was the hallway!'

'You were expecting to walk through into a mansion?' He folded his arms. 'And what would Jennet want with a big house? This suited her.'

I could feel the dreams of a smart flat in a converted factory draining away as fast as the hope of a quick sale. From what I could see as the bleak single bulb rotated overhead in the draught from the open door, the sale of Jennet's house would just about fund a room in a damp basement. And I'd probably have to share that. With rats. The bulb swung again. The ceiling was so low that the light almost clipped my forehead and its constant movement meant I couldn't see anything properly, everything was angles and shadows and partly lit corners of things. A fireplace, over there at the far end of the room, a stone floor, and then, as the bulb oscillated in the opposite direction, a stack of what looked like wood, a cupboard door.

'But, aye, there are windows, over there.' Magnus seemed reluctant to move any further into the house, he was still behind me, his hand hovering close to the light switch. When I turned, I could see him outlined by the afternoon light which shone through and made it very obvious that, yes, beneath the darkness, his hair was, indeed, red. 'They'll have boards over them, we've been spending the last fifty years trying to stop the place falling down and there's nothing like a broken window for letting the weather in, so we covered them all.'

'We?' I walked a very small circle, carefully still in the daylight that was sneaking in past Magnus. 'You're not old enough to have been doing that for fifty years.' Then I stopped and looked at him. 'You're not, are you? It's not now that you tell me about the family curse and then crumble into ashes?'

He laughed. 'Don't be daft! No, it's a family thing. Look, Great-Aunt Jennet was *our* great-aunt too. We – you and me – are something like third cousins. When she died, she left half the land to her brother's son Johnnie, and the house and this piece of land away to the loch to her sister, Morag. It's stayed in the family. Tor and I are Johnnie's grandchildren, and you're down from Morag's side. The land, and the house, stayed in the family, but no one has lived in here...' he held out a hand and indicated the bleak little room, 'since Jennet died.'

'Because she cursed the place?' I asked waspishly. Despite Magnus' faith in Innis' cleaning routine, there was a distinct odour of lack-of-caring about the little place. A cold, deserted sort of smell, like the dungeons in old castles or neglected sheds.

'Well, no, more that it's tiny and a bit shite, and there was no water or electric until we put it in.,' Magnus said, in a sudden blurt of honesty. 'So we used it to store stuff, mostly hay.' He looked down at his boots, and I saw a stray stalk caught between the air inside and the wind outside, tumbling and twitching. 'Sometimes the feed for the sheep. In really bad weather, come to think of it, actual sheep.'

I took a deep breath. My brain metaphorically rolled up its sleeves. Okay, so sale of the place wouldn't buy me a beautiful flat, not outright. But it would give me the deposit for somewhere, and, with a clear-out, a good scrub and open windows, maybe the place could be sold as a potential holiday let? I tried not to think about the lack of access, the bogland that surrounded it, and the primitive facilities. There were people who liked isolation, liked a holiday without all the trappings of modern life, weren't there? People who camped on hillsides? This house would be very like camping, only with firm walls.

I could do this. I really could.

'Right then. I presume there's no point in a tour.'

Magnus grinned. 'You'll not be needing a map, no. Open a couple of doors and that's about it.'

'Then I think I'll just bring my bag over from the car and settle in.'

Another hesitation. He really was behaving as though the house was carnivorous. 'You'll be needing a hand?' He took a couple of steps back into full daylight. 'Only I ought to be heading home. I've got to get to Kirkwall.'

'Before dark?' My tone hadn't lost its snippiness. Kirkwall was, by my estimation, no more than a twenty-minute drive away, and it was only early afternoon.

'There's a cruise ship in tomorrow. I'll be needing to open the shop.' Magnus backed off a few more steps as though he were preparing to turn and run. 'And I need to do a stock check before that, so.'

I felt suddenly ashamed. *Why* was I being so edgy with these people who'd been nothing but welcoming to me? It wasn't *their* fault that my mother couldn't be bothered to do this herself, that my dad had MS and couldn't travel and that I would rather have been sitting in front of spreadsheets in an office that looked across the racecourse to the river.

'I'll be fine here,' I said, pleased to note that my voice was now far more reasonable and even slightly warm. 'Thank you for opening the place up for me.'

Magnus twisted his head in acknowledgement, dropped the key and the padlock onto the narrow stone ledge by the door, and turned away.

'Oh, is there wi-fi?' I half called after him, fully expecting him to laugh at my city-girl assumptions, but he paused on the first of the flagstones.

'Of course there's wi-fi.' There was a half-laugh there, but more at my presumption of primitive conditions. I didn't know why, after all I was standing in a cottage with one window and an outhouse toilet, primitive seemed to be fitted as standard. 'You'll be able to access the wi-fi from the house. Password is "simmer dim". All lowercase. We're a lowercase type of family, as you'll no doubt have figured.'

'What the hell is "simmer dim"?' I hated to admit it, but I was a little bit reluctant to be left here alone. The cottage felt as though it was waiting for something, and it would probably turn out to be some kind of awful accident involving archaic bathroom fittings. Keeping Magnus talking was postponing my inevitable confrontation with the internal fixtures.

'It's what we call the light in the evenings. Never gets properly dark from now until August, just simmer dim.' At that, he raised a hand in farewell and began the trot across the flags back out to the bogland that separated me from civilisation.

I had no alternative now. I had to go into the house proper, that, or stand just inside the door for a fortnight and that was going to get uncomfortable after the first hour or so.

I propped the door open with the wooden bucket. I told myself I was doing it to let fresh air into the place, but really I was a tiny bit suspicious of that ivy, and wouldn't have put it past it to try to slam the door and seal it shut with me inside. Sentient undergrowth was something I was sure had featured in some of the Orkney folk tales that my mother had used to scare me into staying in bed at night. Who needed long-haired princesses and porridge-loving bears, when you'd got terrifying weeds and sea monsters to keep your child awake and too frightened to poke a toe from beneath the covers?

By the time I'd got the door secured, as much ivy cleared from the entrance as I could, and I'd watched Magnus get into a Isuzu Jeep and drive away, I had done everything in the doorway that I possibly could and had to finally go inside Jennet's house, where the thin light from the bulb rotated in the draught and there was an air of still anticipation.

What? I stopped, foot raised in the act of stepping further into the room. Anticipation? Had I really thought that? It seemed a rather imaginative notion and I wasn't used to needing imaginative thought, not when my daily life consisted mostly of numbers, reliability and being there for my parents. But wasn't anticipation a natural result of my being about to start sorting out all the things that had been in here for years, untouched apart from a swipe of Innis' cloth and a squirt of Pledge?

Except that it wasn't me that felt anticipatory. I could quite cheerfully have locked the place up again, headed to Kirkwall and handed the keys over to the first estate agent I saw. House clearance firms would be a thing, even up here, surely? They'd have it emptied, contents auctioned and the house up for sale without me having to put my career on hold and leave clients dangling in a kind of tax-allowance related limbo. And – I had the uneasy thought of my parents sitting silently together in their living room – without my being on call to help out with domestic tasks and companionship. But the house... somehow it felt as though – and I had to laugh at myself for the whimsy – as though it were *waiting*.

Should I ring my mother? Maybe I ought to check up on them both, I thought, as that mental image of the living room swelled to encompass my father struggling to finish his crossword whilst my mother fretted about the plot line of one of her soaps. They both liked to talk to me about their pursuits, Mum monologuing about her favourite male character – 'such a nice, clean-cut young man' – and Dad worrying about whether it was time to get the onion sets planted in his garden. What would they be doing, without me there?

But then the silence whistled in my ears, broken only by the wind hushing through the grass and the gentle sluice of the loch waters against the reeded margins, and I decided to leave my parents to their evening boredom. It was their fault I was here, let them feel my absence in their misunderstandings of TV plot points and lack of anagrams.

I started talking to myself as I moved out of the sunlight and wind that reached through the open door and into the gloom beyond. 'Well. I suppose this is mine now and I ought to make a start.' My, well, Innis' boots tapped a hollow sound on the stone floor as I reluctantly stepped further in. 'Smells a bit funky in here, but then I suppose it's been closed up for so long. Let's find a window and see if we can get a through-breeze.'

Clump clump went my feet.

In the wall opposite, my groping found two tiny windows set into the thickness of the walls. As Magnus had said, they'd been covered over with sheets of hardboard wedged into place and when

I tugged these free, light streamed in and I got my first proper look at the inside of Jennet's cottage.

To call it tiny made it sound cute. 'Tiny' was for kittens and babies, small but appealing; all the right things in all the right places, just concentrated. This place wasn't just concentrated, it was *reduced*. It was one single long room, with a cast-iron fireplace and range at one end, what I'd thought was a cupboard turned out to be a bed, built into the thickness of the wall near the fire, and a tiny passage right by the door led into an extension which housed a miniscule kitchen and, off that, a toilet. When they'd run water and sewage to the place, they'd clearly only catered for this outhouse, tacked on as an afterthought. It looked like the old stable. In fact, in the toilet there was still a drainage channel in the floor, and the beams in the kitchen looked more suitable for hanging harnesses than the picturesque bundles of herbs I'd envisaged.

I stopped suddenly at the thought and stared out of the small window in the kitchen, only half noticing the view around the loch or the three-quarters-submerged boat tied up at the edge. Then I pulled myself back and gazed around at the mismatched kitchen cupboards, the elderly oven with its bottle of gas, and the obviously new kettle. It was the walls, that's what it was. These dry-stone walls, combined with the beams, had made me think of those magazines that I secretly browsed in my lunch hour. Country cottages, beams, bare stone walls – they'd almost all had racks of herbs drying over the Aga, hadn't they? Mind you, they had almost all been 'skilfully renovated' by people with lots of money and an aesthetic. This place looked as though if you'd tried to bring in an aesthetic, the ivy would have strangled it before you'd got over the step. It looked like a working house, everything designed to be functional. No 'playful touches', no 'living walls', unless you counted that ivy. This was a house hunkered into the landscape; a house that did what it did without fuss or flourish. And, evidently, without herbs or a decent bathroom.

There was another door in the kitchen, latched carefully closed. I looked at it for a moment with that half-hopeful feeling that it could lead to a four-bedroomed extension with a whirlpool bath and all the rural country touches that those damned magazines had led me to expect. Then I opened it, and screamed.

Inside was a tiny stone-flagged larder, with a raised slate slab shelf running along one wall. On the slate slab was a bird, and that bird was regarding me with an expression of distrust, suspicion and a tiny hint of eye-removal.

4

After I'd slammed the door shut, regained control of my breathing and discovered that the outhouse toilet flushed with the sound of a thousand Niagaras in spate, I crept back. This time I went around the outside of the cottage, tracing the walls with one hand against the ivy, until I found the larder. The window was broken and whatever had boarded it over had collapsed into a soggy brown mass, so I could stand on tiptoe and peer in through the missing pane.

It had not been a hallucination born of lack of sleep and unfamiliar surroundings. There really was a bird, a large one, now squatting confrontationally in the middle of the floor. It was brown, with an orange beak and an eye of such ferocious antipathy that I withdrew from the window, hoping it hadn't seen me.

A few squashed feathers and a splatter of bird poo told me that the creature had been coming and going through the broken window. Right. I could put a stop to that immediately. As soon as the bird went out again, I'd block the window off. That would do it. Bird out, weather out. All right, the larder would be as dark as midnight, but as I didn't anticipate using it as storage for anything other than items that were going to remain in the house during the sale, that didn't matter.

All I needed to do was wait for the sound of the bird leaving. Fine. I could do that.

I went back inside and left the door that led through to the outhouse open. The missing window was quite small, and the bird was huge, so it would, presumably, make sufficient noise squeezing itself out that I could act swiftly. Good. I propped that door open with a sack of twisted brown stems, presumably kindling for the fire, as the wind that was coming through from the front was threatening to slam the doors shut hard enough to knock the chimney off the roof. To Innis' credit, there didn't seem to be any dust caught up in the minor hurricane, but papers rustled in corners I hadn't explored yet, and the single-glazed deep-set windows made the occasional rattling noise.

I paced the length of the cottage, the borrowed boots making the sound of rubber-coated doom against the flags. Stone walls. The fireplace huge, with a small metal stove fitted in the centre, and a grubby old pan still sitting on its burnished top. Two wooden chairs pulled up tight to what must have been the only source of heat when Jennet had lived here. The walls were whitewashed, presumably to make the room look larger, which wasn't working, and an ancient wooden dresser took up most of one of them. The other side was almost entirely the built-in bed, concealed behind cracked wooden doors and barely large enough for a person to stretch out. I poked it thoughtfully and wondered if Jennet had died in bed, most particularly in *this* bed, on *this* mattress.

At the other end of the room was a small table, a tiny kitchen chair and some wall shelves which held empty bottles. There was a rag rug under the table, in some feeble gesture towards homeliness and comfort, and that was it. My entire estate. Stone and wood and rag. My heart sank a little further and downgraded my future accommodation purchase to a three-roomed flat in a converted railway worker's house, somewhere in the arse-end of York. *And* I'd need a mortgage, the sale of Jennet's place might just raise enough to bump my savings into the decent deposit category, rather than enable an outright purchase.

Oh, bugger.

I trudged back and forth to my car a few times, carrying my luggage through the swamp, with a few wellie-sucking moments of horror, and trying not to peer in through the windows of the house to see what Innis and Torstein may have been up to. Their kitchen looked directly out to my new abode, albeit with a large stretch of tussocky marshland between us, and I didn't know whether that made me feel better or not. They could watch my comedic attempts to carry laptop, suitcase, rucksack and a carrier bag of food and drink down to the cottage, but they were also close enough to hear me scream, should the roof fall down on me during the night. On the whole, I thought, it balanced out.

The entire building seemed to contain only three power sockets, and two of those were in the kitchen, so I perched myself uncomfortably on the floor in the main room with my back against the rough wall to plug in my laptop and connect to the internet. There were fewer emails than I'd been expecting. Panic clearly hadn't yet set in among my clients, although HMRC was requesting some updates which would soon change that status. Mum had messaged me to say that she hoped I'd had a safe journey and had arrived at the cottage, but I didn't reply to her. Not yet. I had to think of a way to phrase my annoyance and disappointment that wouldn't upset her but would let her know that 'Jennet's Cottage' was not the adorable, fully fitted holiday destination that she'd been leading me to believe, nor would it sell 'almost overnight'. Unless to a particular sect of monks, stringent adherents to the no possessions, no comfort end of the religious spectrum, eagerly seeking isolation to further their ascetic ends.

I looked up, and the change of brightness from the screen to the huddled darkness of the room made it feel as though the shadows were closing in around me and reading over my shoulder. It wasn't quite claustrophobia, but a close cousin to it, a feeling that the walls were gathering themselves to squeeze all the oxygen out of the air, and I glanced over at the still propped-open door to reassure myself that I wouldn't suffocate.

As I looked up, there was a sound from beyond. A rustle, like the noise of silk skirts sweeping over stone, which made the small hairs on the nape of my neck prickle, and dragged me to my feet. Then came a soft padding sound, followed, to my relief, by the unearthly but once-heard-never-forgotten noise of a large bird squeezing itself through a wooden-framed window.

The bird, whatever it was, had gone.

I tiptoed around the walls and through the little doorway to the extension. I didn't want to make any sudden noises in case the bird had changed its mind, or was perched there on the outside of the window, waiting for me to appear so it could attack. After a moment's hesitation in the larder doorway, I slid far enough around so that I could see inside but still be within easy reach of safety and the ability to slam the door hard on the beak of attack.

The bird had, indeed, gone. Unfortunately, it had left behind a nest, built casually of a collection of loose items from the floor of the larder, bits of hay and straw, some old sacking and feathers. In the nest were three eggs.

Oh, bugger.

If I blocked up the window, I'd shut the bird away from its eggs and they would die. But then, birds laid eggs all the time, didn't they? And people collected them and ate them, and they weren't usually fertile eggs, so maybe these were the same?

On clonking wellies, I crept into the larder and bent down to the nest. Cautiously I reached out and touched one of the eggs; it was warmer than I could have imagined, almost like a living thing in its own right. *And it was moving*, pulsing with a kind of internal pressure, and making a very faint peeping sound. These eggs were about to hatch, and I couldn't shut the mother out without condemning a brood of three youngsters to death, unless I wanted to take on the job of rearing them, which I definitely didn't.

Still cautious, I bent lower and ran my hand over the closely bunched clutch. Only one was peeping, but they were all warm and all had a kind of vitality, in a dreadfully creepy, horror-movie way. I had images of *things* bursting out of the shells and attaching themselves to my face, which rocked me back on my rubber heels with momentary disgust, and then there was a violent kerfuffle at the window gap and I found myself being swooped at by a bundle of beating feathers and hard beak.

'Get *off*!' I put my arms over my head. Trying to protect my face with one hand and use the other to beat off the attacking bird, I groped my way backwards, rebounding off the slate shelf with a degree of force that bruised my arm. The bird was leaping from the ground, hissing and honking, wings thrusting towards me and neck snaked out so that the main point of contact was the brick-hard bill, which was setting about my legs and any part of me it could reach. There suddenly seemed to be much more bird in here than I could cope with, and I reached the empty space of the doorway, bolted through it and slammed it in the face of the angry bird with a degree of relief that I would never have believed possible.

I leaned against the closed door for a moment, letting my heart stop its attempt to batter its way out of my ribcage, and listening to the hearty thumping which was presumably the bird trying to worry its way through the woodwork to get at me. Adrenaline was firing all my nerves into sickening pops of thwarted action and I knew I had to move or do *something* or I'd burn my way back through into the larder again with the sheer force of it.

Pausing only to pile the sack of fire kindling against the larder door, just in case the bird somehow managed to batter it open and come looking for me, I went back through. Ignoring my laptop on the floor, I went outside to breathe heavily, and surprised Magnus, who was just about to sweep enough ivy aside to allow his head to fit through the doorway.

The big, sudden presence of a man, at first unrecognised with the light behind him and the ivy tendrils draping over his shoulders, following hot on the heels of the bird attack, was too much for me and I screamed for the second time in one day.

'Are you all right?' Of course, as soon as he spoke I realised who it was and felt more stupid than I had in years. 'I came over to make sure you were all settled in.'

'There's a *bird*...' I gabbled. 'In the *larder*. And it tried to kill me,' I added, when his lack of surprise made me suspect that he was enjoying my evident upset.

'Oh, aye. Greylag, I expect. They get in sometimes. Shouldn't think Innis has been in the store for a while, no need, y'see. Is it nesting?'

'Yes! And the eggs are all warm and it's disgusting and I can't shut it out but I don't want it in here and I...' I trailed off. I'd been about to say that I wanted to go home, but then realised that I didn't want to sound completely pathetic. 'I don't think my larder is a suitable place for a bird,' I finished, managing to sound prissy instead.

Magnus had retreated, with me in pursuit, around the building to where the broken larder window showed as a dark square in the stone wall and a smatter of white feathers across the spiky grass. He peered in for a moment, then withdrew and nodded.

'See?' I pointed an accusatory finger at the window. 'This one wasn't boarded up properly and the glass has fallen out and the bird has been getting in and out – I mean, *anyone* could have got in!'

Magnus turned around and looked at me steadily. 'And who would want to do that, now?'

'Well, I don't know, do I?' I sounded a little bit shrill, the panic from the bird attack was making me defensive. 'Squatters?'

The head-on evenness of his expression was disconcerting me almost as much as the bird had done. He was looking at me as though I were a little bit mad, but then, I was still wild-eyed and crazy-haired from running away from the bird and I was still wearing rubber boots two sizes too big.

'Squatters.' He looked pointedly around. Behind us, the little loch twinkled in the evening sunlight, the water ran up to the edge and hit the submerged boat carcass with little 'patting' noises. Far away a cow bellowed and there was the noise of a distant car. 'Here.'

'I don't know, do I?' I even sounded crazy, my voice was too high, my words too sharp. 'Burglars or... or...' The unlikelihood of there even being a passer-by out here in this field, with no track or any way of approaching the cottage that didn't involve rowing or squelching through bog, was beginning to strike me. 'You padlock the door! You must be trying to keep something out.'

'Only the weather.' Magnus had turned back to me now and his expression was almost pitying. There were lines around his eyes that looked weathered in, as though he spent a lot of time squinting into the sun and rain, and his eyelashes were a shade lighter than his hair. 'The wind can be dreadful fierce, that's why we board up the windows too. Only to keep the rain out.' He took a deep breath. 'Nobody has told you about the cottage, have they?'

I looked at him suspiciously. A statement like that, with the almost sad weight he gave the words, sounded as though it was going to be followed by some kind of awful confession about dreadful killings, wailing white ladies at midnight or lack of proper planning permission.

'And what, exactly, are they supposed to have told me?'

'Look, let's get in, out of the wind.'

We went back inside and Magnus moved the bucket I'd had propping the door open. The heavy wooden door closed behind us, instantly reducing the wind noise to no more than a rattle of window, and the light levels to 'dusk'. I sat in one of the chairs beside the cold and empty range, but Magnus prowled around with oddly quiet footsteps.

'D'you know what they call this place?' he asked, from somewhere over by the enormous dresser. I inched the chair around, grinding wood on stone, until I could watch him and, incidentally, keep an eye on the whole room.

Condemned? I thought, but had enough self-possession not to say. 'We've always just called it "Jennet's Cottage",' I said warily, in case the phrase 'Infamous Murder House' was going to be next past his lips.

'It's "The Witch's Cottage",' he said, and his eyes caught a stray gleam from the tiny window, so they almost shone for a moment.

'Okay.' I thought, processing fast. 'Is that "witch, apostrophe, S", as in, belonging to, or witches, plural?'

'Does that make a difference?'

'It might. I'd like to know how many pointy hats and broomsticks I may be dealing with here.'

Apart from the whole 'witch' thing, which I couldn't take seriously, I was distracted by the way the light on his eyes was highlighting the reddishness of his eyelashes and the curiously intense nature of his stare.

The intensity broke when he laughed. 'Och, it's only the one. Whoever lives here, they're the witch. It's tradition,' he added, with the amusement still heavy in his voice, making it sound as though he didn't believe a word of it either.

I looked around at the thick white walls, lumpy with lack of plasterboard or decent paint; at the tiny windows set so deeply into those walls that they were more like medieval arrow-slits than actual windows, and the sparse furniture which looked as though it had been less constructed and more just felled and roughly shaped. 'I'm surprised they didn't call it Insanity House,' I said dryly, 'for the same reason.'

'Jennet was the last witch.' Magnus drew up the other chair now and sat opposite me. 'So, when she died, the place was closed up. Your great-granny Morag should have been the next witch but she married and moved to Rousay instead. Your granny left for Scotland, and your mother never came. The place has been waiting for its witch for fifty years.' He looked at me expectantly.

I left a good, sarcastic pause, before I said, 'And it's going to go on waiting. I'm only here to clear it out and sell it, not become the new incumbent.' Now I sighed. 'Look. I have as much respect for local tradition as anyone else. If someone wants to buy the place and set themselves up as the local witch, then that's fine, I don't care. It won't be my cottage and it won't be my problem. I am not a witch, and have absolutely zero interest in witchcraft; I am an accountant in York and I have clients and spreadsheets and people who rely on me to tell them whether ballgowns are tax-deductible expenses!'

I could hear my voice going up the register towards bird-bothered levels again and made a conscious effort to drag it back down to sanity. 'Which, for the record, they aren't,' I finished, quite proud of the fact that I sounded more normal now. 'My father has a disability, my mother needs me to help her, and I have to spend most of my evenings and time off providing them with company and socialisation. My life is barely my own, let alone providing me with the opportunity to swan around in wafty black garments pretending to be occult, even if I had the inclination to do so. I am here to sell the place, not run around it sprinkling herbs and chanting.'

Out in the extension, a door slammed hard.

'There'll be a fair draught from that broken window,' Magnus observed. He didn't say anything about my lack of witchiness, though. 'And it's a greylag goose in there, brooding her eggs. She'll likely be off as soon as they hatch, and we can mend the window then. Will you be here long?'

'No.' The word sounded wobbly, the door-slam had made me jump. 'As long as it takes to sort out any bits and pieces and get it on the market. We'll deal with the paperwork back in York.'

Magnus stood up and I smelled that pleasant, citrusy smell from him again. He wasn't wearing his overalls now, it dawned on me. He'd got on a thick navy jumper and jeans and no longer looked as though he'd walked out of an episode of *All Creatures Great and Small*.

'Aye, well,' he said. 'You might find it's not as easy as all that.'

The light, which had been on since we'd opened up the building, flickered. 'I can see that,' I said. 'But if Innis and Torstein want to buy it from me and turn it into a permanent feed store and have the extra grazing, I'll take a reasonable price.'

Might as well put it out there, I thought, watching his face. Save them from trying to frighten me off any further with ridiculous stories about witches. Realism, that's what we needed here, an acknowledgement that this place and the few acres of weedy, marshy land and the loch were probably more valuable to the farmers who already lived here than to a holiday house business.

Magnus shrugged one shoulder, in a dismissive gesture.

'Oh, and is the bed fit to sleep in?'

This time, he pulled a face. 'I dunno. I suppose. I think Tor's had a few nights over here when Innis has put him out of the house.' He scratched at his chin and it rasped, nails on stubble. 'They're a wee bit volatile, those two. But things have been better since Freya was born, so I don't think he's been over this last two years.'

Well, that explained the half-full bottle of gas, the kettle, microwave and slow cooker that the kitchen contained. I stood up and went to the bed-cupboard. 'That doesn't really answer my question, though. Can I sleep here?'

Magnus looked at me as though he was trying to sum me up. 'Jennet had a stroke,' he said. 'She died in the field there, you've no worry about yon bed. We put a memory-foam mattress on it a while back, when Tor complained about the damp.'

The bed looked thick and well-blanketed, covered in linen sheets and woven blankets with what looked like a handmade patchwork quilt over the top. It was the most picturesque thing in the entire cottage, shades of faded blue and green cut into curiously curved shapes, like the sea, and exquisitely stitched. I poked it and the mattress did, indeed, seem to be foam. I had worried that it might be stuffed with horsehair or some other itchy and probably hazardous material.

'Well. Good,' I said.

'And you're right, it's late. I should let you get some rest.' Magnus moved towards the door. 'You'll be tired with the travelling.'

'Is there – I mean, what do I do about a shower? There's no bath or anything?'

He kept looking at me in a curious way. It was hard to put my finger on it, but it looked a little as though he expected a second head to burst out of my shoulder, or me to start speaking in tongues. The way he was standing by the door, with one hand on the latch and watching me, made me wonder if he thought I was about to go up in flames or something.

'There'll be a tin bath around somewhere,' he said. 'And there's a hot water boiler, aye.'

And then he was gone, closing the door so the latch fell like an executioner's axe into its socket, leaving me alone with my itchy sweatiness and a larder still full of goose.

5

I didn't sleep much.

There were several contributors to my sleepless state. The bed, although comfortable, was unfamiliar and basically a cupboard with a mattress in. Then there was the relentless daylight, which muted gradually to the 'simmer dim' I'd been warned about by Magnus before eventually becoming dark just in time to start getting light again. Unfortunately, when I tried closing the cupboard doors to darken my environment, I fell into dreams of premature burial and woke to absolute terror and propped them back open again. The goose in the outhouse came and went amid soft honking noises like a four-year-old experimenting with a vuvuzela. Around the point when the darkness looked as though it was going to let me fall into unconsciousness, rain started, blown against the windows with the savagery of handfuls of grit against glass.

It was endless. It made my night-time complaints in York about noisy neighbourhood parties and fighting cats feel trivial. At least the parties stopped eventually, even if that was accompanied by yelling, police sirens and flashing lights. The cats wandered off. *This* – I pummelled the pillow, which seemed to have been formed from brick dust and concrete – was never-ending.

Around 4 a.m., as the sun began to rise despite my entreaties to it to 'give it a rest and go back to bed', sliding in through the windows that overlooked the loch and blurring the entire land-scape into a festival of spear-sharp edges and white light, I stopped trying to sleep and got up.

My hastily packed pyjamas were no protection against the early chill and I wrapped myself in my coat and made a cup of tea in the tiny kitchen, ignoring the sounds of restless goose in the connecting larder. Then I went and paced around the cottage again.

With the sun high above warming the indoor air, I felt a little less hopeless. There was a certain charm to the rustic nature of the bare stone walls and the rough wooden furniture. The warmth was bringing out a smell of old polish, ancient peat smoke and a vaguely medicinal tang, and the wind seemed to have dropped for a moment. My heart lifted a fraction from its 'rat-infested hovel' depths and I wondered if I could maybe paint a couple of walls a more interesting colour, put down some more rugs and hang some curtains, fit a lampshade to the bare bulb and get some additional lighting. It might make the place look more lived in. Or with the potential to be lived in. Then I could go to an estate agent and beg them to take the cottage on.

Yes. A plan. I worked better with a plan. I planned profession-ally. Accountancy was basically just organising figures, and my parents relied on my ability to sort and out and direct their lives. Planning I was good at. I started to wander around again, making notes on my phone. It needn't cost a fortune, but a bit of carpeting would make the place less echoey, a spot of colour would tone down the 'inside of a barn' feel, and some proper lighting would also help. I'd need an extension block to add extra sockets, but that could all work.

I wondered if moving the furniture would help, but a few seconds of attempting to drag the heavy chairs away from the fireplace, then staring at them in the middle of the room like Goldilocks awaiting the arrival of the bears, and I returned them and added 'furniture' to my list. A few small cushions, maybe a little sofa – I didn't want to spend money, but if it helped Jennet's cottage to sell quickly, it would be worth it.

All I needed was a shop, and, so far, all I'd seen was a large Co-op on my way out of Stromness and some village store-cum-post office places along the road. Tears of resentment and anger pressed behind my eyes for a moment until I realised that I was probably still tired and took a deep breath. *Organise, Brid, it's what you do.* This was all manageable. There must be furniture shops and decorators on Orkney somewhere, the locals didn't all live in bare houses. Innis had a lovely kitchen and that had to have come from *somewhere*. Torstein didn't look like a man who would know a Philippe Starck from a B&M Bargains.

Although there was Magnus. I stopped suddenly in the middle of the room. There was something about Magnus that made me think he knew things. As though I could have asked him about anything from Farrow and Ball colours to sofas, and he would know how to source them. He had an air of creative practicality and I wondered what on earth had made me think that – until I remembered that Innis had told me he made jewellery in Kirkwall and I was giving professional designer attributes to a man I'd only met twice.

I paced around a bit more. The sun moved higher and the light became wider. When I opened the front door and peered out, the air was as sharp as lemon juice and the sky vanished into the distance, travelled by a few clouds of fluffy innocence. There were no trees, nothing to the far horizon but Innis and Torstein's house up the slight hill and, in the other direction, spiky grass and reeds down to the edge of the loch.

In the foreground, however, was the goose, gobbling at the few patches of lusher growth. It stopped grazing when it saw me and raised its head menacingly.

'I'm going,' I said, backing away. 'You carry on.'

Then I felt stupid for talking to a goose, and slightly lonely. I never thought I'd miss the sound of Annie singing in the shower in the morning, or the noisy York streets on my walk to work. Or even my ever-present work colleagues, chatting about their weekends or football or cats.

Here there was nothing but the wind and a goose.

I set my shoulders. Right. I'd better get on. In York, I was needed. I had people who were relying on me to finish this what-ever-it-was, and get back to sorting out people's financial messes and helping Mum fold Dad's wheelchair down to fit in the back of the van so they could go to Tesco. I had two weeks *max* to get this place sorted, on the market, and hopefully sold, so I needed lists, I needed a plan of campaign and I needed some shops.

* * *

'Shops?' Innis asked, in a tone that implied this was a foreign concept. 'You want Kirkwall for that. They sell all the fancy fabrics and gear that the tourists like to take home; we use the builders' merchant away to Thurso. Tor did all the work in here and I ordered all our furniture from John Lewis.' She looked at me over the mugs of tea. 'But it can take a while to arrive, mind.'

'I haven't got a while.' I sipped at the tea and pretended to myself that I wasn't enjoying sitting in the warm kitchen while various children rioted in the hallway. 'I need to get the house fit to be sold and I think some rugs and curtains and things will make it look more – homely.'

'Aye, well.' Innis stood up again, heavily. Nobody had said anything, but I had begun to wonder if she was pregnant again, she moved almost weightily, even though she was slim and neatly dressed in jeans and a jumper. As though something was pulling at her. As she climbed over the barrier that kept the small children from invading the kitchen and eating everything remotely edible whilst taking the oven to pieces, and dealt with a minor border skirmish that was establishing over the dressing-up box, I watched her. Her face looked a little drawn and there were shadows under her eyes – maybe she was just tired. It must be a hell of a life out here, constantly on edge with children and a precarious existence eked out from the farm. Maybe they couldn't *afford* to buy Jennet's cottage.

Innis directed me to Kirkwall's main shopping street, and I drove the rise and fall of narrow roads, feeling like a solitary blood corpuscle travelling a set of veins, threading through the landscape. As instructed, I parked in a windswept car park between supermarkets, and found that the proximity of huge illuminated signs, and offers posters, tattered by the wind, made me feel slightly less far from home and claustrophobic. Here were unattended trolleys and women with shopping bags chatting on the side of the street, and it felt a long way from the wind-combed isolation of the cottage.

I found the shops, opposite the huge cathedral of St Magnus, which sat with a very resigned air in the middle of the town, its edges buffed and rubbed by the constant wind. There were, indeed, cushions in many of the shop windows and I felt my heart rise a little more at this obvious sign of civilisation. Some paint, some soft furnishings and a bit of colour, and Jennet's cottage would sell in no time. Of course it would.

With the wind buffeting at the back of my head, I looked along the shopping street, with St Magnus behind me like a brooding father whose only daughter is late home from her date with the local rake.

As I stared in some shop windows, distracted by cushions and fudge, I wondered idly whether Magnus was named after the saint, and what a shame that would be. There was something... not unholy, but a little bit... yes, *pagan* about the man, I thought. As though he lived on the edge of wildness. And then I laughed at myself for the whimsy, because of *course* he lived on the edge of wildness. Everyone on Orkney did. It was practically their defining characteristic, that and owning, from the look of it, an abundance of cushions.

A movement distracted me. From a tiny, crooked-fronted shop, someone was waving at me, and when I realised it was Magnus my forehead started to sweat, despite the wind. Almost as though I'd called him into being just by thinking about him, here he was, leaning across a window display of woven silver bracelets on a background of heather stems, and beckoning to me. I hesitated for a second. Then I saw, inside the shop, a woman, talking to Magnus, one hand on his arm as though she was trying to hold him down. She had gorgeous golden hair, sweeping down over the collar of her coat, which was red and dramatic, touching the tops of her black leather boots, and a pregnancy bump that jutted beyond her slender body and made her look like a python that had swallowed a goat. He'd been looking up and through the window at me, but now his head was lowered, as though he were listening to her with close attention, her lips close to his ear.

I felt intrusive just looking at them and didn't want to go into the shop and ruin the tableaux of concern they were forming. But the wind was cold and there was a threatening spatter of rain coming in on it that foretold of more to come. The rain here was horizontal, so cautiously I pushed the door and walked under the ping of the bell into the shop.

The girl kissed Magnus on the cheek and squeezed past me in the doorway, wrapping the red coat around herself as she went, highlighting the bump.

'What?' I asked him, slightly irritably, although I wasn't sure why. I didn't want to allow myself to think it was because of the pregnant woman and her evident closeness to Magnus.

'Good morning.' He didn't remark on my edgy tone. 'Innis phoned and said you were in search of things to do up the cottage?'

I looked around the inside of the shop, forgetting the pregnant blonde as the smallness of the sales floor crowded her out. It was minute. 'What is it with you lot and your tiny buildings? Are you all secret hobbits or something?'

Magnus wandered back behind the counter and perched on a stool. 'Small buildings, less air to heat,' he said, picking up some silver wire. 'It gets fair fierce in the winter in Orkney.'

'Given that it's supposedly summer and still about ten bloody degrees out there, I am not surprised.' It was warm in the shop and downlighters brightened the gloom in a subtle way. I made a note.

'Aye, this is no place to come for the sunbathing,' he said equably, and began looping the wire around itself, concentrating hard on it, so that I could see those lighter eyelashes contrasting with his hair again. 'Anyhow. Would you like me to show you the best places to shop for the paint, now? I can help you carry it to the car, if you need.'

'Oh.' I was taken aback by his offer. I'd been verging on rude to him, but he was still willing to help me. 'That would be... I mean... you don't have to.'

Now he flicked his gaze up to my face. 'Aye. I know.' Back down went his eyes, as though my nose was embarrassing or my somewhat startled stare was capable of bleaching his skin. 'But it's quiet the day.'

'I thought you said the cruise ships were in.' Innis had told me, whilst making the tea, that the tourist business that the ships brought was how most Orcadians made their living through the summer. And, judging by the fine silverwork dotted around the shop in illuminated cases, Magnus wasn't immune to appealing to the visitor market.

'I've got Mhairi here training, she can mind the place a wee while. The cruise people'll not be in before eleven.' He put the silver wire down and gave me another very level look. 'If you want me to help, of course.'

'Your jewellery is beautiful.' Somehow I couldn't quite bring myself to admit that I did, very much, need his help, as I hadn't contemplated how I was going to get several tins of paint and some potential soft furnishings back to my car.

'Thank you.' He dipped his head in acknowledgement. 'I trained over to Glasgow.' Now he slipped off the stool he'd been sitting on. 'Tor says it's a prissy wee way to make a living, but I like it and it beats the sheep. Indoors, no heavy lifting and you don't get your nose broken by the ram twice a season either.'

Now he grinned and I felt better. I hadn't been sure if he'd been teasing me or pretending to want to help because Innis had guilted him into it, but the smile was genuine and made him look less dour. He had a lot in common with the cathedral opposite, I realised, an imposing build that looked as though it had been tapered around the edges by the weather, although thankfully the building wasn't wearing a startlingly striped tank top, because that would have been bizarre.

'But you're a farmer too?'

'I help out here and there.'

Magnus called a very pretty young girl through from the back room, and pulled on a coat. 'Right. Let me show you what town has to offer in the way of interior design. I warn you, round here country living isn't a magazine, it's literal truth. I am seen as dangerously cosmopolitan for living in a flat above the shop in a town so small that we can't afford suburbs.' Another grin. But now he'd got a coat on over the knitted top, the grin held a little more charm. The slight note of teasing was still there, though. 'Let's go.'

He took me to shops that sold paint, knitted throws, furniture and cushions. Sometimes these were all the same shop, but not often, and we staggered back to my car carrying boxes and bags and with the promise of a sofa and table delivery next day. 'Although it'll only come as far as the house,' I was warned. 'We'll not go up to the cottage.' And eyes rolled in Magnus' direction.

'Why won't they deliver to the cottage?' I asked, as we pressed the cushions down in the car boot to make way for the rug.

'Well, you're the witch, aren't you?' Magnus hurled another bag on top of the resilient mound, which bounced back up to meet it. 'They won't come onto the witch's land. Oh, that and the bog between the cottage and the road that you can't drive a van over.'

I had a sudden memory of stepping over that bog for the first time. 'This is where Jennet's property starts,' he'd said, and there had been that – *thing* woven from old barley stalks and set on the ground at the periphery. 'And you mark that boundary?' I asked, with sudden inspiration.

'*I* don't. I'll no believe in any old wives' tales, even if Innis is the old wife in question, but, aye. Some of the locals think it's only right to...' He trailed off for a moment, scrubbing a hand across his chin. 'To demarcate,' he said, having clearly struggled to find the right word. 'To show they remember. To show respect. To show they're waiting.'

'Well, they can carry on waiting.' I hoisted another bundle across into the boot. 'Once I'm gone they can come over as *Wicker*

Man as they want and it will be between them and the new owner.'
I rubbed my hands down my legs as though to erase the feeling of
those odd, rotting stems. 'I just want my furniture.'

Magnus slammed the boot shut. 'I'll call up later and have a
word. I'm sure I can persuade them that you're not warty enough to
be a proper witch.'

A very large coach edged a cautious bumper around the corner
of the narrow road and pulled up beside the pavement. 'Oh, that'll
be the cruise passengers. I'd better get back to the shop and sell
them lots of handmade silver jewellery to remind them of their trip
before they head out to Skara Brae.'

He set off at a vigorous trot, hands in pockets and not a backward glance towards me, still trying to feed a large rolled-up carpet
through the passenger door and get it to bend around the gearstick
into the back seats.

'What a very strange man,' I said. But he was too far away to
hear me now, heading up towards the main street, where I could
just see the top of St Magnus poking its way into the blue of the sky
between the roofs. The wind had a quick rifle around in the inside
of the car and then hurled off to worry the little knot of people
who'd just got off the coach, flinging hats from heads and causing
coats and jackets to be clutched to throats.

The wind was ever present as my little car was beaten and
tweaked by some enormous gusts on our way up the road. Orkney
seemed to be all wind and sky, with no trees to break either, a few
hills and a lot of sea. Not at all like York, which was largely flat and
filled with greenery which strained the weather before it reached
ground level. Alien. Odd. No real points of contact, which was
probably why I felt so relieved when I got back to the cottage and
hauled the easier-to-manipulate purchases out and across the
rough ground. A house was a house, whether you were in York or
Orkney; roof, walls, windows. Although *this* house might lack a

certain something – well, no, it lacked lots of things – it was still, recognisably, a house. Being inside it stopped that dislocated sensation that I had wherever else I was on the island, that feeling that the water was too close and the horizon too far away, almost as though I were on another planet.

Indoors, when I dragged the door shut against the growth of ivy and it latched into place with a satisfying click, this was just another house that I had to turn into something approaching a home. I'd chanced a few glances into estate agency windows as Magnus had dashed me past on our way to investigate furniture or floor coverings, and the pictures I'd seen hadn't filled me with hope for a speedy sale of Jennet's cottage. Apart from a few derelict buildings, which seemed to only be for sale for the land, everything had looked immaculate. Tiny places, 'with holiday let potential', had had cutely curtained windows and little loft rooms, lots of exposed wood and descriptions like 'offering unique sea views' and 'access to sites of historic interest'. My cottage looked like the 'straight to video' version. It didn't meet any of the standards, had none of the attractions, and was only coming in as a cottage because it had an actual working toilet, otherwise it was just a storage shed with a kettle. I needed to make it look like somewhere Instagram-worthy. The sort of place that people searched for on Pinterest. A show home. Once people came and saw the view across the loch, perhaps they'd be seduced into buying, or at least, not running away screaming into the mist, quoting the Trades Descriptions Act.

I unfurled a rug across the stone floor. In the shop the rug had looked huge, its 'deliberately worn' blue patterning charmingly distressed. On this bare stretch of flagstone, though, it looked as though someone had dropped a napkin. There wasn't a single angle at which I could place it that gave it enough coverage to appear anything other than a tiny bit of carpet to try to flatten out the bleakness. Ah, well. Maybe when the sofa arrived it wouldn't look so out of place. I could use it to zone a seating area, as some of my friends had done in their otherwise featureless homes. Yes, I thought, as I stood back into the doorway and rebounded off the bin liner full of cushions which sagged dispiritedly against the wall waiting for their moment, some 'zoned areas' would do it. Seating, dining, sleeping – I could use rugs and paint to make them all separate. Of course, in a real house, these areas would have been separated already by the walls and doors, but here I had the one room to work with.

I was about to set off back to the car for some of the paint tins, when the door latch rattled and Innis appeared, backlit and clutching a toddler in each hand.

'Hello,' she said, sounding slightly breathless. 'I'd got the kids out for a play, thought I'd drop by and see how you're managing. Magnus says you've been shopping.'

To her left, the bag of cushions gave up its slump and fell forward, spilling its contents onto the floor. The toddlers lunged, but Innis had them in a firm grip, and they only managed to rotate through their wrists, thwarted in their aim of bouncing onto my newly acquired décor.

'Archie and George, you two go and play with the others for a minute.' Innis shook them free and bowled them out of the door. 'You can get the little cars out, if you like.' The toddlers bounded off and Innis came slightly further inside. 'Well.' She eyed the lonely rug. 'You're getting on with it, then.'

'Yes.' Now we both looked at the rug, in its tiny solitude. I finally bent and rolled it back up again. 'Thank you for keeping it clean and sorted for me,' I said, with my eyes on the floor. 'It won't take me long to get it on the market.'

From outside, there came a hollow honking sound, and one of the toddlers flung himself back into the shelter of the cottage. 'Big bird!' he said, pointing over his shoulder towards the noise, which was increasing in frequency. 'Big bird bit George!'

'George! Go with the others and leave the bird alone,' Innis called, mildly, as the goose came strutting into view and stopped, staring in through the doorway. It was, as far as I could tell because one goose looks exactly like any other unless it's been roasted and served with vegetable accompaniment, the bird from my larder. It pecked at a couple of strands of grass and eyeballed me.

'It's the goose from my larder,' I said, feebly, above the sound of George wailing. 'It thinks it lives here.'

Innis looked interested. 'Oh, you've got a familiar already, have you?' She disentangled the toddler that was clutching her coat and gave him a small encouraging push towards outdoors. Bearing in mind that 'the goose that bit George' was hovering around just behind her, I thought the child was extremely brave to let go and hurtle towards his compatriots, taking bitten George with him as he went.

'No, it was just nesting in there.' Familiar? What was she on about? I hardly knew the bird.

'Aye, she'll be yours now.' Innis nodded, seemingly approving, as the goose seized her chance to escape from the children, who had tooled up with a couple of twigs, and wandered past her into the cottage. Behind her came three fluffy goslings, walking in line and looking like a Beatrix Potter illustration.

'Oh, bugger.'

'So, what are you calling her?' Innis persisted.

At the moment, I thought, I am calling her a bloody nuisance who is tramping her flat muddy feet all over the floor that I am trying to attractively bestrew with quite eye-wateringly expensive rugs. But I couldn't say that, because the toddlers were massing outside the door and I didn't want to swear any more than might be occasioned by the goose, and also I didn't think Innis actually, despite her lovely house, really approved of my decorating plans.

'Er,' I said, looking for inspiration and lighting on the only thing I could really see that wasn't an armed toddler or Innis herself, which was the toppled bin liner. 'Cushion. I mean,' I corrected myself hastily, 'Cushie. Yes. She's called Cushie. I haven't named the goslings yet.'

The goose, now apparently known as Cushie, pecked at the floor, with the noise of a very hard beak rebounding off rock. There was a vague threat to the gesture.

'Yes,' I said again, more definitely now as the goose raised her head and fixed me with an orange eye. 'Good, Cushie. Just, er, go back to your larder now.' I made shooing motions with both hands. With considerable dignity, the bird turned her head, gathered her feathers, and led her brood through the living room and out through the door to the larder, which she then hit with her beak. The hollow wooden sound was an imperative. 'I'll, er, I'll just go and open the door for her,' I said, sounding as feeble as I felt. 'They must have come out of the window.'

'Aye. We'll be off for playtime.' Innis wheeled around. 'Magnus said he'll be over to help with the painting tomorrow, if you'd like. He's no ships in and the shop will be shut.'

Discombobulated was too short a word, I mused. There needed to be something with more syllables, more punch, for how I felt right now. 'That would be very kind,' I said weakly, lacking access to anything with more than a single syllable. 'Thank you.'

'Och, he'll love it.' Innis herded several small children before her, all of them tiptoeing back across the bog. 'He's the kind that likes that sort of thing, y'know. The painting and the art and such.' She ended up calling over her shoulder as she and the children reached the solid ground of the field in front of the house, and the wind tugged her words apart and threw them at me as though she held her brother-in-law's jewellery making in contempt. Although, to be honest, there had been more of a note of slight condescension in the words as they'd come from Innis; an undercurrent of censure, as though enjoying art was only one step away from molesting goats.

I closed and latched the door again, because the wind had come in for a look round and was busy flipping fabric like a dissatisfied seamstress. The cushions resettled themselves and I swept them up into a pile against the wall and went to hunt down a cloth to clean up after the avian invaders, whom I could now hear honking and cheeping amongst themselves out in the larder.

I ran the hot tap, which caused the boiler to flare into terrifying life, and put some water in the bucket which I'd at first thought was an attractive rural decoration but now looked essential, then I got down on my knees and began wiping over the floor in a rather desultory way. I was *definitely* going to give my mother a piece of my mind, I thought, wringing the cloth out with a level of ferocity it didn't deserve. I was *supposed* to be putting this place on the market. I was *not* supposed to be providing a nanny service for birds, or looking at the sharp end of several weeks' worth of decorating. *This wasn't how it was supposed to go!*

'I'm an accountant,' I muttered to myself, swiping over the smeared flags again. 'I have *clients*. I offer a *service*. People depend on me to...' I rubbed hard at what I'd thought was a smear of bird poo, but appeared to be something ground into the stone. 'To be reliable. To offer advice and to turn in paperwork on time.' I leaned back on my heels and realised I still had Innis' borrowed boots on and that I'd gone round town in noisy, ill-fitting wellingtons. 'I'm clever!' I told myself, trying to ignore the tears that were pushing at my eyes from behind. 'I've got a degree. I've got qualifications. I know how to make all those little columns add up properly, and what to do with the results. My parents rely on me for company and helping out. I am *someone*. I am *needed*.'

The tears fell itchily along the sides of my nose and I absentmindedly raised a hand to wipe them away, then realised I'd still got the floor cloth in my grasp. 'Oh, *bugger*.' I flung the cloth away and it slithered down the opposite wall, leaving a muddy streak in the whitewash. The cushions, which had seemed like jaunty additions to a colour scheme in the shop, now sprawled like hopeless drunks across the floor, and the rug had come unrolled and flopped, doubled over, in the corner. The two tiny windows, which were the only way light could come in, showed me that the weather looked set to change, yet again. The wind rattled the door behind me and crept in underneath like a stray cat.

'Oh, *bugger!*'

Not enough. Not nearly vicious enough for the emotion that was coming down my cheeks now and pooling under my chin as I leaned back and clasped my knees to my chest in a well-worn posture of defeat and powerlessness. 'Bloody eternal *fuck*.'

There was no reassurance from the cottage. Only a pool of cold hardness under my bottom, the rough rattle of the door behind me and the sound of a goose and her offspring settling down in my one useable cupboard.

6

I managed a decent wash before bed, which made things look up a bit. I'd also heated one of the ready meals I'd brought with me, pinging it in the microwave until it steamed and made the place smell properly lived in, then I carried it through to the main room and sat at the table with it, in splendid isolation as the sky darkened further and a splatter of rain swept across the windows. From outside I could hear the distant sound of cars on the far-away road, and then the bleak, stretched silence of nobody caring for hundreds of miles. It was just me and this little stone building. But at least I'd got out of the wellingtons, and with the rug tucked under the table providing a layer between my socked feet and the bare stone, there was a measure of comfort.

I checked my emails again. Nothing urgent. My boss had shared my workload among some of my co-workers while I was away, so the only people really needing me were those for whom I was the first port of call at the office.

I decided to email my mother and sat with my hands poised on the keyboard, trying to frame sentences that would encompass the amount I would have to do to the cottage and the sheer futility of

trying to sell this bleak little section of the island that the Orcadians called Mainland. To me, 'Mainland' was miles away and
contained my life, to the locals this, the largest island in the
archipelago, was the mainland. That summed it all up.

I couldn't think of any words that would illustrate this austere stone
box, or the desolation of these treeless islands in ways she would
understand. If I said 'isolated', she would read 'attractively quiet'. My
mother was always one for putting a positive spin on things, perhaps
that was what happened when you were born an Orcadian; you looked
for the plus side to prevent you from throwing yourself off the nearest
cliff. I typed a few banal words, reminding her that Dad had a hospital
appointment coming up and that I'd written it on the calendar, and
telling her that there was plenty of food in the freezer, but she needed
to remember to defrost it before cooking. Then I signed off, shortly,
refraining from mentioning how I was getting on. Let them read
between the lines, even if it did mean Mum might worry. It had been
her idea that I come here, and I wasn't feeling particularly inspired by
the Herculean task she'd sent me to, so a little worry would be payback.

I finished the chicken stew and some tinned peaches. The
showers had blown past and the light now glistened in at the
windows. Maybe I could get some blinds? Something to shut out
these ridiculously over-elongated days, which only served to illustrate how little there was to do out here, apart from stare at walls
which seemed to have been built out of leftover bits from the
construction of the islands.

The walls were so thick that the windows were deeply sunken,
like eyes in a very old face. I stared at one for a moment. Someone
had at least taken the trouble to put wooden sills beneath the
windows, which made the phrase 'window seat' pop into my head
for a second, until I realised that nobody was going to want a seat
that could only be accessed by climbing onto a chair. They were too

high to be useful, too deep to be practical. I supposed I could stand some candles on them, if I wanted to look as though I were signalling to smugglers on the other side of the loch, in a *Famous Five Go to the Middle of Nowhere* look.

I walked across the room to check the integrity of the possible shelving. It was about chest height, wide at first but tapering to the small window, which didn't appear to open, and through which I could feel a distinct draught, air carried straight over the water and through the reeds directly to my indoors. It wasn't double glazed. It was barely single glazed, in fact, if half glazing had been a thing I would have sworn Jennet had cut costs by having it fitted. Any candles standing on this shelf would be extinguished in the first gust.

The windowsill was wobbly too. The wooden surface, when given a bit of a shove, lifted. To my astonishment, the whole thing hinged up and left me looking down into a dark, lined cavity under the window, like a narrow box. It seemed to be filled with paper, which didn't surprise me as I suspected that any insulation this cottage had was formed from old newspapers and straw. Still. It was useful storage space, and the place was desperately short of that, so I began pulling the paper out to try to establish the dimensions of the hidden cupboard. Maybe I could use it to put the paint tins in, because they were currently just inside the door and I tripped over them every time I went past.

It was mostly brown paper, I saw, as I pulled another ream out, useful for making attractively homespun decorations in a kind of 'cottagecore post office' way. Annie, my housemate, had a penchant for Pinterest and was given to doing variously decorative things with household items, if not prevented. She'd wrapped some boxes in plain brown paper and tied them with string last Christmas, to hang around the windows, and it had looked attractively festive if you didn't mind being bopped over the head every time you checked to see who'd rung the doorbell.

I had to stand on a chair to completely empty the space, as it went right down to the floor, inside the wall. I had a brief horror-movie moment, where I envisaged falling into the cavity, the lid slamming and trapping me like a Poe story, until I realised that I could just stand up and open it again. Right at the bottom, under the industrial quantities of packing paper, my fingers touched something hard, yet slightly warm. It felt, at first encounter, like a lizard, and I shot back up out of the gap with a squeal of disgust and horror. I went to fetch my phone so I could shine the torch down into the depths, and the long-handled broom from the kitchen, so I could poke it.

It was a book. Bound in leather, which accounted for the weird feel, cracked and peeling. I prodded it up and down the space a bit, and nothing dreadful fell out, so I bent back in and retrieved it, keeping the light in my other hand just in case the peeling leather was the result of some kind of infestation.

Once I had it in hand, I got off the chair, closed the lid and scuffled my way through the piles of brown paper over to the table, where I put the book down. A few flakes of leather covering came away like old skin, and I pulled a face at its blackened surface. It was A4 size, quite thick, and still with that odd almost-warmth, as though it had been down the back of a radiator and had soaked the heat into itself.

I flipped the cover open with the tip of a finger, almost reluctant to touch it. There was something scabrous about the peeling surface that felt dry and warm, almost as though it were a living thing, and as the only other living things in the cottage wanted to take my eye out with a beak, I wasn't sure how I felt about that. The first page was smooth, yellowed around the edges as though it had been dipped in tea, and in the centre, written in sloping, cautious letters in ink that had faded to the palest blue, were the words *Book of Shadows*.

The next page was covered in what looked like the same handwriting, cramped and squeezed, with asterisks and arrows pointing to footnotes, and a quick flip through the pages showed that this filled the entire book, except for the odd page which was covered in pencil drawings. It looked like a school exercise book of someone with an attention deficit disorder, very tidy handwriting and a penchant for afterthoughts.

I went back to the first page and squinted at the opening lines. 'If people come to you, remember they are already at their wits' end,' I read. 'Keep calm, even if they have a wound the size of your head, and also remember that they may not tell you what the problem really is. It's your job to find out, and it might not be the obvious.'

From the larder, Cushie made a kind of strangled snorting sound and there was a moment of distressed peeping. I left the book and went for a guarded look, just in case the goose was choosing now to finally pack up and leave, so I could whip a quick board over the window gap, but all that had happened was that one of the goslings had gone for a wander and got itself stuck under the bottom shelf. Almost without thinking, I lay down on the floor and reached in to scoop it loose, because the cheeping had reached car-alarm levels and Cushie was paddling her feet in an unhappy way, whilst sitting on the other chicks.

The little gosling was nothing but fluff and bone. I'd never touched a bird before, and it surprised me how little there was to it, as I swept it from under the slate shelf. Just a morsel of not-quite feather and the most fragile of joints, tiny wings flapping at me and a small beak pecking at my attempts at rescue.

'Just shut up and sit still.' I got the bird into my hand and then released it to the freedom of the rest of the larder. 'And don't do it again.'

The chick ran to Cushie and crawled its way into the reassurance of her feathers, whereupon she snaked out her neck and pecked me really hard on the arm, her beady eye swivelling around to fix on me with an almost serial killer regard.

'I was only trying to help,' I said, rubbing my arm. 'Next time they can all get stuck under there, and see if I care. Oh, great, now I'm talking to the bird that is squatting uninvited in my cupboard.'

But then, who else was there to talk to? I supposed I could have wandered across to the house, visible from the kitchen window on its slight rise where the meadow met the road, downstairs windows bright with illumination despite the fact that the day hadn't yet faded into twilight. I briefly thought about wading across the flag-stoned bog with some excuse, to be invited inside where there were people. Maybe Magnus was there, discussing the evening milking, or talking about my choices in paint finish and rug design?

I was halfway out of the door when I realised that I'd got my pyjamas on, that despite the brightness of the light it was quite late, and that Magnus lived in Kirkwall and likely wouldn't be here anyway. And then I gave myself a stern talking to. Magnus might be helpful and really quite attractive in a windswept and rugged way, but he was as temporary an acquaintance as the man who'd sold me the table or the lady who had persuaded me to buy half the cushions. And, I reminded myself, he'd been the one to tell me about 'The Witch's Cottage', even if he didn't seem to buy into the whole occult thing. As far as I could tell, everyone else seemed to believe in witches, as though they were as inevitable and perpetual – and *real* – as the rainswept sky or the battered landscape. Even the otherwise down-to-earth Innis had called Cushie a 'familiar', which had been so bizarre I'd had to look it up and found that it was an animal associated with witchcraft.

The whole lot of them, I thought, were bonkers. Or credulous. Or, possibly, both.

But then, I thought, squaring my shoulders and propping the hardboard half across the windows to block most of the light but leaving enough trickling through to prevent those nightmares, I'd only been here a day and a half. I was still dislocated. Still wrapped around in the difference between York, with its somewhat overpopulated nature, and this wild, lonely, isolated place. If everyone here wanted to believe in witches and fairies, it was not my concern, or my business. I was here to do a job and go home.

I climbed up into the cupboard-bed, leaving the doors wide open, and crawled under the patchwork coverlet so that my feet could thaw out. From the extension beyond came a faint peep and the replying of a truncated honk.

'Night, Cushie, goodnight, babies,' I half whispered. Then I banged my head hard on the pillow for my sentimentality, and fell asleep.

7

The next morning, I decided to have a proper wash. The lack of ablutionary facilities had meant that, thus far, I'd settled for sponging myself down with a bowl of water in the kitchen, but I'd was tired of that now. I needed a bath.

The bath was a tin thing, hanging from a nail on the back of the toilet door, where it clanged like a peremptory alarm every time the door was opened or closed. I took it down, squeezed it onto the tiny space available on the kitchen floor, and began filling it from the hot tap by means of the bucket, whilst the water heater boomed and gurgled at the unexpected demands. Then I drew the flimsy curtains across the window, just in case Innis or Tor might be peering out, found the expensively scented body wash I'd brought with me in case the four-star accommodation I'd been expecting had been light on lovely fragrances, took off my pyjamas, and got in.

The water felt wonderful. Even though I was scrunched up with my knees jutting like a mountain from beyond the bubble lowlands and the rim of the tin bath was sticking into the back of my neck, being immersed in warm, nice-smelling water made me feel a bit less primitive. The bruise on my arm where the goose had pecked me was a blueish stain with a red, pinched middle, and I rubbed it thoughtfully with body wash, mapping its extremities and wincing. 'Bloody goose,' I muttered, swooshing myself with another double handful of hot water. 'You're out as soon as, well, as soon as the goslings are... well, soon.' Slosh, slosh.

Rattle rattle. And then a voice. 'Hey now, are you indoors?'

Magnus. Letting himself into the house, as confidently as though he owned the place. I shrieked and tried to cover myself in bubbles which, in a tub that only really contained my arse, was an impossible feat. 'I'm in the kitchen, in the bath!'

Silence. Then, 'Oh. Shall I go away and come back again?' And the tread of boots along the stone floor.

I was filled with the fear that, if he went away, I might be left doing the decorating by myself, which would take me at least twice as long. 'No! Just wait there, I'll be out in a minute.'

I arose, like a soapy Venus, the bath making tinny noises as it slid along the stone floor when I stepped out, and wrapped myself in a towel. I hadn't brought my clothes in with me, so I had to go out and face Magnus, wrapped in the enormous Pokémon bath towel that my parents had bought me for Christmas when I was twelve.

'Good morning,' Magnus said brightly, obscuring the entire doorway. 'D'you feel better now you're clean?'

'I'll feel better when I'm dressed,' I muttered, trying to bend down to sort through my bag for clothes without letting the towel gape. 'You're early.'

'Och, we finished milking and there's no point in going home to come out again.' Magnus leaned against the doorframe. I hoped he wasn't waiting for a towel-drop moment. 'What's this?'

He'd seen the book that I'd left on the table. For some reason, some proprietorial reason, I didn't want him to touch it, so I swept across to grab it, with an associated dropping of knickers and bra as

I failed to keep the clothes, towel and book sufficiently within my clutches.

'It's mine,' I said, parcelling the front of the towel around the book and trying to kick my underwear ahead of me so that I could get into the kitchen to dress.

'Oh, aye.' He was watching my attempts to play keepy-uppy with an underwired bra with a raised eyebrow. 'I wasn't thinking it was mine, y'know. You can put it down, I'll not steal it.'

'No, I...' I booted my knickers along with my instep.

'I just saw it and I wondered. Jennet must have left a few things behind in the cottage.'

My bra strap got tangled in the edge of the rug as I strode along like a Man United striker aiming for goal. 'I have to get dressed.' With a final punt, I dribbled everything around the corner, scrabbled the towel and outfit, bra and knickers all together in my arms, and kicked the kitchen door shut with a slam that made the goose honk a protest from the adjoining cupboard. I really hoped that Magnus wasn't going to shout something like 'Don't bother on my account!' or whatever the Orcadian equivalent was, but he didn't, and when I emerged from the kitchen, decently covered, he was sorting out the paint tins and made no mention of my recent nakedness.

'We'd better get on with the painting, if the sofa is arriving today,' Magnus went on, as though a previous conversation had been interrupted by my disappearing to wash in a metal tub. 'You won't want to be having to paint around it.'

'I'm going to put the greyish purple on the end wall, there.' I pointed with the handle of a paintbrush towards the range. 'And the rest in this – what colour is it?'

'Says "Gull's Wing" on the tin.' Magnus held the paint up and looked at it dubiously. 'But it looks like "Dishwater" might be more appropriate.'

He was wearing overalls again today, I noticed. Big dungarees in a blue canvas material like a toddler that meant business, with pockets all over the place. 'I just want to brighten it up in here,' I said, slightly feebly, because he was absolutely right and the paint really did look like slightly dirty water. 'Have you got a drill? I might hang some curtains too.'

'Curtains.' Magnus stared at the tiny windows. 'Are you not thinking that it will make the place look like a pig in a wig?'

It would, indeed, make the windows look smaller and curtains were completely unnecessary when the only people who could have looked in at that side of the house would be bobbing in a boat on the loch and therefore presumably having other things to think about than trying to catch a glimpse of me in the altogether, but I was damned if I'd admit it.

'Curtains will make the room look finished,' I said confidently.

'It's already got all it needs,' Magnus observed, stirring the off-white paint with a stick that he'd had the foresight to bring. 'Roof. Walls. Doesn't need any extra to be finished round here.'

'Do you live in a shed?' I asked, somewhat acerbically.

'Nope. Flat over the shop.' Magnus threw me a look and I was slightly surprised to see that he was smiling. 'Very nicely done too, I'll have you know. I'll show you sometime. But it's all neutral shades, I'm not having with all this fuss about whatever the current trend is, I've got it how I like it and that's how it's staying.'

'Well, this place has to be fit to sell and I've seen those pictures in the estate agents' windows, so let's get painting.'

Magnus made me feel awkward, that was it. As though he knew a joke that I didn't understand and he was laughing at my inability to grasp the punchline. It gave him an air of superiority that I was *almost* sure he didn't mean to adopt, but it scratched my nerve endings anyway. He swept the walls clear of generations of cobwebs with the conveniently placed broom that I'd left propped against a chair, while I grabbed the storm-purple paint tin and a brush in a way that showed I was serious about this decorating thing.

'So, what do you know about our Jennet?' he asked, scuffing bristles along the top of the wall.

'Absolutely nothing. I think my mum only met her once and that was when she was very small, before Granny left the island.' I watched a series of small spiders tightrope their way clear of the brush and hasten down the wall to hide behind the range. 'That was in the early sixties. Mum didn't come back much, and she never mentioned coming here again.'

'Oh, aye.' Magnus finished sweeping detritus onto the floor and bent to brush it into a little pile. 'I can imagine the witchcraft wasn't a topic of constant conversation.'

I half-laughed, not sure if he was serious. 'Neither Mum nor Granny have a witchy bone in their body,' I said, very definitely, then had a moment of memory-shock. *Mum, sitting at the table. Years ago, I can't have been more than ten. Cards spread out in front of her and Granny saying something about it being a shame, it looked like Brid would be an only child. I'd only noticed because they'd mentioned my name, but when I came over and asked, they'd said they were playing a game and Mum had shuffled all the cards back together and put them in her bag. But they'd not been the cards she'd used to teach me to play Patience, or that Dad played with his friends when they came round, for pennies. These cards had had pictures on. A tower and people falling, lots of naked figures all in bright yellow and red.*

I tried to cover my sudden confusion by rearranging the paint tins, but I didn't miss the look that Magnus gave me. It was another of those odd looks, almost sympathetic, as though I'd been diagnosed with an illness nobody would tell me about.

'I imagine they wouldn't,' he said. 'Jennet was very well regarded. People came from Scotland to consult our Jennet.'

As I considered Orkney to be part of Scotland, whilst it was clear that, to the locals at least, 'Scotland' was a distant and foreign country, this probably didn't have the impact he'd intended. I levered the lid off the tin, wielded my brush and began to apply it to the lumpy whitewashed stone. 'Family history is all very well, but I'm selling the cottage,' I said firmly. 'I need the money.'

'So you've said.' He gave the tin of greyish-white paint a dubious look and then loaded his brush.

'Do you think Innis and Tor would buy it?' I had my back to him, slapping the paint, which looked a lot less impressive on my wall than it had in the room in the shop, as far up as I could reach. 'For the land?'

'They already use the land. We put the sheep down here, in winter. Close to the house, you see. And nobody will be wanting it, when you've got to come right past their house to get here, the access is so bad.' A moment of sloshing. 'So they've kind of taken informal possession. Plus, it's mostly bog,' he added, practically.

'Oh.' I definitely wasn't going to admit to having checked out land prices online earlier and getting my hopes up. I hadn't thought about access or the fact that the wetness of the land would put people off. 'I just thought they might want the extra grazing. Make a bit more money – after all, childminding can't bring in a lot, and with another baby on the way...'

I stopped suddenly, unsure of where that had come from. I mean, yes, I'd suspected Innis of being pregnant but I neither knew enough about her and Tor to even know whether that was a possibility, nor should I have mentioned any such thing to Magnus.

Magnus was silent. I turned around and he was staring at me with an unreadable expression. 'What?' I asked, finally.

'How did you know?'

His tone was... yes, unreadable, like his expression. Very level, but with an undercurrent of something else. Wariness.

'I don't. Of course I don't. I'm only assuming – probably

wrongly... I mean, I...' I gabbled and then stammered to a stop. 'I just thought she looked different,' I ended, feebly. 'Oh, come on, you're not going to tell me I'm right?'

Magnus had his head on one side. His eyes were a pale hazel that was almost yellow in the limited light of the cottage, and even from my position by the newly purpling wall I could see the widening of his pupils. 'Tor told me this morning, while we were milking,' he said, his voice very quiet. 'Not certain yet, she's not done a test, but she thinks she might be.'

I was a little alarmed to see that the paintbrush in his hand was shaking. 'Female intuition.' I tried to sound light and dismissive. 'That's all.'

'Aye.' Magnus turned back to the wall now. 'Yes. That'll be all.'

'Seems like everyone on Orkney is pregnant,' I said, trying to sound cheery and not at all as though I really didn't want him to think about how the hell I knew about Innis. Even *I* didn't know how I knew about Innis. 'I saw you talking to a pregnant girl in your shop. Before I came in,' I added, as though he may have thought I was somehow staring into a crystal ball to watch him at work.

'That's Kizzie.' Magnus was concentrating hard on the wall now.

'Girlfriend?' I thought about the way she'd kissed his cheek, almost proprietorial. The hand on his arm.

'She was.' He was painting the same spot, over and over. I wondered if he was trying to work out how to spin the relationship, then I remembered that he had no need to spin anything in my direction. He was helping me paint a wall, not proposing marriage. 'A long time ago. We were at art school in Glasgow, a couple for a while. We broke up and she followed me back to Orkney.' Magnus lowered the brush and turned to face me. 'We're still friendly, mind, and she pops round now and again, but I'm really not sure why she's stayed.'

He'd gone a bit pink. It contrasted well with the paint. I wondered if he thought that Kizzie had stayed for him, to try to rekindle their relationship. Whatever reason she had for still being here seemed to give him the kind of guilt that made him drop his head and avoid my eye.

'Is it your baby?'

'Only if it's a medical miracle. We broke up over two years ago.' Now he grinned. 'Nobody knows who the father is. Lovely woman, Kiz, very artistic. Wee bit of a tendency to act first and worry about the consequences after, but she does some lovely paintings. Of the sea and suchlike. They're in a few of the shops.'

I absolutely was not going to examine what his admission made me feel and whether that slight lift of my spirits was relief. I was being stupid, that was all; it had been a long time since I'd had the chance to date or flirt and while I was not thinking of Magnus as a target for flirting with, finding out that he didn't have a pregnant girlfriend in the wings definitely improved my day.

We silently painted for a bit. Out of the corner of my eye I saw him give me occasional glances, almost as though he was expecting me to fling down my brush, whip out a pointy hat and a besom and cackle, 'Fooled you! I *am* a witch!' before flying off over the loch, and my lack of any movement in that respect was slightly disappointing him.

'Well, that looks better,' I said, aiming for, and hitting, banality as I stood back from my wall after completing the first coat.

'Looks like someone hit it really hard.' Magnus broke off from his painting to join me. 'Bruised, like.'

'It does, a bit, doesn't it?' We continued to stare at the blueish purple of the wall. It did, indeed, look very much like my upper arm, where the goose's beak had left me with a dull ache. 'But it's on now. I'll learn to live with it.'

'Will you, aye?' Magnus was looking at me again.

'Figure of speech. When someone buys the cottage, they can paint it whatever colour they like. This makes it look as though someone has decorated in the last century, that's all.' I stood back a bit further. 'And it looks nice with the grey.'

The colours didn't clash. They toned, that was the best you could say. They went together well and gave the walls a kind of outdoorsy, heather-meets-the-elements sort of look. Being indoors, in a cottage with almost no natural light and stone walls, made it look as though we had tried to make a torture chamber look hygge. Magnus jerked his head up.

'That'll be the van with your sofa and table,' he said. 'I'll go and give them a hand bringing them in.' Then, to my relief, because he'd been looking a bit dour and suspicious, 'They'll make the place look a bit lived in when they're in.'

He gave me a grin which made him almost good looking. 'To fool the estate agents.'

With that, he was off to greet the white van which had pulled up alongside the house and where two delivery men were beating off the toddlers.

I watched him go and wondered. Why was he being so helpful? What did Magnus have to gain by painting my walls and sorting out furniture deliveries? Was he just being nice? Or was he hoping to sabotage my attempts to make the place look better and therefore get a higher price from the holiday home market than I'd be able to ask Tor and Innis for? All that stuff about the unsuitability of the land – had they asked him to convince me that the place was unsaleable, so they could get it for a knock-down price? Then I remembered Innis' look of relief, almost excitement, when I'd told her I was here to sell. Yep, she'd be glad to get rid of the place and not have to come over regularly to wrestle the cottage from the grip of entropy.

I stood at the kitchen window, supposedly putting on the kettle but mostly because it looked out up to the road, unlike the other windows, which were all giving views of the occasional sun scintillating off the water of the loch. Magnus and Innis were chatting idly to the delivery men, with Magnus leaning against the house wall whilst Innis and her accompanying band of young children peered into the van. The two young men sent to bring my sofa and table hulked around, conspicuously not unloading.

They all looked as though they'd been friends for life. Which, I reminded myself with a sudden pang of loneliness, they probably had been. The few school friends I'd had had drifted off to bigger cities, apart from one who worked in a racing stables further north. My workmates were all somewhat distant, although I knew that they had work nights out to which they'd stopped inviting me, because I'd never go, my evenings being occupied with helping out my parents. There was nobody with whom I had the kind of relationship that was being re-cemented out there on the short grass of the rise by Innis' back door.

The knowledge followed me around the grim little kitchen, where the kettle was steaming a boil that condensed along the beamed ceiling in droplets which fell back on my head. It even bloody rained indoors here.

Then I caught sight of the peeling cover of the book that I'd wrapped in my bath towel. It probably wasn't good for it to be damp, I thought, and pulled it free with an uncomfortable snatch and snag of the leather against the towelling. Had this belonged to Jennet? Or had it been lost by someone who had been in here for some other reason in the intervening years? I flipped it open with a finger and the book creaked and flopped a double-page spread over the chipboard work surface.

Listening will do more good than treatment, and you can't beat a bit of a massage. Pop some comfrey leaves in some oil, rub it in

and mutter – they'll feel you've done something and go away
happy, but watch out for babies and horses; there's no substitute
for the doctor and the vet unless you're sure.

Then there was a recipe for something, which seemed to
involve lard and some kind of seaweed. I wasn't sure if it was for
massage or dinner and I didn't get chance to read it because there
were noises at the door. I flipped the bath towel back over the book
again for reasons I didn't dare consider, and went through to see
the new sofa grumbling its way across the stone floor, propelled by
Magnus.

The two delivery people were standing outside, peering in
through the door as though they half-feared a large cauldron and
cackling. A table was suspended between them.

'Bring it on in,' I said, 'and put it over there next to the dresser.'

The long-haired delivery man, who was wearing a hoodie,
glanced at his shorter-haired mate and the pair of them dithered
about on the step.

'It's fine,' Magnus shouted over his shoulder. 'She'll not curse
you, if you're being useful.'

More table-juggling and almost balletic attempts to look as
though they were moving forward without notable advancement.
The table got a corner in and then retreated.

'For heaven's sake, just get it inside,' I snapped as a ferocious
gust pounded the door back against the ivy and all the windows
rattled. 'And don't listen to him. I'm no more witch than either of
you are.'

The man with all the hair, which was being swept forwards by
the wind, cautiously took a step inside, and, when he didn't immediately burst into flames, his mate followed. The table jiggled
across the floor and made a horrible hollow sound as they put it
down. I watched them both glance around the inside of the cottage

and appear reassured by the tins of paint and collapsing bag of cushions, while Magnus wrangled the sofa single-handedly into place near the range.

'See?' I held up my hands. 'No witchery here. I'm getting it ready to sell.'

Both gazes had travelled to the kitchen door and frozen then, with a kind of inevitability that I was beginning to get used to, I turned to see Cushie marching her flat-footed way out of the larder, where the door had rattled itself open in the intrusive wind. She led her little band, with fluff and feathers swept every which way in the breeze, through the kitchen doorway, across the living room floor and, as the men moved aside, past them to the great outdoors.

Nobody said anything. I didn't know whether it was better to acknowledge the fact that I had a goose living in a cupboard or to pretend that they'd hallucinated the whole thing. In the event, I didn't really have time to do or say anything, as the table was abandoned and the two delivery men had shot out, back across the bog and up to their van as though Cushie was a waddling forerunner of the hounds of hell.

'Oh,' I said, and stared at the table.

Magnus laughed and gave the sofa a last shove. 'Aye. That'll be all round the district by morning.'

'Oh, no.' I cupped my hands over my face.

'Och, don't worry.' He straightened up and came over. 'No one's *really* thinking you're a witch. This is modern-day Orkney, not the fifteenth century. We've got TV and broadband and money and everyone's educated here now, not like it was when Jennet had the cottage. It's just a wee superstition that we all play up to, more for the fun of it than anything. And for the tourists,' he added. 'They all like a wee bit of the history, and to think that we're a backward community and them visiting is like a breath of the twenty-first century for the poor, primitive locals.'

There was the smallest undercurrent of bitterness in his tone, as though this was a prejudice he'd been fighting for years.

'Is it really that bad?' I found I was interested, despite myself.

'Glasgow was not kind,' he answered. 'I had to prove myself. Be better than the other students, just to show that I had talent and wasn't knocking rocks together to make fire and considering myself an original thinker.'

'Your jewellery is lovely,' I said spontaneously. 'Anyone can see you've got talent.'

Magnus turned away for a moment, pushed the sofa another couple of centimetres and then, with his back to me, said, 'Thank you,' rather gruffly.

I wasn't sure if he felt I'd patronised him. After all, I'd also arrived on Orkney thinking that this was the ends of the earth, so maybe I was also tarred with the 'tourist' brush. In an attempt to change the subject, I rotated the table and put it against the long wall opposite the dresser, fussily and taking far longer than it needed. After a pause of a few seconds, during which the table legs made a monumental amount of noise on the bare stone, he came to help me and we fidgeted it into place, then stood back.

'Well. It makes the floor look fuller, anyway,' I said, hands on hips. We'd now got the range inset into the purple wall, with the two chairs and the sofa grouped around it as though a sewing circle had just got up and left, the dresser and bed and, against the other wall, the table. At the far end, the small table now looked pointless and in the way. I took the dining chairs and put them at either end of the new table, which made it look as if the butler was about to serve dinner to a couple who never spoke to one another.

There was still about an acre of empty floor in the middle of the room, unadorned apart from the miniscule rug.

'Curtains,' I said firmly. 'It will look better with curtains.'

'Twenty tonnes of loose sheep feed and forty bales of hay,' Magnus said, unhelpfully. 'That's what we used to fit in here.'

We stared at the newly painted walls. The light bounced off the 'Gull's Wing' and made it look depressingly flat. 'No,' I said firmly. 'We've not gone to all this trouble to decorate a barn. I'm going to sell it as a house.'

Cushie wandered back in, the goslings trailing like a kite-tail behind her.

'With a sitting tenant?' Magnus asked.

'The goose can bugger off. Would you like a cup of tea?' It suddenly struck me that I hadn't offered him so much as a Hobnob, and he'd done a morning's milking and then painted my wall. He must be starving and I was desperate for tea.

'That would be lovely.' A grin that illuminated his pleasant features and made his eyes twinkle. 'Have one yourself, we've done a good day's work here.'

'How often do you work on the farm?' We went through to the kitchen and I studiously ignored the sounds from the larder of Cushie settling down on her three goslings, who were peeping and pecking at the floor.

'When I'm needed. Tor mostly runs the place, with a couple of lads not long out of school who fill in with the donkey work. But we've just bought in a few Jerseys and they're calving now, so he needs an extra pair of hands to help in the milking shed. He's looking to go into the local ice cream market.' Magnus leaned back against the cupboards, which gave a groan of woodchip under pressure. He leaned a lot, I observed. As though he spent too much time standing.

'That sounds nice,' was all I could say, thinking that ice cream out here, on these wind-scoured islands where the temperature rarely seemed to be sufficient for me to remove even my coat, was probably ill-advised.

'Tor bought me out of the farm, y'see.' Magnus seemed hellbent on giving me his whole family history and I was too busy trying to find the biscuits to stop him. 'Dad left it to both of us, he got it down from *his* dad, who was Jennet's nephew. And splitting a farm is never a great idea, you end up with daft little pockets of land too small to make a living from. So I used my share to buy the shop.'

The worktop groaned again and I still couldn't think of anything to say. I really wasn't sure why he was telling me all this, I was only here for a few weeks and hardly needed the entire family history.

'And you're an accountant, you say?'

The question surprised me. I turned around, away from the high cupboard, and a packet of biscuits rolled out and bounced off the worktop to land on the floor at my feet. 'Yes. In York. I work in quite a large team, we deal with a lot of farmers and racehorse owners.'

I bent down, picked up the biscuits and, as I stood up, hit my head on the still-open cupboard door edge and bit my tongue. My mouth filled with the iron taste of blood and my vision clouded amid a burst of white lights. I put out a hand to steady myself and the first thing I grabbed was a fistful of Magnus.

'You should sit down,' he said, his voice coming from a long way off. 'I'll finish the tea.'

I couldn't let go. It was as though my muscles had seized up with my hand clutching at his shoulder, the coarseness of his over-alls covering moving flesh and then hard bone beneath. Woozy, I moved forward, cannoned off his chest and stopped dead, muffled against his body and smelling that warm, non-dairy-related smell again. A smell that made me think of – home?

'You've knocked yourself daft,' Magnus observed mildly, as I stood just under his chin. 'Let me see. Och, your eyes look fine.' He ran a careful hand over the top of my head. 'No depressed fractures.

Go and try out the new sofa. I'll finish here.' A gentle push to my shoulder turned me around, and I was probably still half-hallucinating because I *thought* I heard him mutter, 'That's enough now, Jennet,' as I shuffled my way out of the kitchen and back to flop onto the sofa with its forgiving cushions.

As soon as I sat down, I felt better. My vision had cleared, and, apart from a sore spot on the top of my head where the door had connected, I was fine. I retrieved a few of the new cushions from their black bag and scattered them behind me. At the same time the sun came out from behind whichever cloud had been concealing it and beams slanted in through the small windows to line up in blocks across the floor.

Instantly the whole room looked cheerful. The paint looked subtle yet colourful, the sofa seemed right at home. The bare stone of the floor lost the chilly, outdoor feel and gained a charming, magazine-like quality and even the rug seemed to magnify and become a floor cover rather than an object of derision. Magnus, walking in with two mugs of tea and the packet of biscuits jutting out of his top pocket, added to the pleasant effect. The sun rippled over his hair as he moved and laid auburn stripes amid the darkness, and highlighted a scatter of blonder stubble across his cheeks.

It was, momentarily, an appealing, homely image.

'Feeling better?' He flopped down beside me, looked surprised, and then bounced on the sofa surface beneath him with one hand. 'Comfortable, aye?'

'Have you never met a sofa before?' I took the mug he handed me and tried not to notice that he was sitting very close to me, in overalls he'd milked cows in. I wondered if the cushions were washable.

'At home I sit on nothing but wooden chairs, bolt upright. Comfort is for southerners,' he said into his tea.

'Are you taking the piss?'

'Aye. Little bit. But you're behaving as if you've watched one too many episodes of *Vikings*,' he replied, holding out the biscuits.

'I'm sorry.' I meant it too. 'It's just so... so *different* up here. So much sky and water, and it's either too bright to see or horizontal rain, and I feel...' I stopped abruptly, not sure what had caused this outpouring.

Magnus sipped his tea for a moment. 'Well. It's nice to know you feel something, anyway,' he said. 'You were a wee bit robotic for a bit back there.' He shook the biscuits at me again. 'Go on. You need sugar, you've had a shock.'

Robotic? Was that what he'd thought of me? I took a biscuit. Then, so as not to appear robotic, I took another one. 'I didn't want to come,' I said, and before I knew it, I was pouring out the tale of my mother telling me I could have the proceeds of the house sale if I sorted it out, my desire to get out of shared housing, my job needing me back soon. I even touched on Dad's illness and his reliance on Mum and *her* reliance on me, and having to be around to help out, and we ate most of the biscuits in the interim.

Magnus sat quietly and listened. He didn't try to leap in and tell me what I 'ought to do', as so many ex-boyfriends had, he just nodded now and again and, when I finished talking, he let a moment of silence carry the last of my words.

'Sounds like you have a great sense of duty,' he said at last.

'A lot of people rely on me.' My tea was nearly cold. I'd talked longer than I thought.

'Do you have any fun?'

'Fun?'

'Aye. Y'know, going out, running about. Doing stuff. Fun. Not a strange concept.' He flashed me another of those sudden grins.

I opened my mouth to list all the fun things I did in York, realised that these mostly consisted of the odd evening in watching

TV with Annie and Steve, and closed it again. Finally I managed, 'We get passes to the racing. Because of working for the owners.'

'Oh, aye.' He was looking down into his mug, but he was laughing at me, I could tell. 'Can you not leave the city then? Like, some accountancy-related force field keeping you trapped?'

Now I just shrugged. Anything I could say would sound defensive, and anyway, he had a point. When *had* I last been anywhere outside town?

'Do you not go on holiday?'

'I've been studying.' Now I sounded sulky. 'For accountancy exams. So I've used my holiday time for reading and revision.'

Magnus shook his head. 'You poor wee soul,' he said softly.

'You can cut out the patronising,' I said sharply. 'It's my choice. I could go away if I wanted to, I've just been busy. Anyway, I've come here, haven't I?'

'That you have.' He stood up so suddenly that the sofa bounced. 'Come on then.'

I stared at him. He was standing in front of me with a hand outstretched. 'What? Where?'

His hand made beckoning motions. 'No point in coming all the way up here if you're not going to see the sights. And there's no ships in, so it'll be quiet about the place, it's as good a time as any.'

8

The bang on the head must have still been affecting my judgement, because I let him grab my arm and pull me up, and the next thing I knew we were bounding across the bogland to the cab of his Isuzu, and then driving off across Mainland, following the sun.

Magnus took me to Skara Brae, the Neolithic village preserved under sand, where we got in with a nod to the girl on the admissions desk, and we wandered amid the sunken, long-gone houses. Then back in the truck to a ruined Viking settlement across a still-wet causeway, the sea draining from its edges and swooshing under our tyres. We visited a broch which had been fortified in the Iron Age and stood at the edge of the water looking across to another of the islands when a black fin broke the surface and Magnus, with a commendable lack of excitement, said, 'Orca. They come this far south sometimes.'

I was astonished. The memory of that black skin, coasting along just under the surface of the chilly waters, stayed with me as Magnus drove us across a thin slit of land, white-tipped waves playing on either side, and then pulled the Isuzu over into a car park beside the water.

'And this,' he said, with a wave of his hand, 'is Brodgar.'

The stone circle sat on the horizon, pointing at the slate-black cloud. Unfamiliar birds circled overhead. It looked like something out of a supernatural TV series.

'It's very... old.' It was all I could think of to say. The stones squatted on the hilltop, huddled against the savage wind, giving the sky something to loom over. There was absolutely nobody about, but given the force that the wind had behind it, they were probably all currently bobbing about in the loch with surprised expressions. The vehicle rocked.

'Aye.' To my relief, Magnus didn't open the door, he just put the Jeep in gear again and drove off slowly. 'We'll take a proper look another day. I just wanted you to see.'

The shiny-dark stones, the black sky, the slippery shadowed shapes of the orca, the sea draining before us; tide and wind and cloud, all merged together in my head to form a kind of existential impression of wildness, a feeling of things that should be touched lightly. *You'll know what to do*, a voice in my head whispered, *when the time is right*.

I hadn't realised I'd been dreaming until Magnus shook me awake. 'Hey now. Are you sure that bump on the head wasn't worse than you thought?'

Woozily I surfaced, the dream breaking and leaving me with nothing more than an impression of reassurance and a background of darkness. 'What? Mmm, no. Sorry. I'm not sleeping well in that cupboard.'

'Well, we're back now. I need to head home, do some work. If you're sure you're all right?'

I opened the door and the wind instantly tried to snatch me out and fling me to the ground. 'Yes. Yes, I'm fine, thank you.'

'If you take badly, go to Innis. She used to be a nurse.' He shuffled his hands on the wheel. 'Before Freya was born.' He tapped his fingers. 'I ought to go.' He sounded almost reluctant.

'Of course. Yes.' I climbed down onto the grass, hearing the sound of small children shrieking, even above the noise of the wind in my ears. 'And thank you for showing me those places.'

Magnus let out the clutch. 'You needed to see,' he said, with the van moving forward almost before I'd closed the door. 'What you're letting yourself in for.'

I latched the cottage door behind me with a slight sense of relief. The rain had begun again, hurling itself at the little low building like a rugby player practising his tackling skills, and it was – yes, *nice* to close the door on it and breathe in the aroma of new paint and soft furnishings. Cushie honked what I was going to assume was a greeting from the larder, and I made myself a cup of tea and stood and looked at today's handiwork.

Colour *had* made a difference. The pale blue of the sofa went with the rug and the walls nicely, I thought, standing in the kitchen doorway. Of course, in most houses you couldn't appreciate the entire décor of the house from one place, but, well, the cottage was what it was, to quote my mother. I wasn't quite trying to make a silk purse out of a sow's ear – another of her expressions – but it did feel rather like trying to make a silk purse out of two bits of inexpert knitting, a bent bit of wire and a ball bearing, with instructions printed in Japanese.

I flopped down on the sofa with the black book I'd rescued from the window seat. My laptop lay beside me with its little green light winking an invitation to open it and attend to all the things I'd missed, but I didn't want to, not just yet. Work felt like a million miles away today. The stuffy office with the constant background hum of voices and electronics, occasional shouts of laughter or admonishment and the men in their ties and jackets didn't bear any resemblance to this constant quiet and the steadiness of stone.

None of the men I'd seen in the last few days had worn suits or ties, it was all overalls and warm clothing, defence against the weather which changed on the turn of a breeze.

All those places Magnus had shown me. All the history, which had meant nothing to me in York, suddenly seemed very up close and personal. Not a school lesson or a reluctant trip, with a guide droning about Romans and Vikings, but rather quiet places of stone and conjecture, where no one living knew what had really gone on.

My head was drooping. I really needed a good night's sleep. For a moment, I wondered if I could sleep on the sofa, but it had been constructed more for style than comfort and I'd bought it simply because it would make the cottage look as though someone actually lived a life in it rather than squatting audaciously. No. An early night would be more use than a nap. To keep myself awake, I flipped the little book on my knee, and skiffled the pages at random.

It fell open at a page of drawings. A leaf, wearing the spring in every pencilled line. A hare stretched out languidly as though resting and then again, captured in coiled movement. An orca, carefully shaded to give the impression of light on firm skin, and water breaking beneath its weight. Jennet had written something beneath each, but in letters so faintly drawn that it was impossible to read them in this light.

I flipped the page again. *Someone at the door*, the words in bold blue ink swam into view at exactly the same time as a knock at the front of the cottage, and I jumped so hard that the book slid off my lap and fell, sprawl-paged, onto the rug.

When I cautiously lifted the latch and opened the door, it was the long-haired delivery man, jittering his nervous dance on the threshold. 'Er,' he said.

'Have you made a mistake? This *is* the right sofa, isn't it?' I glanced over my shoulder as though the neat blue two-seater had somehow become a corner settee with footstool, although they would never have got that through the door.

'Er. Aye. I just... *wanted a word.*' It was whispered so quietly that his voice was almost inaudible beneath the wind. I didn't know why, the only living things within hearing distance were a small rabbit, which was showing no sign of evident interest, and Cushie with her goslings in her cupboard.

The nervous man's name was, apparently, Nathan, although as he was reluctant to raise his voice above a tense hiss or come further into the cottage than the front step, it was hard to tell. He carried on his St Vitus Dance and kept hitting his elbows against the latch.

'I've got a bit of a problem,' he undertoned. 'You... you *are* the witch, aye?'

Saying no to a man who had obviously had to steel himself considerably to return and come indoors would have been cruel. Like someone believing you to be the local Mafioso and having to inform them that, actually, you ran a newsagent's and helped at the cat rescue home.

'Yes, all right, let's say I'm the witch.' I aimed for sympathy but seemed to come down more around annoyed. 'Why are you here?'

He didn't speak, just clasped his hands together in front of his groin and jittered.

'Look, come in and sit down. I'll put the kettle on and you can tell me what you want, all right?'

He followed me into the kitchen and loomed, head nearly touching the beams. Gradually, as I filled and boiled the kettle, put teabags in mugs and fetched out more biscuits – judiciously placed in a low cupboard now, I didn't need any repeats of the head-banging incident – he stopped the nervous movements and looked around with evident wonder.

'It looks like my gran's place,' he said.

'Yes, well, we don't all live like Maleficent,' I said tartly, because his boggle-eyed staring was getting to me. 'It's just a kitchen.'

'Aye, but...'

Cushie, hearing voices or, more probably, hearing biscuits, because she and the babies had had the Hobnob crumbs, snaked her head out of the larder door. I left it open now. I hadn't really examined why, because the draught was fierce, but somehow it was nice to know that there was something else alive within half a mile that I could actually talk to. I didn't count Innis and Tor and the children, because I couldn't address them directly, and even if talking to the goose only resulted in angry honks, at least she was there. She rolled an orange eye at Nathan, who suddenly stood very, very still.

'It's all right. She doesn't eat people,' I said, then, feeling the bruise on my arm from yesterday's peck, 'not whole, anyway.' I picked up the mugs and shoved one at Nathan. 'Let's go and sit down and you can tell me why you're here.'

I watched him as he stared his way back into the main room, eyes bigger than a child's meeting Father Christmas, then I sort of poked him down onto the sofa where, hunched over his mug, he blurted out his reason for coming.

It was sad, sweet and funny. Nathan, who always felt like the weird geeky guy at school, had met an incomer and wanted me to make him a potion to give him the confidence to ask her out. That was what it boiled down to. I sat on one of the hard chairs opposite the sofa and wished I knew how to light the range, as he gradually gained fluency, with the smell of new paint tickling our noses and the occasional short rustle from the kitchen reminding us that Cushie was still there.

As soon as Nathan stopped talking, I eyed him seriously over the rim of my mug. 'Why – what did you say her name was? Sofia? What's so special about her?'

Nathan went red and stared down the front of his hoodie. 'She's gorgeous,' he muttered. 'And she's not known me forever like everyone else. She doesn't know they used to call me Worm, or that I wet myself in front of the class when I was five.'

I had sudden visions of myself at school. Where I'd been taller than most of the boys right up until sixth form, even in the flattest of shoes, and I'd had to wear boys' shorts for PE because the girls' ones weren't just 'shorts', they were 'indecents' on my height. They'd had names for me then. They probably had names for me in the office; I'd heard one of the team call me 'Madame Maxime' quietly behind my back, but I knew my Harry Potter and it wasn't a compliment.

Nathan was wobbling a knee now, but the rest of him had settled down and there was an urgent look on his narrow face. He couldn't have been more than twenty, stray wisps of a beard he hadn't learned to deal with were beginning around his chin and he was pale and looked mostly like a ferret that someone had stuffed down their trousers for a bet.

'Look, Nathan.' I put my mug down on the floor. I was about to launch into my 'not a witch, not so much as a potted parsley plant, never even seen *Wicked* and about as much idea of how to do a spell as how to perform abdominal surgery', but his expression was just so... so... *hopeful* that I couldn't do it. I thought of all the random bits I'd read in that little black book with the crumbling cover. People just wanted to believe in something, didn't they? And those words, *people only come to you when they're at their wits' end*. 'It sounds to me as though you're fixating on Sofia just because she hasn't known you since you were born. Aren't there any girls a bit more, um...'

Nathan had made Sofia sound like a cross between Heidi Klum

and Victoria Coren and, even given the exaggeration that infatuation was prey to, I couldn't help feeling that he might, just possibly, be punching above his weight there. She'd also, and I only half admitted this to myself because she reminded me of all the plastic girls at school who'd made my life miserable, sounded a bit of a cow.

'Girls you've been friendly with for longer?' I finished, rather weakly. 'Girls you've got something in common with? I mean,' I went on hastily because Nathan was beginning to squint alarmingly, 'Sofia sounds lovely, very... um... very...' *Aware of her own physical loveliness? A bit of a show-off? Like the sort of girl who mows men down in swathes and doesn't even bother to go back and tidy up the offcuts?* 'Attractive,' I went on. 'But it doesn't sound as though you could have many things you could do together. Does she like anime and *The Rings of Power*?'

It was a wild stab. Nathan was wearing a T-shirt under the hoodie, with a character from an anime series and, thanks to Annie and Steve's TV addiction, I knew what he'd been talking about when he'd dropped Halbrand and Gil-Galad into his monologue. But Nathan clearly regarded this as more evidence of my 'witchy' powers.

'How do you know that?' He jumped to his feet. 'How do you know what I like?'

I sighed, wearily. 'Witch, remember?' And I wasn't going to point out that, even without the T-shirt and the name-dropping, he was precisely the right demographic and age group for those to be among his interests.

'Aye.' He subsided back onto the sofa. 'Aye. Right. I just – they said you were the new witch but...' He scrubbed a hand through his hair. 'I mean, the oldies, they believe but, well. I've never been sure, myself.'

And you keep it that way, sunshine. I wasn't quite sure whether the thought came from myself or whether it had been another pithy sentence from the book that had popped into my head at the right moment. 'So, is there anyone else, apart from Sofia? Someone who may be a little bit more approachable, just in case you and Sofia don't have a lot in common?'

'There's nobody. Well, there's Old Morag, she and I used to hang about together, and she knows her way around *Lord of the Rings*, and she used to be nice to me, but... we've known each other all our lives and I really, *really* like Sofia.'

I held up a hand. '"Old Morag"? We're not talking about someone's mum here, are we?'

Nathan stared for a moment and then his expression cleared. 'Och, no! She's known as Old Morag because she was very poorly when she was fourteen and got held back a year at school. So when she came back she was a year older than the rest of us in the class.'

'You weren't particularly imaginative with the nicknames, were you?' I noticed that I was sounding acerbic; carrying all the tones of how I'd always imagined – when I'd imagined it at all – a wise woman would speak to those without her acquired intelligence. I blamed those stories my mum had read me at bedtime, and cleared my throat. 'Morag's not exactly ancient, then.'

'They called me "Worm",' Nathan reminded me, muttering into the front of his hoodie.

I had it on the tip of my tongue to say that it was probably only because they'd never seen a weasel, but kept my mouth shut.

'So, can you help me?' Nathan straightened again, brushing off the unwanted soubriquet and pretending to a degree of confident self-assertion. 'Give me something so I can... I only want to ask Sofia out... nothing bad.' Nathan had a gleam about him now. Clearly my subtly telling him that Sofia probably wasn't the girl for him hadn't worked. Oh, well. I'd never been very good at the psychological chats. But how could I let him down now, when I'd brought it on myself by letting him think I was a real witch? After all, if he asked her out and she said no, well, at least he'd *asked*. I wasn't responsible for his life thereafter, although I had a momentary wish that I could bring Sofia out in the acne that had also plagued my teenage years and, from the small scars on his cheeks, Nathan's too.

But that wasn't fair. I was pushing my own past traumas onto a girl who might be perfectly lovely. Just because I had taken against her for being pretty and perfectly proportioned and a little careless with male emotions – well, that was on me, wasn't it?

'Look. I'll...' Wits' end. *Anything is better than nothing.* 'I'll see what I can do, all right?'

'Now? I mean, have you got something? Only, there's a big do in Stromness tomorrow night, that's where we live, Stromness, and I'd like to – well, it's a good chance for me to see her. She'll be there, cos the older lads will be hanging around.'

Oh, bugger.

'Give me a minute.'

I snatched up the book from the floor by the sofa, where it still lay, tumble-paged, and dashed into the kitchen. I closed the door and leaned against the worktop for a moment, then leafed furiously through the pages in the hopes that some kind of recipe for confidence would spring out at me.

Apart from a rather beautiful line drawing of a dock leaf, and step-by-step instructions on polishing a wooden table with homemade beeswax polish, I couldn't see anything helpful and I didn't have time to read every page. I clattered a few cups together to make it sound as though I were doing something useful, then, in desperation, I tipped the coffee out of its small jar into the sink, made a cup of raspberry and lemon herbal tea in a mug, added cold water and put it into the coffee jar. As an afterthought, I took the coffee label off and added a spoonful of honey. Shook the whole thing until it frothed in an unappetising way, and took it back through.

'Here.'

Nathan took the jar, which was uncomfortably body-temperature, and looked at the yellowish liquid dubiously. 'Did you wee in it?'

'No, I did not!'

'Oh.' He held the jar at arm's length. 'Looks like wee.'

'Take...' What sounded like a reasonable amount? '...a tablespoonful before you ask Sofia out.'

'Will it give me confidence?'

'Yes,' I said, with a ladleful of confidence. 'It will.'

After Nathan had gone, I slumped on the sofa with my cooling tea and wondered what the hell had just happened. Why had I played along? Why hadn't I told Nathan, Magnus, Innis, *everyone*, that the witch thing was as stupid as living in The Captain's House and pretending to be able to sail a schooner? Or living in Bay Tree Cottage and being, you know, an actual *tree*. I was no more witch than anyone else on these islands, and just because I'd inherited Jennet's place...

The thought struck me. Perhaps even *Jennet* hadn't been a witch? I mean, obviously, witches weren't real but there was the whole Female Empowerment stuff and wise women and local healers thing, so perhaps Jennet hadn't so much *been* a witch, as had witch-hood thrust upon her? Perhaps she'd taken on the cottage as a place to live, and got so sick of people coming to her for help that she'd adopted the persona as the easiest way around it?

After all, Nathan had gone away happy. I hadn't needed to do any more than listen to his worries and make him a jar of herbal tea.

People want someone to listen to them. To take their worries seriously. That's what I did at work, too. Even when it was obvious to me that HMRC weren't the devil incarnate, creeping around in farmers' barns and cellars in search of minor tax infringements, people still rang me two minutes before the office closed on a Friday afternoon to offload their fear that, somehow, the tax man would find out that they'd been selling eggs from the yard hens to locals for cash, and I would have to reassure them that, as long as they were honest about the few hundred thousand pounds in stock and equipment and a further few million in land assets, the tax man really wasn't going to be bothered about thirty quid's worth of under-the-counter eggs. But I didn't laugh. I didn't dismiss them. I *listened.* I reassured.

And maybe that's all it was.

With that realisation, the cottage suddenly seemed brighter. It shouldn't have done, because the sun had crept over the rooftop and was no longer illuminating the loch in shades of blues and deep browns, but instead threw the shadow of the cottage long and low into the water, as though a submerged creature lay just offshore. The memory of the orca, gliding beneath the surface, fin splitting the waves into tumbled cascades, rose in my mind. This was a place where killer whales slunk between islands. Where improbable rocks pointed the way to the sky, and villages more ancient than anything I'd ever seen lay, pitting the earth like an enormous crazy golf course. Where people believed in witches.

And I couldn't wait to go home.

9

For several days, I didn't see anybody. Not to talk to, anyway. I occasionally waved to Innis as she marshalled children on the slope beside the house, but she was obviously busy, so I didn't go over. I drove to Stromness and Kirkwall and bought food, having come to the end of my temporary supplies and Cushie had found her way into the low cupboard and eaten all the biscuits.

Kirkwall had been crowded on the day I was there. A cruise ship had disgorged its passengers, who were standing around taking photographs, or chatting noisily amid the ruins of the Bishop's Palace, competing with the rooks who seemed annoyed at the disturbance. I wandered slowly down the main street, half thinking of popping into Magnus' shop and buying something. A bracelet for my mother, perhaps, for Christmas? Or a necklace, for me, a reminder of this strange time for when I got back to normality. Something to show off in the office, 'Oh, just a little thing I picked up when I was on Orkney,' and they'd admire the handiwork and be quietly jealous that these things couldn't be bought online.

But when I'd strolled casually past the shop, it had been full of tourists. Magnus was a head and shoulders amid the crowd, opening cabinets and putting things in gift bags. I hadn't wanted to intrude and he hadn't looked up for a moment so I could catch his eye through the window.

So instead I found a feed merchant at the bottom of the hill and bought a sack of duck and goose pellets, in the hope that, if I fed Cushie and the goslings proper food outside, they might get the message and move on. The salesman and I had a chat about rearing poultry and then, when it turned out that he'd moved from Sheffield, we talked about Yorkshire for a bit and he told me he'd never been happier. He waved a hand at the cluttered, dusty-smelling floor of his shop and said, 'You'd not get owt like this in Yorkshire,' with a broad grin of bliss and I wondered about his financial situation and had to agree.

Back at the cottage, I looked up greylag geese and found only depressing reports of the family group staying together until the following breeding season, about the geese mating for life – Cushie's lack of an obvious mate had led me to even more depressing reports about the legal culling of greylag – and their increasing tendency to stay in their breeding grounds all year.

'How am I supposed to sell this place with you living in it?' I asked her, as I sat on the sofa in front of my laptop, whilst she and the goslings pecked around the remains of my dinner. 'Why don't you go and live on the loch with all the others?'

Cushie twisted her head and gave me a single-eyed stare. Then she glanced over her shoulder at the goslings, one of whom was trying to attack the fork I'd left on the plate.

'Well, yes, but they're your responsibility. They need to be out on the water, taking their chances with... with... I dunno, whatever eats them. Rats or really big fish or something.'

Then I looked at the fluffy, blameless little chicks, whose tufty softness brushed against my legs as they hunted under the sofa for any more dropped goodies. I knew Cushie took them to the loch,

I'd seen the family paddling about among the reeds only this morning. I just wished they didn't have to come wading back to shore, and my cupboard, with such regularity. I was getting tired of mopping wet webbed footprints from the flags.

'And keep the noise down. I'm working.'

Actually, there seemed remarkably little for me to do. I'd anticipated worried phone calls, desperate emails and having to spend evenings scurrying about through my records trying to help those who couldn't find details they urgently needed, but there had been none of that. And I couldn't work out why. Even my mother hadn't rung. Admittedly, she wasn't big on the phone; being slightly hard of hearing meant that she didn't really like phone calls and usually relied on my almost nightly visits to update me on how my father was irritating her beyond her capacity to say, 'Yes, dear,' and how the cast of *Strictly* were getting on. But I'd been here for more than ten days now, with only a couple of cursory emails and a text.

I pushed the laptop to one side. People were busy, that was all. They knew I was tidying up the cottage, getting it ready for sale, they didn't want to bother me with things I could do nothing about.

The front door was propped open with the bucket again, in the hope that Cushie would go out and never come back, and I could see a sliver of that midday sun poking through the gap to lay a knife-slice of light across the floor. It highlighted the new grey of the walls in a pleasant way and I made my mind up to get to the estate agents in the morning. Now I'd worked out the best arrangement for the furniture, put a second coat of paint across all surfaces and given the kitchen a good clean-up, the cottage was as ready as it ever would be.

A shadow insinuated itself into the room and fell long and lean across the flagstoned floor. 'Hello?'

My skin prickled, but not in an unpleasant way. It felt as though my spine had been gently stroked by a finger. 'Oh, hello, Magnus.'

It was nice to see someone, that was all. After several days with nothing more than a conversation about the nutritional composition of duck pellets and shouting at geese, seeing someone I knew was making me feel part of the world again.

'Hey there. Innis sent me over to see if you want to come up to the house? For a cup of tea?' Magnus came into the room and the goslings instantly ran to hide under their mother's feathery body, trying to tuck their increased bulk invisibly beneath her wings. She did her best, bless her, but looked as though she'd detonated.

'Oh.' I looked around the room, as though the table might leap out and shout, 'No, no! You have to stay here!' Which it didn't.

'I think she wants to find out how you're getting on.' Magnus came over and sat on the artfully arranged chair by the range. 'She's nosy, that's all. And we've not seen you about much, we need to check you're not dead and decomposing.' He shoved up his sleeves and ignored Cushie's savage eyeballing.

Had a tiny part of me been hoping that *he* wanted to see me? Was that why I felt this curious dropping sensation in my stomach? The thought that he'd only come over because Innis had told him to? Or was I upset that my plans for an afternoon of vague sweeping and tidying so I could get a flying start on visiting estate agents had been thwarted?

'And your lack of cries of delight and immediate donning of boots leads me to believe that you would rather stay here.' Magnus looked up now and met my eye. His expression was unreadable.

'No, I...'

'If it helps you decide,' he was holding my eye now, making me feel slightly uncomfortable, 'her friend Donal is here too. He's an estate agent.' He grinned. 'I saw you up to Kirkwall the other day, peering in the windows. He'll likely be able to give you a valuation, if you play your cards right.'

'That's not fair.' I put the laptop aside. 'You're going to make it sound as though I'm only coming to talk to the estate agent.'

An eyebrow raised. 'And that's not true?'

'No!'

'Aye. If you say so.' He stood up again and lounged across the room. 'Paintwork's looking good. Sorry I couldn't come over and give you a hand with the second coat, but we had the boats in, so.'

'Yes, you looked busy in the shop.' If he'd admitted to watching me, then I could admit the same, couldn't I?

'And you? Have you been busy?' Magnus nodded towards the laptop. 'All those farmers and racehorse people fighting for your advice?'

I glanced at the laptop myself now. There was a spreadsheet on the screen, but it was my own expenses; money I'd spent on getting the cottage looking liveable and a list of items I still needed. 'Yes,' I said firmly. 'Lots of work on. I've been answering emails all day.'

'Aye.' He knew I was lying. I had no idea how he knew, or how *I* knew he knew, but he did. 'So, come on then. Boots on and away, before Donal gets fed up with fighting off the tiny terrors.'

* * *

Donal was a short, plump man with a hairline that was receding so rapidly that it almost made a noise. While Innis put the kettle on and Magnus and Torstein leaned against various walls and talked about something dairy-related, he twinkled at me in a professional way. 'So you're wanting to sell?'

'Yes. As soon as possible, actually.'

Donal had a rather high-pitched voice, with an Edinburgh accent. It sounded hard-edged and urbane against the soft Orcadian tones of Magnus and Torstein, now onto something to do with sheep. 'Well, I could come over the day after tomorrow and take some pictures, do you a valuation? Would that suit?'

'Don't rush the girl, Donal.' Innis brought mugs over and put them on the table. In the little room off the hallway there was the sound of plastic beakers hitting the floor; a toddler wailed and Innis seized a mop. 'You're not in that much of a hurry, are you, Brid?'

I watched with interest, mildly concerned that she was going to use the mop to wedge the children apart, but she only needed it to clear up some spilled juice that had been causing the ruckus.

'I can't stay much longer,' I said. 'I need to get back home.'

There was a moment of quiet. Even the fighting toddlers resumed their squabbling in a purely physical form, and the farm talk had stopped. Finally Magnus said, 'She knew about the baby, Innis.'

Innis had been coming back over the child gate, with the mop held out like a jousting lance. She stopped, straddling the gate and the head dipped, as though paying tribute.

'I didn't!' I felt obliged to defend myself, although what I was defending myself against, other than a blackcurrant-soaked mop head, I wasn't sure. 'I thought that... I mean, I assumed...'

'I only suspected myself, last week.' Innis' voice was very low. 'Did the test yesterday.'

They were all looking at me now. I narrowed my eyes at Magnus. This was *stupid*. 'Anyway.' I tried to make my voice firm. 'That's got nothing to do with anything. I need to sell the cottage and get back to York.'

'Oh, aye, that's why we asked you up to the house.' Innis laid down the mop and began shuffling through a drawer. 'We found...'

'*I* found,' Magnus put in mildly.

'All right, Magnus found some old pictures he thought you'd like to see.' She handed me a small folder, the sort my mum still fetched back from Boots when she'd had her film processed. Mum was rather 'old school' about technology. 'There's some of Jennet in there.'

There were photographs in the wallet. Varying vintages, judging by the different sizes and colourations; some black and white and small, as though taken by those old-fashioned cameras like the one my grandma had had, some large and garish.

I flicked through while I drank my tea. Tor, Magnus and Innis grouped at my shoulder and looked at the pictures with me, interjecting occasionally, whilst Donal stood on the other side of the kitchen, looking out of the window across to my cottage.

There were lots of photos of the cottage, looking smaller amid overgrown reeds and grasses, with the loch a dull mirror in the background. General scenic views, populated with cars from the seventies. A boat out on the water – 'That's your grandad, with your gran and our Uncle Allie' – a fishing fleet bobbing on steel waters, and then – 'There's Jennet.'

Two photographs, clearly taken moments apart. A woman in a long dress with an apron tied around her middle, hands on hips. Eyes challenging the camera, no trace of a smile on her face, just an expression that seemed to be judging the taker of the picture and finding them not only wanting, but desperate. Behind her, the door to the cottage stood slightly ajar and I found myself, ridiculously, tilting the picture to try to see further inside.

The woman looked capable. The type to milk a cow with one hand whilst stitching a wound with the other and carrying a baby on her back at the same time. A kind of ferocious independence had worn a little crease between her eyes and her expression seemed to dare the photographer to come any closer or she'd poke him with a broom handle.

Donal came over and took the photograph from my hand. 'She looks a bit like you,' he said cheerily.

'No, she doesn't,' I said quickly because this woman was elderly, grey-haired and, despite her direct gaze, slightly hunched.

'Aye, she does, a bit.' Magnus was peering over Donal's shoulder at the photograph. 'It's the expression.'

'Take no notice, Brid. He's being a bastard on purpose.' Innis took the sheaf of pictures from me and swiped Magnus around the head with them. 'What's rocked your boat, Magnus? You seen that wee kite Kizzie today?'

Magnus went a bit red around the ears and muttered about needing to get back to Kirkwall. Donal shuffled his feet and chinked mugs on the worktop. I wondered if he felt as embarrassed as I did.

'She's bad news, that one.' Torstein made one of his rare, non-agricultural pronouncements.

'She came to Orkney for me,' Magnus said, shortly. 'And now she's stuck.'

'You never asked her to come, though,' Innis observed, tucking the pictures back into the little wallet. 'You broke up with her. It was her decision to come here, and if she's finding it hard she can always go back.' She gave her brother-in-law a shrewd look. 'No need to feel guilty on that one's behalf.'

At this point, Donal must have swallowed some tea the wrong way. He had a sudden coughing fit and Innis had to give him several hefty thumps on the back before he could stand up straight, eyes streaming, apologising and with his sleeked-back hair flopping forwards over his high forehead. I silently thanked him for the interruption.

'Yes, well.' I cleared my throat. 'Excuse me for breaking up this edition of *The Orkney Soap Opera*, but I ought to get back and make sure the cottage is looking its best, if you're serious about coming to take pictures the day after tomorrow, Donal.'

'Oh, aye.' Donal raised his head and met my eye. His voice was raspy and hoarse from the coughing fit. 'I'll be round at ten.' He still had hold of the photograph of Jennet outside the cottage, as though it was a valuable antique that the rest of us just hadn't recognised yet. I wondered about asking him for it, but decided not to. It was just a picture, after all.

And she looked nothing like me.

I trudged back over the bog in my borrowed boots, vowing to make the cottage look like the best prospect for purchase on the whole Mainland. Maybe I could get some of those old photographs blown up and framed on the wall, I mused, picking my way over the dotted stones, almost unconsciously avoiding the suckier mud now. Then I shook my head. No. That would make the place look like it was trapped in time. As though I wanted to keep it as it had always been – it could only be more obvious if I put hay on the floor and took out the toilet. No. It needed to look like a house. Like a home.

The home in question smelled more strongly than ever of paint when I went in, with just an undercurrent of goose, so I left the door open and sat on the sofa with Jennet's black book on my lap. The wind had retreated from its usual full-on attempt to remove the walls and was a gentle, tickling breeze that occasionally brushed my cheek and the sun slithered in to decorate the floor with artisanal gleams of mica amid the sandstone slabs. For the first time, I wondered what Orkney would be like in the actual summer, with softer winds and warmth to the bright early dawns highlighting the red cliffs. Being able to walk upright and not squint into squally rain. Seeing the sea as a calm blue surround rather than viciously huge waves trying to wash away the scenery.

It was probably quite nice.

Then I shook myself. Nice it might be, but it wasn't for me. There was nothing here for me. Home was York, work and Mum and Dad; people needing me for tax returns, company and shopping expeditions. The crowded little house near the river, with Annie banging doors and Steve revising on every flat surface.

I sighed and went to unhook the tin bath. I needed a good soak and to plan how to show the cottage off to its best advantage for Donal and his camera.

10

I got up early the next morning amid a sneezing fit. The smell of paint didn't seem to be lessening, even though I'd left the door propped slightly open all night. I needed to make the place more inviting, to persuade Donal that it was worth a decent price, and so far it was giving off shades of industrial warehouse with undertones of barn and storage shed. What was it you had to do to make a place sell? I was sure I'd read somewhere you had to bake bread and make coffee or something? Well, I couldn't make bread and I certainly wasn't going to dash out and spend a fortune on a coffee machine, even if there had been somewhere to buy one.

A quick look in the cupboard didn't inspire me either. A microwave curry wouldn't give the air of homeliness I wanted, unless someone was hankering to move into a slightly seedy takeaway. Cooking had never really been my thing and I was wishing I'd paid more attention to my mother's attempts to drill the recipes for sponge cake and biscuits into me on wet Sunday afternoons. My mother had been trying to brainwash me into housewifery since I was twelve, and my resolute lack of success with the opposite sex, my affiliation for numbers and my avoidance of anything which involved an oven had been a source of disappointment to her ever since.

I looked at Jennet's book. From its place on the floor under the sofa, it had flopped open again, this time at a page listing ingredients for a 'skin tonic' which seemed to be mostly herbs and didn't seem to involve any cooking apart from gentle heating of a carrier oil to infuse the herbs. It didn't look as though it contained any elements I could burn or undercook, so I made an executive decision, kicked on my boots, and headed to Kirkwall.

Almond oil, that was easy enough. Calendula and chamomile were available from the little health food shop. Apparently I needed some nettles, but apart from nettle tea I couldn't find any, and I didn't even know what horsetail was, apart from the obvious, and I hadn't seen a single horse since I'd been here. Okay. Maybe fifty per cent would do. Less of a skin tonic and more of a condiment, but I'd just have to live with that, and anyway it was only so that I could make the place smell nice, I wasn't trying to open a spa.

The street was crowded. One of the enormous cruise ships must be docked, disgorging its city-worth of passengers on a shopping and culture-grabbing expedition, although it looked as though many of them were eschewing the culture part for the shopping opportunities. People stood outside shops admiring window displays of Orkney gin and local artwork, and I could see Magnus' shop door practically revolving with the stream of customers.

Someone caught at my elbow and, in a roundly American twang, asked me the way to the Bishop's Palace. I pointed and gave vague directions – to be honest, the ruined building loomed opposite the cathedral in an unavoidable way – to which the woman raised her eyebrows at me and said, 'I thought you'd be local. You sure *look* like a local!' before tripping her way off to where my pointed finger had waggled at the entry.

I clasped my purchases to my chest and breathed indignantly. I did *not* 'look like a local', whatever that might mean! The locals all wore sensible coats and probably did their shopping over the internet rather than stomping about in the elements. Then I looked down at myself, in my borrowed rubber boots, and the jacket that had got a streak of paint down the collar from close contact with a newly painted wall, and realised that, whilst I might not look like a local, I didn't exactly look like a qualified accountant with a string of clients and an encyclopaedic knowledge of tax clauses either. In fact, I looked more like a bag lady who'd dressed up to go out.

A small shop down a narrow side street caught my eye. In the window was a mannequin, wearing a smart 'city meets country' kind of dress. The sort of dress that I could imagine wearing to waft around my, as yet unknown, house in York, with a lot of skirt and a bodice that showed off any curves I might have. Which wasn't very many but the dress was making the plastic model look as though *she* had a bust, and I was fairly sure I was more shapely than a window dummy.

I went into the shop. The cruise brigade had clearly already been through because two women were hard at work replenishing shelves and refolding dropped sweaters. The inside of the shop smelled of tastefully diffused perfume and was filled with a 'seascape' soundtrack from, presumably, a hidden CD player, gulls calling and waves rippling. The walls were decorated with paintings of the sea amid the racks of clothing, large canvases daubed with greys and blues that managed to suggest the wash and swirl of eddies and currents so successfully that I had a momentary recurrence of seasickness. One or two of the paintings had clearly sold and been taken by recent customers because there were stretches of bare wall behind the cashmere department.

One of the folding women turned around on my entrance. 'Good morning!' she said brightly. It was the pregnant lady I'd seen talking to Magnus. Kizzie, had he said she was called? 'Or it might be afternoon now, I lose track. Can I help you?'

She was younger than I'd thought, younger than Magnus and me by some way. She had strawberry-blonde hair piled high on her head, wide blue eyes and the kind of clear fair skin that looks as though it is bathed in milk.

'I'm just looking,' I said.

She came in closer, arm arcing into her lower back for support. 'Are you the new witch?' she asked, and I wasn't sure whether to feel charmingly disarmed or horribly disgruntled. 'You've moved into Jennet's cottage up at Midness?'

'Is there a flashing sign on my head or something?' I settled for 'mildly annoyed'.

'No, no. Just Magnus mentioned you a few times. And you're wearing Innis' boots.'

I looked down at the yellow wellies with the blue ducks on the ankle. She had me bang to rights on that front. 'Well, I'm just staying in Jennet's cottage while I get it ready to sell,' I said. 'Donal's coming over to value it tomorrow.'

I didn't bother to explain who Donal was. It would have been a waste of breath in a place this small.

'Lovely!' She had an English accent and I'd clearly already been here too long because it sounded strange to my Orcadian-attuned ears. 'So.' She looked me up and down. 'Are you looking for something to wear? Or a picture? This one would look good in the cottage.' She went to the wall and, after a brief struggle, pulled down a small painting. 'It's a view from the coast near Midness. I've been commissioned to do some pictures up there, and this is one of the first.' She turned it towards the light and frowned. 'I don't like this one, though. So it's for sale.'

I ignored that. 'Did you paint all these?' I remembered Magnus saying that Kizzie was an artist just too late to keep the disbelief from my voice.

'Mmm. I like painting the sea.' She looked down into the picture that was currently resting on her bump. 'Lots of blue. I sometimes do the sky too.'

I wasn't quite sure whether the slightly simple thing was an act she was putting on for my benefit, or not. Kizzie had a high-pitched, sing-song way of speaking, almost childlike, and the wide blue eyes didn't seem to hold any guile, so I had to assume that she was always like this. 'They're lovely pictures, you're very talented.'

'I am, aren't I?' She twisted the picture to and fro. 'I can't do much else, though. Oh, apart from this.' She pointed at the bump. 'I'm going to be a mummy.'

I absolutely did not know how to react to Kizzie. She seemed to combine the talents of J. W. Turner with the mind of a Teletubby and it was not a combination that I'd ever dealt with before. I wondered what on earth Magnus had seen in her, and then berated myself. She was very pretty, verging on the beautiful, and, apart from the bump, slender. Magnus was, no doubt, as capable of having his head turned by long hair and a winsome expression as any other man.

Plus, she clearly did have artistic talent. Maybe they'd bonded over techniques. I tried not to think about it. 'I need to buy some boots,' I said firmly. 'I can't keep wearing Innis'.' Well, not if people could recognise me by them, I couldn't. I tried not to think about the fact that I'd put off buying wellies because I wasn't staying long enough to need a pair of my own. Big rubber boots were a necessity I was getting used to.

'Oh, we've got lots.' Kizzie, light, despite the pregnancy bulk, danced me over to a corner where a selection of boots ran from the pragmatic rubber through to eye-wateringly expensive leather.

'And you could get some proper trousers to go with them. Your legs must be freezing!'

They hadn't been, but I still staggered out of the shop carrying two new outfits and a boot box containing a pair of what I had been assured were stylish, yet practical, full-length boots.

Whatever else Kizzie may be, she was one hell of a saleswoman. I'd also bought the little picture of the sea, although where or how I was going to hang it on walls that were only perpendicular by accident I wasn't sure.

11

The smell of paint seemed to have intensified when I got back. I put Jennet's book on the worktop and followed the instructions to put all my scented ingredients in a pan to infuse gently. Cushie and the goslings came to see what I was doing, pecked up a few dropped herbs and then went out, meaning the cottage immediately smelled a lot better.

I stood in the kitchen and stirred. Then my phone, which I had taken to generally ignoring, buzzed a message. Work.

You haven't answered the email. Please do so before close tonight.

That didn't sound good. I opened my emails and there was the work one. A question that was so banal and unimportant, regarding the filing of accounts for one of my clients, that it seemed designed only to ensure that I was actually checking my mail daily. I answered, a quick one-line mail to confirm that everything had been completed and turned in on time, and then added:

I am on annual leave. Questions should be addressed to the
team.

Then I felt a momentary pride. I was needed. I was the person
they turned to. There was a quiet comfort in that, in knowing that
things didn't just roll on without me, obliterating my presence
under the steamroller of HMRC's constant demands. I had a place
in the York accountancy world.

I looked around the little kitchen, where steam from the
warming oil was beginning to make the windows fug up; tiny worktop, strangely antiquated cooker and kettle and a microwave that
seemed to have been made out of wood and aluminium. Barely
enough floorspace to move around. Why hadn't someone just
knocked through into the larder – it would double the floorspace
and mean that there was another window? Or knocked the whole
of this extension down and built another, larger and more practical
one, with a proper bathroom and a functional kitchen?

I took the warm oil and herbs off the hob and set it aside, next
to my phone, which sat on the worktop, silent now and almost
threatening. I decided to text my mother, as I hadn't heard from her
for so long that I wondered if she'd forgotten I'd been exiled up
here. Or, horrible thought, maybe there had been an accident? Or
something had happened to Dad, and she hadn't had the chance to
let me know, being absorbed in hospital routines and dashing
about? Without me there, keeping her organised and Dad enter-
tained, they tended to go to pieces a little. She may even have lost
her phone.

Hi Mum!
How are you getting on? Did you manage the shopping on
your own?
Bx

I usually took her shopping on a Tuesday evening, helping her find the best bargains and carrying the heavy bags. Before I'd come up here, I'd taken her for an extra big shop which would hopefully take her and Dad through until I got back, and she could pick up bits at the little local shops in the small town where they lived. They'd never got the hang of internet shopping and relied on me to keep a list of what they needed from week to week.

There was no immediate answer. I tried not to worry. Mum, in common with many older people, didn't keep her phone in her hand, alert for any incoming messages. She was quite capable of putting it down on the side and leaving it there for an entire day without even looking it, and then I had the horrible thought that that was exactly what I'd done with mine, and slipped it into my pocket. It wouldn't do for me to start living like an elderly semi-recluse, just because I was occupying the cottage of an elderly semi-recluse. Work needed me to be reachable. Mum and Dad needed me. Everyone was just assuming I was too busy marketing the cottage to talk. They knew I'd be back sooner if I was uninterrupted, that was all.

The kitchen smelled lovely now. Of warm oil and herbs, like the kind of smells they puff out at expensive hotels, the smells that make you feel relaxed just by sniffing – that give the illusion of a Mediterranean garden in summer, even when you're sitting in a foyer in Birmingham. Lovely.

I carried the pan through to the living room, doing a kind of 'wafty' move as I went to try to get the smell as far as possible. I waved the pan over the sofa, and was trailing it past the windows to try to infuse the smell into the walls, when I glanced out and saw a boat on the loch.

For some reason it gave me an eerie feeling, with a tightening across my shoulders and a prickle of the hair on my neck, which in itself was odd. It was a loch. Big body of water. Seeing a boat on it wasn't strange. But the way the little rowing boat drifted along, coming closer whilst sticking to the edges of the water so closely that it clipped the stiff reeds, made me wonder whether I was looking through history.

Then the boat came closer still and I could see that it was being rowed by a woman who was struggling with the oars in a decidedly un-hallucinatory way. She didn't look as though she'd ever previously been in charge of a boat that didn't bob amid bath time bubbles, and the way the older man, who was the boat's only other occupant, was evidently shouting at her wasn't helping.

I went outside, surprising Cushie, who'd been basking against the wall of the cottage while the goslings grazed, and around to the back where the loch lapped only centimetres from the wall, just in time to intercept the boat putting in on a sandy spit, and the woman clambering out.

'Can I help you?' I asked, in my iciest landowner tones. I really did not now want to find out that the loch was some kind of public right of way and everyone and his dog was entitled to pitch up outside my windows.

'It's my dad,' the woman said breathlessly as she tugged the boat closer onto the shore until it beached with a grinding noise against the pebbles.

'Aye,' agreed the elderly man, who was still sitting like a minor royal in the boat, watching his daughter dragging without any attempt to help. 'Come to see the witch.'

'And roads and cars are out, because?' I was still being chilly. This was getting ridiculous.

The sun, temporary at best, went and hid behind a big cloud and the luminosity died from the scene. The liminal stretch of water became sullen and grey, the wind twisted the surface into trails of white until the loch began to look like a used ashtray. The woman shivered.

'You'd better come inside,' I said grudgingly, mostly because the breeze was getting down my neck and I didn't want to have to stand here through yet another rainstorm, trying to convince yet more locals that I was no more witch than they were.

'I'm Margaret,' said the woman, more middle-aged than her efforts with the oars had made her look. 'And Dad is Fergus.'

'Mr Flett to you, witch,' said the man.

'And Dad insisted that we come to see you, but we had to come the old way.' Margaret examined her blistered hands ruefully.

'Over the water,' Fergus Flett said lugubriously. He had very blue eyes in a lined face, but his cheeks were sunken and there was an ominous yellow tint to his skin. 'There has to be effort put in, otherwise it's not right.'

'That would carry more weight if it was you rowing,' Margaret said snippily. 'It's not me that needs treatment.'

'Aye, well.' It didn't sound like agreement. 'I'm not long for this world.'

By the looks of it, his daughter would probably see him off if whatever was pulling his cheeks inwards and giving his eyes that distant look that meant pain was perpetual didn't get him first. She shot her father a look of mingled exasperation and desperation, but there was a fondness in the way she helped him from the boat that made me think of my own dad, currently in a lengthy remission from symptoms but still prone to tiredness and unable to walk far. Mum hadn't replied to my text. I was going to have to ring them.

'I hope that Donal won't mind us using his land to launch the boat,' Margaret said, sounding a bit worried.

'It's the old way,' Fergus grunted with the effort of climbing onto the bank. 'He'll just have to get used to it, people coming over the loch to the witch. If he didn't like it, he shouldn't have bought that shoreline.'

I led the way around the cottage and in through the door,

noting that Cushie had taken herself off somewhere, although the goslings were happily chirping around in a puddle.

'Oh, it's lovely!' Margaret stopped just inside the door.

'Yes, yes, very *Homes and Gardens*, now get in out of the wind, girl.' Fergus hobbled past her and into the living room where he promptly sat himself down, uninvited, on the sofa.

'But it is. It's so... relaxing, somehow.' Margaret hovered about, until I pointed her towards one of the chairs. 'And isn't that one of Kizzie's paintings?'

I just could *not* get used to the way everyone seemed to know about everyone else here on the islands. York isn't exactly a huge city, but I regularly met people who'd lived there all their lives that I'd never come across before. Hell, I'd even gone out with the brother of a girl I'd been at school with and he and I both swore we'd never set eyes on one another before the night we met at her birthday party. Here, on Orkney, it was like there were only a dozen or so people, all circulating in different jackets and rubber noses and trying to pretend to be a population.

'Look, I'm rather busy,' I said, trying to pretend I was, 'so if you could tell me why you're here?'

Margaret looked uneasy, but Fergus launched happily into his story. 'I'm diagnosed, bit of liver, bit of kidney, bit of pancreas, whatever that is. I'm like a bloody casserole, not a human. But it's all failing and there's not much the doctors can do.'

'Then I really can't see what I...' I tried.

'I'm not asking you to cure me. You're a witch, not a bloody saint. I just want something to make me a bit more comfortable. I get these pains, you see.' Fergus talked right over the top of me. From Margaret's expression, this was his usual means of communication. 'All over. Hands and feet swell. Bones hurt, that kind of thing.'

'Dad remembers the old witch,' Margaret said.

'Aye. Jennet. I was at school with her nephew, Johnnie. We used to come by here after school and she'd chase us off with a clothes prop.' He gave a happy sigh. 'Och, those were the days.' Then he fixed me with a stare that was surprisingly intense. 'We've been waiting a long time for the new witch,' he said, and his voice was strangely urgent. 'So we're glad you're here. Even if you are English,' he finished, curling his lip over the word as though it was synonymous with 'feeble minded and ineffectual'.

'Look. I'm just here to sell the cottage,' I said. 'I'm not a witch. Not even a bit. I'm an accountant.'

Fergus settled himself complacently against my new, toning, cushions. 'You're in the witch's cottage,' he said evenly. 'You're the witch.'

Margaret caught my eye and looked pleadingly at me. Don't try to fight him, her expression told me. Just go along with it and maybe he'll be happy. Or as happy as he ever is, which isn't very, but he might stop making my life a misery.

I thought about Nathan, happy with a jar of raspberry and lemon tea, and wondered. But then I looked at Fergus and decided against anything internal. I had no idea if he was on a special diet and I didn't want to give him something that might work against any conventional drugs he may be taking. So I fell back on the only other avenue open to me.

'I'll see what I can find,' I said and hurried into the kitchen, closing the door behind me and surprising Cushie again, this time with her beak in the herb bag. 'Bugger *off*,' I hissed at her, poking her with my toe. She honked and pecked at me, but with no particular ferocity, and I scrabbled through the cupboard in search of a vessel.

All I could find was a small plastic pot, half full of salt. I tipped the salt out onto the work surface in a grainy pile, rinsed out the pot and then tipped in a little of my almond oil and herb room fragrance. The bits of chamomile floated to the surface while the calendula sank, forming a kind of 'oil sandwich'. I contemplated sieving them out but then thought that they gave the mixture a herbal integrity and left them in, put the lid on the pot and shook it vigorously.

It was still warm. 'Get someone to help you rub it into your hands,' I said, because this was as far as Jennet's book had advised. 'And anywhere else that hurts.'

'How often?' Fergus held the little pot up to the light dubiously.

'Er. Twice a day?'

With stiff fingers, he unscrewed the lid and sniffed the mixture. 'It's a bit girlie,' he said. 'I'm going to smell like a bloody footballer.'

'If it helps, Dad...' Margaret now threw me a thankful glance.

'Yes, yes.'

I made them both a cup of tea. The wind was increasing. I didn't want Margaret to have to start rowing back in a storm; I had visions of her doing a Grace Darling through massive waves, although it was unlikely the loch would go to such extremes. The least I could do was wait until the weather passed, which, around here, usually only took about ten minutes.

The sun duly reappeared, and Margaret carried the cups through to the kitchen, while I persuaded the grumbling boiler to part with enough hot water to let me wash up.

'Thank you,' she said quietly and almost shyly. 'He means well, you know.'

I raised my eyebrows, about to ask her if she had any kind of life away from her acerbic father, but, before I could, she saw the salt I'd tipped onto the work surface, and gave a little squeak.

'Oh! Are those... *runes*?' Her voice was a breathy mixture of shock and awe.

I looked. Cushie had clearly hopped up onto the top and had

an experimental peck after I'd ejected her from the herbs. The salt was spread about, and there were big flappy footprints in it.

Margaret was looking at me with huge eyes and her mouth open. I didn't know what to say. Admitting that a goose had been prodding around in my foodstuffs was going to make me sound like the worst housekeeper in the world, so was letting her think that I knew anything about magical symbols better, or worse?

'Um,' I said.

'We thought... I mean, *I* thought, I'm never sure whether Dad believes or not, but, well, when the word went out... when it started to spread that you were the new witch... I thought it was all bullshit, you know?' Margaret still sounded slightly winded. 'In this day and age and all. But...' she waved a hand at the salt-strewn surface, 'you really *are* doing magic. Salt, that's for protection, isn't it?' A shy smile. 'I was interested, as a girl. We all went through a Wiccan phase, didn't we? Oh!' A hand went over her mouth. 'I'm sorry! I didn't mean to insult your beliefs or anything!'

I didn't know whether I should laugh or cry. I settled for making some noncommittal noises and internally vowing to lock that bloody goose out of the house next time she set webbed foot beyond the larder. Margaret and Fergus left, him still complaining broadly and her sighing heavily, but at least the wind had dropped sufficiently that their little rowing boat wouldn't be breasting the waves like an Atlantic icebreaker.

When I was quite sure they'd gone and weren't going to pop back for something else, I sat down heavily on the sofa and put my head in my hands.

This was *stupid*. No, more than stupid. It was *ridiculous*. Why was I going along with everyone believing that I was a witch? *Why?* Was it really so difficult to shake my head and tell them all to stop being silly; that I was turning the cottage around for a quick sale and then heading back to the overheated office by the racecourse to sit and smell Damien's cheese and onion crisps and listen to Dymphna arguing quietly but vituperatively with her boyfriend over the phone?

I found myself staring out of the window. The sun was poking shyly out from between veils of cloud stretched as taut as violin strings, slices and streaks of light formed corridors across the surface of the loch, highlighting the water into pools of green across the leaden surface. The far horizon faded down into the distant sea and the wind bent everything vertical into complicated shapes. Then I shook my head and went to tidy the kitchen.

12

The next morning, I threw the door open wide to greet Donal, who was standing in the grass looking dubiously at Cushie and the goslings.

'It's all right,' I lied. 'They just like to peck around out here. Come in.'

Fortunately the morning had chosen to be bright and dry and the light was twinkling in through the windows, deflected from the mirror-glass surface of the loch. I'd rewarmed the herb-and-oil mixture, pulled all the furniture into the most appealing positions, and placed Kizzie's painting on one of the broad ledges.

The doors to the cupboard-bed stood open, with a titillating peek at the quilt inside, the kitchen was immaculate and I'd hidden the tin bath round the back of the cottage. Jennet's home looked cute, smelled delicious and I wasn't, therefore, quite ready for Donal's immediate reaction.

'It's a wee bit restrictive.'

'Restrictive? Only if you're going to hold ballroom dancing competitions. For one person...' I quickly corrected myself, 'or a couple, it's a lovely place to live.'

I saw him notice Kizzie's painting, propped on its shelf. He moved, as though to have a closer look, but then seemed to think better of it. 'Hmmmm.' Donal poked the wall next to the picture. 'Typical farm worker's cottage, early- to mid-eighteenth century, I'd say. Have you had anyone else to look at it?'

I didn't want to admit that all the estate agents I'd looked at had had windows full of cottages that were a lot bigger, and better decorated, for, what looked to a York resident's eye, giveaway prices. 'Er, no, not yet.'

'Well.' He suddenly sounded perkier. 'Let's see what we can do, shall we? I'll take some pictures, while the sun's out.'

On his very shiny shoes, which had clearly suffered during the crossing of the bog, he began poking around, with me following behind like King Wenceslas' page, ostensibly to answer any questions he may have, but really to stop him opening any difficult doors.

Donal said 'hmmm' a lot. He prodded a pen into gaps in the woodwork, took a few pictures with his phone, said 'hmmm' again, and then turned to me with a radiant smile.

'I think I can shift the place for you,' he said, brightly. 'Of course, it won't be easy. No land with it, access is difficult, no real bedroom, you've got damp in the kitchen and that bathroom – well. No bath is what I'm, essentially, saying here.' Another twinkly smile. 'But someone might want it for storage, although it's *quite* far from the road, isn't it?'

Storage? *Storage*? And I'd painted the walls *especially*… 'You don't think it could go for a holiday home?' I asked, feeling a bit feeble.

In answer, Donal crossed the floor and opened the door to the toilet, in its little cubbyhole. 'No.'

From beyond the kitchen came the unmistakable sound of a large goose and three goslings squeezing themselves back in through an as yet unmended window. We stood and waited for the noise to stop.

'It will probably go for a few thousand.' Donal looked upwards into the roof, where, I now noticed, a large spider's web swung like a makeshift chandelier from the rafters. 'Might get them up to twenty, if the roof's sound.'

I opened my mouth to mention the prices being charged at other estate agencies, then remembered the places those prices were being charged for. Places with little bedrooms in the eaves, proper fitted bathrooms and cosy seating areas around open fires. Closed my mouth.

'It's got history,' I said weakly.

'As a witch's cottage,' Donal said sternly. 'Puts people off, that kind of thing. Bit worried they might be cursed if they buy it!' He gave a laugh in his rather squeaky voice that I was beginning to hate.

'Would it be easy to get permission to build a proper bathroom?' I had no idea about Scottish or Orcadian planning laws.

Donal turned his mouth down at the edges and pouted extravagantly. 'Mid-eighteenth-century cottage with history as the witch's dwelling?' He made sad eyes at me. 'I think you'll find it's a listed building. Plus Innis and Tor may object and that kind of thing can drag on for *years*.'

'Oh.'

Inside my head was the plughole-exiting sound of my dreams for my own house in York. At this rate, I'd be lucky to cover my costs for the time off work and the trip up here, let alone the paint and the new sofa.

'But if you'd like to sign here, for us to have exclusive rights to the sale, then I'll see what I can do.' Donal twinkled again. 'You never know, someone may offer for it as a field shelter to put ponies in. Very popular, that kind of thing, I understand.'

'Is it?' I asked dully, looking at the piece of paper he held out in front of me. I'd got the pen in my hand almost before I knew what I was doing and was poised to put my signature on the little line, when there came the sound of breaking china from the kitchen and a ferocious amount of honking and flapping. 'Excuse me a second.'

The cupboard had swung slightly open, and one of the goslings had somehow managed to get in amid the battered old plates and tureens that nobody had cleared out. Two plates were smashed beyond repair on the kitchen floor and a young goose was standing on one leg, the other held up and dripping blood.

I forgot about Donal and cleaned the goose's leg with a cloth to check the injury. The little gosling, becoming more feathery and less fluffy by the second, lay against the crook of my elbow and let me, nibbling occasionally at the toggle of my hooded top.

'You'll be fine,' I told it, stroking the top of its head, where fluff still outnumbered feather and made it look like a soft punk. 'Just a little nick, that's all. Stay out of the cupboard in future.'

The goose twittered, a strange half-honk, half-cheep that reminded me that Donal was still standing in the living room. I went back out and he immediately thrust the contract for sale at me. I still had goose blood on my hands and didn't want to take it. 'Look, give me a couple of days,' I said. 'I want to get the place on the market before I leave Orkney, but I need to get the geese out of the larder before I go.'

Donal twitched at his jacket, pulling it down over a small paunch. 'But you'll come back to me then?' he asked. 'I mean, I can start preparing the adverts and doing the paperwork?'

I thought about the pathetic amount of money he'd said the cottage was worth and wondered about trying a few other estate agencies first. Then I thought about the cute, accessible little places in their windows, and lost all hope. 'Yes, I'll get back to you.' I began hustling him towards the door. 'I just want to make sure the goslings will be all right first.'

I presumed that Innis had told him about Cushie, because he didn't react as though wanting to eject avian wildlife from food storage was at all unusual. He left with a cheery wave and picked his way carefully back over the makeshift path to where he'd parked his very shiny car out near the farmhouse. I watched him go.

'Well,' I said, to nobody, because Cushie had taken the goslings back into the larder and was making 'settling down' noises in there. Up to twenty thousand pounds for this place. It wouldn't buy me a house outright, but it would add to my savings, go towards a deposit. It wasn't nothing, it was more money than a lot of people had, and I should be grateful. I should sign the contract, leave it all in Donal's hands, and run for the border.

Shouldn't I?

The strange quiet calm of the building wrapped itself around me like a comforting cardigan. Yes. Yes, of course I should. I'd done what I could here, the cottage was presentable and tidy. Someone could buy it and make whatever they wanted out of it – feed store, weekend retreat, let *them* bear the brunt of the cost of planning permissions, building work, architects and decorators. I'd be a few thousand pounds better off, and we wouldn't have it hanging around in the back of our minds like a distant relative that everyone thought should be in a home, but nobody wanted to talk about.

Or – I looked out of the windows across the now-smooth surface of the loch, where fingers of reed broke the cloud reflection into pixelated fractions. Around the margins, bog cotton poked its gosling-fluff into the breeze and flexed into convoluted shapes. Birds waded and argued. Maybe we could *keep* the cottage? For... for weekends? Family holidays?

Then I remembered how far we were from home, and that any

weekends would be almost entirely taken up by travelling; how the boggy access would make the cottage inaccessible for Dad's chair. No. Plus, money. If I scraped everything together, maybe asked for a raise, I might just be able to get a mortgage for a tiny new build on one of the estates going up just beyond the ring road.

Suddenly the thought of my own house didn't fill me with the anticipation that it once had. Perhaps I'd used up all my interior decorating mojo on painting these four walls and arranging cushions. But Donal seemed to think that it might take a while to sell Jennet's cottage, so maybe we could use it *until* it sold? After all, it might take years.

I had no idea why this thought was so cheering, until I saw Magnus looming in the doorway again. Yes, I had to admit it, I'd got a crush the size of the cathedral on this tall, dark-haired man, even though our only contact seemed to revolve around banalities of wall colour and him teasing me over how ill-equipped I was to be here. And yet here he was. Again. I had no idea what he thought of me.

'Well, then.' Magnus stepped inside and I had to turn away from my perusal of the loch and its environs or risk having him tap me on the shoulder. 'How did it go? I should point out that I'm not a massive fan of Donal, but I'm the bearer of family questions. In other words, Innis is nosy as hell about what he said and she's sent me over to find out, "but tactfully" in her words. So, this is me being tactful. How much is it worth?'

'Almost nothing.' I flopped down onto the sofa, with a concomitant squeeze of cushions issuing from underneath me. 'Donal makes it sound as though I'll be lucky to sell at all. Maybe I could raffle it?'

'Och, someone will want it.' Magnus sat beside me and looked around. 'Probably.'

'But it's lovely!' I almost wailed. 'Look at it! In York this would be worth half a million!'

'Really?' Magnus pushed his hands through his hair and stared down at the bare flagstone floor. There was quite a large splash of goose poo that I'd missed. 'I've never been that far south. Maybe one day you could show me this paragon of house prices.'

'All right, maybe not half a million. But quite a bit. A builder would buy it, shove another storey in and a flashy kitchen and turn it around for a huge profit.'

We sat in silence for a moment. The wind hissed through the reeds outside and I could hear the clap and slosh of water lapping against the sunken timbers. A bird cried, long and lonely, into the sky.

'Are you *sure* Tor and Innis wouldn't want to buy it?' I turned to Magnus and surprised him looking at me. 'For whatever they used to use it for? Or, or they could make it into a Wendy house for the toddlers?'

'You've seen the toddlers. Would you trust that lot close to water?' His eyes were dark in the limited light of the room.

'This is Orkney! The whole *place* is close to water!' I was practically wailing now. 'I just want to get it on the market and go back to York,' I added, more quietly, aware that the words lacked a certain rigour now.

'Why?'

'*Why?*' I almost levitated from the cushions at the ridiculousness of the question. 'It's where I live.' I began ticking items off on my fingers. 'It's where my job is – and they need me back as they keep sending me emails to remind me.' Okay, this was a bit of a stretch, but it illustrated my point. 'My mum and dad need me too. They rely on me for – well, for company and shopping, I go round most evenings to chat and make sure everything is all right. Dad has multiple sclerosis and so he's not as mobile as he used to be.

My... friends are there,' I added, hoping he wouldn't quiz me too hard on this because they really weren't. 'It's where I live,' I repeated, in a tone that indicated the finality of the statement.

Magnus shrugged. 'All right,' he said. 'You've no need to go on about it.'

'I'm not!' I protested, and then saw the slow grin spreading over his face. 'You are very annoying, do you know that?'

'Oh, aye. Innis tells me every five minutes.'

He turned the grin on me and I made a disapproving face, even though it was very hard not to smile at the utter audacity of the man.

'So, then,' he went on, settling himself more comfortably. 'How are they managing without you?'

'Who?' I'd been so busy making my expression neutral so he wouldn't see how much I was enjoying his light bantering. Nobody bantered with me. I had to focus too hard at work for banter to feature.

'Your parents. You seem very concerned about them, very keen to rush back. Are they not coping, then?' Magnus leaned back and made a few experimental moves against the cushions, as though he half expected the sofa to collapse underneath him.

I opened my mouth to say that they were all right, then realised that I had absolutely no idea. Our contact had been a couple of messages from me, which had gone unanswered, and yet I wasn't panicking and phoning home or calling the police to do a wellness check. *Why not?* I *knew* how much they needed me, yet I'd been here for days now without a word.

I felt my cheeks go warm. Deep down, I knew why I hadn't been texting, emailing and calling every night, and it made me ashamed of myself to admit it, even quietly in my heart. I wanted them to miss me. My being here was all down to Mum, she'd sent me here and not listened to my objections. She'd behaved as though my work was a mere irritation and pretended that she and Dad would be fine without me. So *let them.* Let them see how much I did for them, how I acted as referee for their spats about fried eggs, how I helped with the shopping and listened to them complain.

It was beginning to worry me more than a little that they weren't begging me to come home yet. Maybe something really *had* happened to them?

'So then, why did you come back to Orkney? After Glasgow? Couldn't you have stayed there and made jewellery, or has silver been banned everywhere with pronounceable names?'

I sounded a little bit sharp, but he'd rattled me. I *was* needed in York, of course I was.

Magnus stretched. 'I thought about it. But, y'know, Innis was pregnant with Freya and Tor needed a hand with the farm and all.' He leaned forward now, elbows on his knees, and he seemed to be looking at something other than the goose-stained floor, something that made his eyes distant and gave his mouth bracketing lines. 'Orkney is in my blood,' he said quietly. 'There's nowhere else I want to be.'

'York is very nice,' I said spiritedly. 'Lots of history and... and... the river.'

He gave a sort of hmmph of a laugh. 'History. You call a bit of Roman invasion and some Vikings history? Skara Brae was built when Stonehenge was just a twinkle in a Neolithic eye, and the Vikings were farming here before they went down to invade you southerners.'

He had a point, but it would have killed me to admit it.

'Would you like to come for a drink?' Magnus asked suddenly, whilst I was still trying to compose a retort. 'A proper one, I mean, in a bar with music and other people, not like another cup of tea while Innis tries to find out how much longer you're staying.'

'A drink?' He'd taken the wind out of my sails, which was odd because there was plenty of it elsewhere from the sound of it hitting the walls outside.

'Yes. We've even heard of cocktails up here, although I warn you now, don't ask Tommy for Sex on the Beach, he's a wee bit literal. Look, I'll pick you up tonight, about seven, aye?'

He was already standing up, leaving a Magnus-shaped dent in the cushions, and then he was gone, letting the door clonk itself back into the latch.

A flat, flappy sound told me that Cushie had come into the room, probably in case the door closing had indicated that I had gone out to spread some more goose feed around on the grass.

'What?' I looked up in time to surprise her eyeing up the sofa. 'Don't you bloody dare.'

A ruffle of feathers and a rolling eye told me she'd be embarrassed to be seen amid my collection of clashing soft furnishings, then she sauntered over and pecked the door until I got up and opened it, whereupon she sashayed her way across the threshold, dolloping a goodly helping of goose poo on the way.

I stared at it, then at my seemingly worthless four walls. How *dare* Donal be so dismissive of the cottage? It was cute, it was adorable; it was the perfect size for one person to live in and the view over the loch was – well. When the sun was shining, it was lovely. Okay, there was a goose in the larder and only one bed, but maybe we could rent it out for honeymooners? Honeymooning ornithologists?

Then I thought of Innis' face if I told her we were going to keep Jennet's cottage and could she manage to clean, tidy and administer the paperwork necessary for a holiday home, and changed my mind again.

Maybe I should ask Mum? My phone sat, still silent, on the window shelf and I felt myself twitch towards it. I could ask for her advice as to what to do with the cottage, couldn't I? After all, this was her family, Jennet had been her great-aunt, maybe Mum had ideas about what could be done with the cottage if it wouldn't sell?

I stared at the silent phone for a few moments. Nobody had rung. If they'd really wanted to give opinions on what to do, Mum would have been calling every five minutes, so I was on my own here. The thought echoed. *I was on my own here.* They hadn't called and they hadn't texted. What if both of them were hospitalised? I took a deep breath and rational thought returned – someone would have contacted me, a neighbour, the hospital. No, Mum was probably not wanting to disturb me, wanting me to get everything finished as quickly as possible so I could go home.

The thought that *I* may have had a dreadful accident and be lying in a hospital far from York wouldn't have crossed her mind. The tiny embers of resentment that I was here at all fanned into a sudden flame of anger again. *Let them see how difficult life was when I wasn't there.*

I closed the door, ignoring the windswept goose on the step, and went to sit down with Jennet's notebook, a cup of tea and a skin scrub, just in case there really *were* cocktails.

13

I squeezed myself into the metal tub again for a bath, so by the time Magnus showed up at the door, as the evening was slanting its long-shadowed path across the field, I felt halfway decent for an outing.

'Where are we going?' I asked, as we climbed up into the cab of his van. 'It had better be worth getting my new gear on for.'

'Yes, I noticed that.' Magnus gave a short, approving nod. 'You look properly dressed. I heard you'd been to Kizzie's.'

I opened my mouth to retort, but realised that there wasn't much I could say, apart from 'yes'. I was wearing a pair of soft cord trousers and a brushed cotton shirt that were warm, practical and, I thought, fairly smart. I'd toyed with the idea of a dress – after all, cocktails – but decided in my post-bath chill that I'd rather be warm indoors and able to function outside than look glam and quietly freeze in transit.

'Kizzie's very... er, she's quite... um, chatty, isn't she?' I didn't want to diss his ex, and she'd been nothing but pleasant to me. 'Very good at selling things.'

'She's fun,' he said shortly.

Oh, I thought. You don't want to talk about her. I wonder why? 'Was it a bad break-up?'

He sighed. 'We'd run our course, but it wasn't easy to split up. Kizzie has attachment issues. We knew we weren't right for one another, but she's had a difficult life and she found it hard to break up. I think that's why she followed me here, not so much that she wanted me back, more that I was what she knew.'

'And now she's pregnant.'

'Aye. No idea who the father is. Someone local, I presume. Look, here we go.' Obviously trying to change the subject, he pointed ahead at a building which stood alone on the roadside, light in every window and the faint sound of music coming from an open front door. People sat outside in the shelter of the wall; groups bent close together, couples wound around one another, a few dancing to the half-heard trails of Dua Lipa, as we parked and climbed out.

Magnus was instantly greeted by just about everyone, while I tagged along behind like a small boat bobbing in the wake of a liner. I was, however, pleased to see that I'd apparently made the right clothing choices, there wasn't a cocktail frock to be seen and apart from a few linen dresses worn with sturdy tights, very few legs on display.

Inside, the low-beamed building was crowded and the air thick with the Orcadian burred tones. This wasn't a place for tourists, obviously, it was a drinking establishment so made for locals that it had a vague *League of Gentlemen* air about it and I was slightly surprised that I wasn't prodded and exclaimed at as Magnus towed me towards the bar. But apart from a few remarks aimed at him, which he brushed off with a casual 'aye' or an inclination of the head, we were left alone.

'Wine?' he asked, and I nodded. The air was thick with the smell of beer, of old carpets and hot wood and I didn't think I'd press the cocktail point, because it might just consist of tipping up all the bottles behind the bar into one glass.

Magnus pointed me to a table and I sat down, banging my knees on the metal underside as I squeezed my way in. He went off to the bar, and the person I'd squeezed in next to leaned across.

'Hello!'

It was Nathan, of the lacking confidence and the raspberry tea. He was wearing an open-collar shirt and had his hair swept back.

'Hello,' I replied, slightly diffident, in case he was going to accuse me of poisoning him or to protest that my 'charm' hadn't worked. 'How are you?'

'Och, I'm grand.' He was almost spilling out of his shirt, I noticed, and looked as though several years of maturity had caught up with him at once. 'This is Morag.' Nathan waved a hand at the girl sitting next to him on the other side. She smiled.

I frowned. Morag? Hadn't it been a Sofia that he'd been wanting to capture with his dubious allure?

He clearly noticed my puzzlement and leaned in close. 'I went to the party in Stromness,' he whispered. 'Took your potion and everything. Sofia wasn't there, someone said she'd got some allergy rash or something, didn't want to be seen out, but I didn't want to waste the spell. Morag and I met up and got talking and now...' he leaned back away and said, in a more normal tone, '...we're a couple. Aren't we, Morag?'

Morag, a girl with winged eyeliner that I could only envy and a T-shirt covered in skulls, smiled shyly.

'So, it worked, your spell,' Nathan said, and now he sounded way too loud. 'I had the confidence to ask Morag out and she said yes.'

Hang on, hang on, back up a bit. 'Sofia had a rash?' I asked and the change of subject made him frown.

'Er, aye, she did,' he said, looking puzzled. 'Brought her out all in spots on her face or something? I dunno. She's gone off with a lad from England anyway, come to work the hotels for the season, so I heard.'

Okay. So the whole 'potion for confidence' thing, that had just been psychological. Nathan had thought he was being given some solution to his shyness, so it had worked. But – I'd wished Sofia to have spots, hadn't I? To feel a little of what it was like to be less than favoured?

Oh, surely not. No. Coincidence, that was all. Yes.

'I got a white wine.' Magnus put a glass down on the table. 'Unless you really want a cocktail?'

Nathan and Morag gave me identical, loved-up grins, and leaned away back into their private conversation, while I scooped up my dropped jaw and tried to concentrate on Magnus. 'White wine is fine, thank you,' I said, a little weakly.

Magnus smiled. He looked relaxed here, wearing a smart grey shirt and navy trousers like an ordinary person. He blended right in, in fact.

I took an awkward sip of wine. I'm not a witch, I was repeating to myself. I'm not. Reading Jennet's book, living in her cottage and catering to the gullible does not make me a witch. Sofia getting an allergy when I wished for spots for her does not make me a witch. I'm an accountant, and accountancy and witchcraft have nothing in common apart from a handful of letters and a way with arcane knowledge.

'So, this the witch, then?'

A young man, with some interestingly sculpted facial hair and a go-faster haircut, stopped by the table, balancing a fistful of drinks.

'No,' I said, at the same time as Magnus said, 'This is Brid, who's here to sell Jennet's cottage. Brid, this is Kerr. He's an estate agent over to Kirkwall.'

'Do you know Donal, then?' I asked, interested for a moment

before I wanted to bite my tongue off. *Know* him? Even given the disparity in age, they were probably best friends who went scuba diving together at weekends. Or whatever it was estate agents did to relax.

'Aye.' Kerr looked at me. He had very blue eyes and sharp cheekbones and I bet he was in demand among his chosen dating set. 'Aye, we all know Donal. You're going with him to sell the place then?'

He and Magnus exchanged a look that made me feel I was being talked about in my presence, only silently.

'I haven't signed anything yet,' I said, stiffly. 'I'm still weighing up my options.'

'Well, if you decide not to go with him, you come and see me. I'll get the place sold for you.' Another eye-chat with Magnus, who frowned and then looked down into his wine. 'It won't be worth a lot, of course,' he went on, dashing any hopes I'd held on to. 'Tiny place and with its history...'

A piece of card was thrust into the hand I wasn't using to hold my wine, and Kerr, his hair and his armful of alcohol were gone, sweeping back out through the door to be greeted with a raucous yell and some cheering. Estate agents were clearly the same the world over.

'What the hell was that all about?' I asked Magnus, in an almost accusatory tone.

'Ah, it'll be Donal. He's probably put the word out that he wants first go at selling your cottage and nobody wants to upset him by interfering. It's an estate agent thing.' He drank some wine and looked around. Various hands raised in greeting and he waved back.

'Do you *all* know each other?' I asked over my wine glass.

'Not quite, but mostly.'

'And you like that?'

Magnus tilted his head and gave me a sideways look. The daylight that reached us was minimal and augmented by a couple of wall lights which made him look darker and taller and, in some strange way, a little unknowable and mysterious. When he opened his mouth to reply, I thought I was going to get a treatise on how the generations had interwoven on these strange, isolated islands; how they had all had to look out for one another when the seas rose, the boats couldn't sail, and Orkney was cut off from Scotland. In fact, all I got was, 'Aye.'

'Oh, very enigmatic.' I drank some more wine.

He raised his half pint of beer to me and smiled. 'You wouldn't understand,' he said, then frowned. 'But maybe you would. I'd guess you tend to stick to the same group of friends – to people you know?'

'I'm not a mad socialite, if that's what you mean. I go to work, I go home, I...' I took another mouthful of wine to cover up the fact that I had no idea what else to say. I really didn't do anything else, apart from take Mum shopping and sit in her overheated kitchen while she and Dad argued lightly about the recycling. For all my haste to get the cottage on the market and head back, when I thought about it, there really wasn't *that* much to head back to. Apart from a sense of duty and a lot of telephone calls to the tax office. It wasn't much, but it pulled at me, a neutron star's worth of guilt-gravity.

'Here it's just like that, only bigger.' Magnus swirled the beer around in his glass and stared down into it. 'And there's a comfort in it. People ask how you are and they really want to know. They ask after your family, because they know them too. I've done my time in the city with different faces every day and a lot of empty questions and pretend emotion and it's not for me.' The glass went down onto the table.

'Maybe Kizzie feels that too,' I said thoughtfully.

'I'm sorry, what?' I heard his chair go back from the table, scudding along the uneven floor as he pushed himself further away.

'Well, you behave as though she's only here because you are, but maybe she actually likes the feeling of being surrounded by people who care,' I went on, having no real idea what I was talking about and trying to shut myself up by drinking more of the wine very quickly.

Magnus was staring at me, his eyes very big and almost black in the odd mixture of natural and artificial light. Over in one corner, someone thumped the old jukebox and Lynrd Skynrd's 'Freebird' started playing, a girl's red skirt flashed as she swirled past carrying a tray of pint glasses, leaving a scent of flowers and just a touch of BO. I wondered why I was noticing these details. To distract myself from the expression on Magnus' face?

'Let's go outside.' He stood up, pushing the chair even further back and grabbing his glass.

'But I...'

'I think outside.' My wine glass was nudged into my hand and I either had to follow him back through the crowd or sit here alone and watch Nathan and Morag play a game of competitive face sucking. People watched us walk out. I could feel the eyes on us as we carefully cradled our glasses out through the door and into the bright outdoors. The wind had dropped and it was almost warm but the shadows thrown by the lazy low sun were long and wavered with the grasses that held them.

Magnus walked us around the building to the side away from the road, where the view stretched like an exercise in perspective, fields with low stone walls dipping down to vanish into a cluster of buildings and more water. Then he stopped me, with a hand on my shoulder.

'What you said, about Kizzie...' he began, then tapered off, like the scenery.

'I don't know, obviously. Just – well, maybe the sense of community is what she's been looking for too? Maybe she came here because of you, but she's staying because of her. And the baby.'

Magnus looked as though he were silently choking. His eyes had gone very round and his mouth seemed to struggle. Finally he came out with, 'You're talking like a witch.'

'Am I?' I stared at my wine, as though it were responsible. 'No, I'm not. Am I?'

'Aye, you are.' He was looking at me in a very concentrated way now. 'I don't believe in the witch thing, before you ask. You came to take back the cottage, all fair play, it's yours to do with as you want – and nobody mentioned that you'd be the witch, until I started hearing it around town once you'd arrived. Well, I just laughed, it's ridiculous, isn't it?' The dark brown stare intensified. '*Isn't it?*' he asked again, dropping the words into what was left of his beer but keeping his eyes on me over the rim of the glass.

'Of course it is,' I said, evenly.

'But there you go, talking like – och, I dunno. Like you've got the knowing of people, somehow. Of Kizzie. I never thought of it, but, y'know, she's a foster child, grew up in loads of homes, no real place to belong. I can see now that she'd find a place here, somewhere to make a home for herself and the baby, somewhere everyone knows her and will keep an eye out.' His gaze dropped down to the short, flower-studded grass at his feet. 'And I feel right stupid now, for not putting two and two together and being so big-headed to think she's only stopped here because of me.'

'I'm sure you're well worth staying here for,' I said, trying not to give the words the sarcastic edge they were striving for.

He grinned. 'Och, no, that sounded fair big-headed of me, didn't it?'

'Wee bit.' I tried not to grin back.

'So you're no witch, but you understand people and they're all spreading it about that you've got the knowing, whilst, of course, not believing a word of it themselves.' Magnus put his glass down at his feet and turned to face me. 'And you've been playing up to them, I hear. So, why's that now?'

I put my empty wine glass down too. 'I have absolutely no idea,' I said. 'It's just easier than keeping on saying that I'm really not a witch. Path of least resistance, I suppose, and it's not doing any harm, after all. If it makes people feel better to be listened to and to pretend to believe that I can do them some good – well, it's like a community service, isn't it?'

Magnus took another small step forward until he was practically standing on my feet. 'Have you noticed,' he said conversationally, 'that all we seem to do is ask questions?'

'No.' I didn't step back, even though I could see every one of his eyelashes, a smooth discolouration of skin on his cheek like a birthmark, the burnished scatter of stubble on his chin. 'Do we?'

He put his hands on my upper arms. 'That's a QED moment, if ever I heard one,' he said quietly.

The whole world went silent. Or, at least, the bit that held Magnus and me did. Beyond us was the normal background soughing and susurrating, cheeping and cheering; bottles were dropped and 'Freebird' mutated into 'Stairway to Heaven'. But here, in our circle of sunlight and cropped grass, Magnus and I stood and stared into one another's eyes in a bubble of hush.

And then, at the same moment, we both leaned in and kissed. Again there was that citrusy smell that I'd noticed around him before, like lemons and limes being detonated just under his skin, a fresh and clean aroma that tickled my nose but brought me in closer. His hands moved from my arms to cradle my face, and mine also moved up, around the back of his neck. It was nice to kiss a man I didn't have to stoop for. Previously – what I tried not to think of as 'back in the real world' – all the tall men seemed to have been taken by willowy blondes like models. I'd been left with the five-foot-six brigade, which had meant that I'd spent most of my dating history with men who'd felt inadequate to my height, whilst I'd had chronic backache from all the bending. Height didn't matter, of course it didn't, but being able to kiss upright was a bonus.

Finally we stepped back and took a breath.

'Well,' I said. 'That was unexpected.'

'Hmm,' said Magnus.

'But I'm going back to York, you know that.'

'Hmm,' he said again. 'Would you like another wine? Or shall we stand here and compare our woeful dating histories whilst commiserating that finding someone we like is going to be snatched away by the desires of book-keeping and inheritance laws?'

I looked at him and again was struck by how well he fitted his environment – slightly wild, very much of this place with his subtly coloured clothes which looked as though they may have been dyed with woad and madder, and then I berated myself for having read too much of Jennet's book and even knowing what woad and madder *were*.

'Another glass of wine sounds wonderful,' I said.

'Or you could have a cocktail?' This was asked with a slight mischievous smile. 'If you're missing home?'

I thought about the sticky bar and how some of the more brightly coloured bottles behind it didn't seem to have been opened since Orkney belonged to Norway, and shook my head. 'Just the wine, I think, please.'

So that was how I found myself walking around the stone circle of the Ring of Brodgar, in a whipping wind, holding Magnus' hand and singing a selected reprise of 1970s prog-rock hits. It had seemed natural, after another couple of glasses of wine, to go for a drive, and we'd ended up here, where the land tilted and threw rocks against the sky.

'What's it for?' I asked.

'Does it have to be "for" anything?' Magnus was watching me, an amused smile making him look as though he were humouring me desperately. 'Anyway, nobody really knows.'

I stood in the centre of the stone circle and looked out over the narrow spit of land which ran away in front of us between two stretches of water, broken by wind-whipped waves and irritated ducks. It was probably the wine, but I had a curious feeling of 'rightness', as though this was where I was meant to be standing, at this moment in time, and with this man. If I'd stopped two glasses ago, I'd have been freezing and wondering why the hell I was standing on a muddy slope surrounded by boulders.

But I'd not been out with anyone in a while and besides, it was Magnus; tall and rangy and dark and watching me with an expression that made me prickle in all kinds of interesting ways.

The sun curved down, touching the horizon like a dropped boiled sweet, the sea turned to fire and the waters stilled and I found myself caught against Magnus in an embrace that kept the wind out but managed to stoke some ferocious fires inside me.

'We could...' I whispered.

'I think you've had a wee bit too much to drink,' he whispered back. 'We need to do this sober, if we do it at all. Let's just appreciate the moment, shall we?'

I rested my forehead against his and looked into hazel eyes that held a lot of mischief now. 'We could appreciate the moment back at the cottage, though.'

He was just about to reply, when I felt a sudden vibration that owed nothing to the circumstances and everything to the pocket of my jacket. It was accompanied by a tinny rendition of 'Oh, I Do

Like to Be Beside the Seaside'. I snatched my phone out and stared at it, as though I'd forgotten that such technology existed.

'Hello, Mum.'

'Hello, love. Just wanted to give you a call to let you know we're all right, your message sounded as though you were worrying a bit.'

Message? Then I remembered the text. 'But that was yesterday,' I said weakly.

'Well, yes, we've been a bit busy, you see.'

I should have felt relieved to hear that they weren't both lying somewhere, unable to move and grasping feebly for a method of communication that was just out of reach. I should have been pleased that my mother wanted to make sure I was still alive up here. I *should*. Instead, I felt annoyed, irritated that she was intruding on the wonderful edge-of-something mood that Magnus and I were in.

And it had taken her long enough.

I transferred my phone to my other ear and followed Magnus as he led the way back down towards where we'd left his van, parked in a romantic spot overlooking the loch which was now far less romantic with the addition of my mother's somewhat self-justifying tones.

'Your father's joined this MS support club and they had a meeting, so we went along, and then we did an online shop, well, you know they always forget bits and there's never any cabbage, so we popped down into town – your father's walking much better at the moment so we didn't need the chair – and we met a couple from the group and had a coffee in Marks.'

Magnus helped me up into the cab, while my mother went into details I would never need to remember about who was who and who lived where and what they'd had with their coffee. We'd driven nearly all the way back before she started to wind down. 'Anyway, Angie is hosting tomorrow, so we're going early so your father can give them some advice about their fruit trees. What have you been up to? How's the cottage selling?'

I wondered how to explain the situation; that I was sharing the cottage with a brood of geese, pretending to be a witch for a quiet life and decorating the place to no great end. I decided that I couldn't. 'I'm fine, Mum. Just sorting stuff out. I'll be back soon.'

'Oh. No need to rush. We are managing fine and the group have put us in touch with some places that can help with your father if he...' her voice dropped away slightly, '...if he starts to relapse, you know.' Then, strengthening again, with a certainty that I wasn't sure I liked. 'Absolutely no need to hurry back at all. Take your time. Honestly.'

We pulled up outside the cottage. Cushie was paddling around in the shallow end of the loch, while the goslings swam further out. 'Thanks, Mum, but this won't take much longer.'

There was a little pause, as though my mother had covered the receiver and was talking to someone else. Then she was back, her voice stronger. 'Brid, we're fine. Everything is fine. There's absolutely no need for you to be rushing through things to get back to us. Take your time. Enjoy yourself!'

I tried to shove a verbal block in the path of her conversational vehicle. 'It's not a holiday, Mum, I'm busy. Doing things. And I ought to go now.'

Magnus just smiled. The mood, which could have taken us indoors at least, had been broken. 'I'm heading back to Kirkwall,' he said, sounding reluctant.

'Is that someone there with you?' my mother, ever alert to the possibility of her daughter actually having a life, asked. 'A man?'

'Well, it's Magnus.' I smiled my apology at him, but he just grinned back and made shooing motions at me. 'So, sort of.'

'Oh, yes, your cousin Torstein's brother. I suppose he's your cousin too, in a way, but I've not spoken to him before, only

Torstein and his wife, she seems a very nice girl, been looking after Jennet's place, I understand, well, that's a blessing otherwise it could have fallen down and you'd be trying to sell a couple of walls and a bit of roof, wouldn't you?'

I stared over at the cottage in question, which was not much more than a couple of walls and a bit of roof. 'Yes,' I said, still sounding pathetic. All this time hoping they were all right and missing me and it sounded as though they'd used my absence to suddenly find a life. 'Look, let's talk later, Mum.'

'It's almost my bedtime,' she said, reminding me that this thick, late light wasn't natural. Simmer dim was well underway this far north. 'I just wanted to tell you not to worry.' Then she rang off, unaware that her 'telling me not to worry' had taken the best part of half an hour and covered almost everyone in York I'd never met.

The sound of Magnus' van was now just a rattle on the edge of hearing.

Oh, bugger.

14

I woke the next morning with the tiniest of wine-headaches, and an itch in the back of my brain, as though I'd inadvertently got myself into a situation that was going to be very hard to get out of. Like making an appointment or an agreement that I'd known at the time had been a bad idea. What the hell had it been?

Then I remembered last night. Kissing Magnus. I bumped my head against the inside of the bed-cupboard and swore quietly to myself. Usually I was rationality itself, and yet last night I'd thrown caution to the, not-inconsiderable, winds. Where had my common sense gone? Well, I knew that, it had vanished under a hot purple haze of lusting after Magnus and too much wine.

Innis turned up at the door while I was still wandering around in my pyjamas, mug of tea clamped between my hands and, no doubt, a vague expression of trying to think up excuses.

'I hear you two had a wee moment last night?' She stepped over the threshold and was confronted by the purple wall.

'Oh, it was just...' I waved an insouciant hand, which spilled tea down my leg. 'Wine. Too much wine.'

'He's a good-looking boy, though, our Magnus. And Jennet...' She stopped talking suddenly and developed a deep interest in the texture of the sofa cushions. 'Well, anyway.'

I straightened up out of my hangover. 'I'm sorry? Jennet? What on earth could Jennet possibly have to do with me? And, or, Magnus?'

'I wasn't supposed to say.' Innis tweaked a cushion. 'Forget it.'

'How am I going to "forget it" when I don't know what I'm supposed to forget? Or even if it's worth remembering in the first place?' I asked, reasonably enough I thought, for a woman with a ringing headache and tea stains on her pink swirly pyjama leg. 'Innis?'

I fixed her with the kind of stare that Cushie used on me. Angled head, principal eye swivelled, beady. It looked ferocious when the goose did it, and apparently it translated into human just as terrifyingly.

'All right! No need to put the evils on me. No cursing the family, isn't that one of the first rules of witchcraft?' Innis bustled her way through to the kitchen. 'Is there any hot water? I'm going to need a cup of tea to make this sound reasonable.'

'First rule of witchcraft is, talk all the bloody time about witchcraft, as far as I'm aware,' I said. 'Like a reverse Fight Club. Cursing has not, so far, been mentioned.'

But I was going to have a sit down and a flick through Jennet's book as soon as Innis had gone, to find out if and when cursing *was* allowed. Because, if geese were mentioned anywhere, I was going to find the cursiest curse that ever blued the air.

Innis flicked on the kettle and fumbled through the tea bags. 'I came to tell you that Tor and I are taking Freya down to Scotland this afternoon for a couple of days,' she said. 'Visiting my grandma, to tell her about the baby. So don't worry if you don't see us about and worry very much if you see lights on in the house and people emptying the contents into a pantechnicon. Have you got any fruit teas? Ordinary's making me feel sick just now.'

'Okay. Now, can we go back to what Jennet has to do with anything?'

'Och, I was hoping you'd forgotten about that.'

'You only just mentioned it!'

Innis sighed. 'I know. I've got baby brain so bad I can hardly remember my own name and I was hoping it was catching. Look.' The kettle boiled and I poked the raspberry and lemon tea bags in her direction. 'Jennet left – letters, I suppose you'd call them. In her will, with all the other bits and pieces. One went to your side, your great-granny, with the inheritance of the cottage. The other came to Tor's side, with the land, he's got it somewhere, in a box or something. But it's along the lines of the cottage witch is meant for the single son, words to that effect, anyway.' She disappeared in a cloud of slightly fruity steam.

I gaped. 'And you take that to mean what?'

Innis shrugged. '*I* don't take it to mean anything,' she said. 'Not my family, I just married in. The shit is not of my making. You need to take it up with Magnus, because I think *he* is taking it to mean that you and he are... well, you know. Destined To Be or something.'

The romantic roses-and-kisses-with-just-a-hint-of-lust thoughts I'd been having about Magnus evaporated in a puff of evil-smelling black smoke. 'Oh, *is* he?' I muttered. To my mind, Destined To Be was only a very short hop from a lot of controlling behaviour and a distinct lack of free will, but then, maybe I'd read one too many Fated Mates paranormal romances in my formative years. 'Well, you can tell him from me that no pre-deceased herb fan is going to dictate to me who I get with.'

'He'll be over later, you can tell him yourself.'

The thought that Magnus had been nice to me, had taken me around the sights and out drinking just because he thought he was supposed to made the hair on the back of my neck prickle. The embarrassment that I'd fallen for it heated me up inside my pyjamas.

'Well, he needn't bother calling in. I'm going out.' I made a very firm decision. Staying away from Magnus and the mortifying realisation that he'd only kissed me because he thought he should was the only way out of this. Perhaps I could avoid him until the cottage was sold? In fact, hadn't I better get the place on the market in double-quick time, so that I could get away? 'I need to go into Kirkwall.'

'Oh. Okay.' Unfazed, Innis sipped at her tea.

'And I'm going back to York in the next couple of days.' If it had been possible, I'd have left in the next couple of minutes, such was my state of humiliation, but I knew that I'd have to book the ferry for myself and the car, once I'd handed the cottage over to Donal to deal with.

'Right.' Innis gave me a look from around the steam. 'Although it does seem something of an overreaction.'

'I don't want to lead him on,' I said, stiffly. 'There's nothing between Magnus and me and there never will be. I drank too much last night, that's all.' *Plus he's the first man in forever to take any interest in me, and it was rather pleasant having him show me the history of Orkney, and help do things around the cottage. He's very easy on the eye. Also, intelligent and kind.*

And putting on an act, my brain reminded me. Because he thinks it's what he's destined to do.

'Fine.' Innis looked around at my painted walls, Kizzie's picture propped in the alcove, the new furniture. 'It's looking good in here. Like a proper house now. I'll always remember it stacked with hay and feed, of course, and it will be nice not to have to keep popping over to clean and dust and check the roof. You're going to see Donal in Kirkwall and let him put the place on his books?'

'Unless you and Tor want to buy it?'

Innis laughed. 'We couldn't afford it. We're farmers, and with two small children I'll not be having the time to come over and do holiday changeovers and all that.'

'Have you known Donal long? He's not an islander, and Magnus said he was a friend of yours.' I used the rest of the water in the kettle to top up my tea, now half of it was soaking into my trousers.

'Och, friend is a strong word. He grew up near my granny, in Leith, so I used to see him when we went down to stay. We hadn't seen much of one another until he turned up here in the spring last year, and opened an estate agency. At the end of last summer, I think it was, he asked about the cottage, if it was for sale and who owned it, so I told your mum that someone was looking to buy.'

'That's presumably why she sent me up here, to tidy the place up so we'd get a decent price?'

'And sign the papers and things. There'll be tax and stuff.' Innis shrugged. 'Easier to do with someone here.'

'He can email us the paperwork,' I said firmly.

There was a noise in the doorway. Fearing that Magnus was already here and I was going to have to face him, I squeaked, but it was only Cushie and her brood, tootling their way in through the still-open door and not even sparing Innis and me a glance.

'They'll have to go.' Innis put her tea mug down. 'You can't sell a place with a sitting tenant. Right. I've told you we're away, I'd better go and start packing. Wee Freya's already overexcited.' She sighed. 'Two under three. I must be mad.'

'Won't be any worse than five under four, surely.' I led the way through to the door, to show her out.

'True, true. While I'm on maternity leave most of the current crop will go off to school too.'

She waved and began the sloshy progress through the low-lying bog, treading carefully over the flagstone pathway, whereupon I tore back inside, dressed and was out in the car in record time.

Kirkwall wasn't busy, no huge coaches full of cruisers nosing their way around the tight corners, no crowds packing into the more scenic of the shops. Just normal people going about their daily business. Locals stopping to chat on corners out of the wind, a few hardy holidaymakers trudging by under enormous backpacks and hats. The town felt as though it had been holding its stomach in until the cruise ships left, and now it was breathing out and letting any unsightly bulges do their own thing.

Magnus' shop was open, I could see the very pretty Mhairi behind the counter, tidying up the stock as I walked past. Further down the road, Kizzie saw me passing as she leaned her bump on a window display to hang another picture, and waved.

I waved back and then lowered my arm. I was going native and this just wouldn't do. I straightened my back and pushed open the door to the estate agency, where I surprised Donal shuffling documents into a filing cabinet.

'I want to sell the cottage,' I said brusquely. 'Now. Today. Well, as fast as possible, anyway.'

'Oh dear.' Donal smiled and slid behind his desk. 'Has something happened?'

I remembered the evening in the bar, the wine and the kiss and then later at the stone circle, and my skin suddenly became too tight.

'No, no, nothing's happened,' I said, far too quickly. 'I just need to get back to York, that's all.'

After all, it hadn't been real, had it? It might have *felt* real, there had been quite a lot about Magnus that had felt real last night, but he'd been acting on an assumption that I hadn't been party to. And that stopped, right *now*.

'It so happens that I have the paperwork right here,' Donal said smoothly. 'Sole agency rights? That means you aren't putting it with any other agencies, of course.'

'No, no, whatever. I mean...' I paused, pen in hand. 'I want a decent price for it, obviously, I'm not giving it away. But it needs to be soon.'

'Of course.' Donal's voice was now so frictionless you could have used it to wax skis. 'I think I gave you the rough price range that I considered feasible?'

'Yes, yes.' I signed on the line, giving the document a cursory read-through just to make sure it was an agency agreement, which it was.

'It so happens...' Donal was smiling at me now. It was a smile that made me slightly nervous and I wasn't sure why, possibly because it seemed to have too much face involved, 'that I've had an enquiry this very morning. If you are really serious about wanting to sell quickly? Someone with the cash to take the cottage off your hands almost immediately? You understand that, in Scottish law, you'll need a Home Report, but I can help you with that. Of course, you've only got nine days to produce one, so we ought to get cracking! Get everything expedited.'

He stood up now. I noticed that his dark suit was shiny, it had a kind of gloss finish to the fabric that made me uneasy. It reminded me of something reptilian, as though he could shed it at will and slither off into the undergrowth. Or maybe it was his unwarranted use of the word 'expedited' that made my flesh prickle.

'Yes,' I said, backing out of the office.

'I'll be in touch!' I heard him call but I banged the door closed just in case he was about to dislocate his jaws and come for me through the gap. But now, of course, this left me with nothing to do in Kirkwall, and not daring to go home just in case Magnus pitched up with an engagement ring and an air of destiny about him.

I got back into the car and drove. Unfortunately, I didn't have a map and the only place I knew to head for was the stone circle we'd been to last night, squeezed between the loch and the sea on a pinch point of land. I sat in the car at the flat little car park and stared at the boulders on the horizon for want of anything better to do.

Overhead the sky swirled, mercury-silver. The stones poked their heads towards the clouds, black as bruises. Vague tatters of mist blew in off the water, occasionally obscuring everything and then parting to frame the scene, loch, stones, hill, in an almost over-exaggeratedly atmospheric way.

'Yes, yes, all right,' I found myself muttering. 'Spooky rocks, long history, rituals, all that. But I've got a life back in York.'

The silence hummed. Then it splashed and vibrated and I realised that it wasn't the silence, it was Magnus' Jeep, pulling in behind me in the car park, as though to stop me from driving away.

There were no other cars. I could have put my foot down and driven off in any direction other than reverse, but his parking on my bumper was clearly meant to indicate something to me.

He got out and came around my car. I kept my eyes front,

watching the hunched stones catching on the low cloud, like cats' claws in knitting.

He tapped on the window.

I didn't look. I just said, 'Go. Away.' But I had the awful feeling that my cheeks were going red, because my reflection in the wind-screen was sharpening and coming more into focus as the back-ground dissolved again into grey fog, like a special effect indicating a new scene.

'I'm sorry!' Magnus' voice came, filtered through the car body-work. He was hopping about. 'I should have told you.'

'I suppose Innis relayed our entire conversation?' I kept my voice level. 'Because nobody around here seems to be able to keep quiet about anything. You probably chart one another's digestive disturbances and outbreaks of acne.' My voice was rising, in both tone and volume. 'On spreadsheets! I bet you do things like... like... say we'd better not go round to Mike's tonight, he's due a recur-rence of his bloat problem!' I finished on a squeak.

Magnus had bent down to look at me through the car window. He was shivering. 'Look, anything Jennet said, it's complete bollocks. You know that, I know that. You can't believe that *I* would believe it, and base anything I did on it, surely?'

I wanted to say that of *course* Jennet's pronouncements were fake. At best, the ramblings of an old woman, at worst, the kind of specious tripe pronounced by people who thought themselves 'mediums' and who believed that their wisdom came from some unearthly source. I mean, I *knew* that was the case.

Except. Except for that tiny tickle of doubt when I thought about Nathan. All right, the raspberry tea and honey thing had mostly been an attempt to build up his belief in himself, but the 'Sofia and the spots' event still rippled through the back of my mind when I tried to fall asleep. And I'd known, somehow I'd known, that Innis was pregnant. Before she did.

But coincidence, intuition and pure luck were still my front runners for all those things. Jennet was not a witch. I, most certainly, was not a witch. In which case...

I wound the window down a touch. 'So what was all... *that* about?' I pointed at the stone circle. 'Last night?'

'Is there any chance you could let me come in?' Magnus moved from foot to foot. 'It's bloody freezing out here, aye, and I can hardly hear myself speak for the clanging sounds of my body parts falling off.'

I pursed my lips at him to show I was acting against my instincts, but unlocked the door and he scrambled round the car and flung himself inside onto the passenger seat, where condensation instantly formed on the sleeves of his pullover and made it look as though the fog was trying to get in here with him.

'Last night,' Magnus began, then stopped. 'Brid. You're a very attractive woman. I like you.'

I gave him a 'dangerous, be careful how you proceed' look from narrowed eyes.

'No, it's true. You blew in here, like a breath of fresh air...'

'...to which there is quite a lot of competition,' I interjected. 'Doesn't the wind *ever* stop blowing?'

'Not really. No, look, you arrived with your determination and your ambition and the way you went about decorating and getting the cottage sorted – you're a woman who knows her own mind and doesn't want to get caught up in anything else. I like that. No, I do. You've got drive and you're fun and I suppose I just fell for that. Got a bit carried away last night and kissed you, and I'm sorry about that but you did seem to be on board with it at the time.'

'I am. Was,' I hastily corrected myself. 'But what makes you think you like me?'

Magnus blinked and looked down at the sleeve of his sweater, sparkling with beads of water. His hair was soaked too, twisted by the wind into dreadlocks of damp and dotted with more moisture that reflected the grey of the piecemeal mist outside. One of my mother's more hair-raising attempts to get me to sleep as a child had been a story about the Selkie; fey beings who wear human skin to entice their victims to come into the water with them, and some of its more colourful detailing swam to the forefront of my brain. Ridiculous, unbelievable, but it was that kind of day.

'Och,' he said, brushing much of the wet off his jumper with the back of a hand. 'I know my own mind. When I like a lassie, there are... *signs*, you know. Do you really think I'd be daft enough to throw my hat after a girl on the word of an old lady who lived with a chemical toilet?' He wriggled a bit and looked at me again. I finally dragged my eyes away from the view and stopped watching him out of the corner of my eye. 'I'm not stupid, Brid,' he said, and now his voice was very serious. 'Not some credulous simpleton. I've lived in *Glasgow*, and that kind of knocks the suggestibility out of most people. Except Kizzie, obviously, but I think you could hit her with a sizeable mountain and she'd still be a naïve wee thing.'

'But you hardly know me!' I almost wailed.

Magnus gave me a stern look. 'Most of the people round here I've known since we were toddlers,' he said. 'And I don't want to kiss any of them. It's almost like we know each other too well.'

I remembered what Nathan had said about everyone remembering your every indiscretion since time immemorial. He had a point. You could, perhaps, know something *too* well. Be too familiar with it.

A tiny shiver ran down my spine at the thought. I wasn't sure why.

'And I think, being honest now, that was part of Kizzie's charm. She's good at what she does and I found her refreshing. She's had a very different life experience to me and that was...' He stopped. Cleared his throat. 'That was all. We had the art in common and it was good to find someone who understands what that's like. By the time I knew that she had attachment issues and that she's not one for deep discussions about things outside her artwork, it was too late, we were a couple.'

Silence descended. The fog danced a tatterdemalion polka around the car. Occasional shreds let a thin sunlight through to shine a milky gleam around the circle, which made it look even blacker and more forbidding.

I looked directly at Magnus. His hair was drying in the warmth of the car, showing wisps of copper red among the darkness, and his fawn eyes were on me.

'I can't,' I said, and the words were heavy with reluctance. 'I really *can't*, Magnus. I like you a lot, but I have to go back to York. Work needs me, my parents need me. I can't shrug it all off and move to Orkney just because you fancy me and a few misguided people think I'm a witch.' Aware that my tone had become a little shrill, I cleared my throat. 'Besides, I like going outside, and "outside" here seems to want to kill me. Or at least stop me having a good time.'

Magnus laughed and the sound made my spine prickle, but not in the same way that Donal had – this was more of a loosening of muscle, a pull towards him. 'You've not seen much of the sun, aye. But summer is coming, Brid, and then this is the best place on earth.'

I raised my eyebrows. The wind rocked the car and the rain fell on us with some force in a bank of thick cloud that splattered all the windows. 'Really,' I said, with exaggerated sarcasm. 'Summer being two days in August, presumably.'

He tipped his head on one side. This made his hair fall clear of his neck and his thick sturdy jumper moved downward. Around his neck was a silver chain with a small pendant design, a spiral inside a fern leaf. I stared at it. I'd seen it before, drawn inside Jennet's little book, where I'd thought it was just an illustration of some local flora, although it had had the look of no plant I had ever seen.

'Did you sneak a look at Jennet's book?' I asked, accusatory and possessive, although I wasn't sure why. 'When you were at the cottage?'

He frowned. 'No. Never seen inside it. Why?'

'That... thing around your neck. It's like one of her drawings.'

Magnus raised a slow hand and touched the pendant, almost as though he'd forgotten it was there. 'This? Och, no, I've had this since I was a baby. It came to me from Dad when he died. There was little else to leave, just the farm and a lot of money owed to the bank, a few books and this. Tor took the books and I got this.'

He pulled the chain to its fullest extent and squinted downwards at the little silver blob with its intricate design. 'I used to stare at it for hours,' he said, his voice distant with thought. 'Wondering what it was, how it was made. It was one of the things that decided me on silversmithing as a career. Well, that and the fact that I hate shovelling cowshit nine hours a day.' He gave me a small sideways smile. 'Do I take it that you don't hate me utterly, then?'

His hopeful tone, his slightly shamefaced grin, the light in his hair and the gleam of the silver against his throat, it all made me weaken. 'No,' I said, on an outbreath. 'No, I don't hate you. I don't dislike you. I might even quite...' I stopped as he raised an eyebrow. 'I might even quite not feel like obliterating you for following me here when I just wanted to sit here quietly by myself. But none of it changes a thing. You love Orkney, I have to go back to York. There is absolutely no point in us starting anything, because it would be no more than an extended one-night stand and I think neither of us is up for that, are we?'

Magnus shrugged one shoulder. 'I don't know,' he said. 'I could lower my principles a bit, I suppose.'

'I *mean*,' I tore my gaze away from him and looked back out across the scenery of water, land, stone and sky, 'that we'd only get fond of one another and then I'd have to head back down south and you'd be here with the cows and the silver and the rain and it would be painful.'

'Are you always this practical?'

'Of course I am. I'm an accountant.'

'So there's no room for some wild nights of fun, throwing caution to the wind and letting the future take care of itself?' He raised that eyebrow again.

'You can't. Not if you have tax bills to sort out, and parents who would otherwise sit silently in front of *The Chase*,' I said, trying to be stern, but his grin was broadening and it was infectious.

'How about a couple of slightly crazy afternoons, with caution put outside on the step and the future carefully seated in the corner with a packet of biscuits and a jigsaw?'

I couldn't help it, I laughed. 'Magnus, you are bonkers! And also slightly offputtingly persistent.'

His grin was gone now. It vanished from his face as fast as the fleeting sun disappeared from outside. 'I'm sorry. I won't mention it again. You know your own mind, of course.'

We sat in silence for a moment, while the wind screamed through the metal bodywork of the car.

'But just maybe...' I said slowly, 'I wouldn't be averse to another drink.'

His grin was back now. 'Och, I think that could be arranged. How about tonight?'

I wasn't sure how I felt about any of this. It was ridiculous, of course it was. But then, so was much of what had happened since I'd arrived here. Witches and spots and spells and a tiny house that was practically sold already, if Donal was right about having someone lined up. I'd be gone soon, as fast as I could sign the paperwork and make sure everything was in order.

And yet. *And yet.* Something deep inside me was buzzing, as though excitement was leaning on its doorbell. Magnus was gorgeous, he was sweet and cute and really, what was the worst that could happen? I'd fall hard and fast and have a few weeks of moping and being off my food when I got back, but as a trade-off I'd have some wonderful memories. I'd forever feel warmly about Orkney and I could hug that slight ache of *could have been* to myself to keep me going during the long hours of spreadsheets and allowance deductions. And when Mum asked if I'd met anyone nice lately, I could smile a wistful, pale smile and make some enigmatic comment about love and distance.

'All right,' I said, making Magnus, who'd clearly been expecting a negative response, jump. 'Drink. Tonight. Tell you what, come round to the cottage and I'll cook us dinner.'

'Are you sure?' He was beginning to behave as though he'd had a rethink. 'Dinner?'

'*Just* dinner,' I said, stern again now. 'And maybe a glass of wine. Don't bring your slippers and pyjamas.'

'All right, I won't.' Another flash of that grin. 'Haven't worn pyjamas since I was a wee one anyway.'

'Don't you freeze to death at night?' My robust pyjamas had felt like iron cladding against the chill dark.

'Of course not.' He opened the passenger door and slid out into the restless air beyond. 'I wear the skin of my previous victims,' he said through the gap of the closing door.

'Well, I've got a fully armed goose, and I am quite prepared to use her,' I said, laughing back at him. 'So don't get any ideas.'

Then, leaving him standing with the air tugging him from every angle, I managed an impressive wheel spin out of the car park and onto the road, wondering where the hell I was going to go to get some edible food to cook for dinner.

16

'Enjoy yourselves!' I waved to Innis, Tor and Freya, all packed neatly into their car, Freya insulated all around by soft toys. They were leaving to catch the afternoon ferry and Innis had come by to drop off the key to the house.

'I've got baby brain well entrenched already,' she said. 'If I take my key I'll only lose it somewhere, and I'm not so daft as to leave it under a flowerpot, so I thought I'd give it to you.'

'What if someone breaks in here and steals it?' I looked around the inside of the cottage, where a break-in would be completely futile unless the thief had a particular attraction for elderly cookware and tins of beans.

'Och, no one will break into the witch's cottage,' Innis said darkly. 'They'd not set foot on your land without permission. Oh, that reminds me. Margaret dropped this off for you earlier today.'

She handed me an envelope.

'Margaret?' I stared blankly at the stationery. 'Who the hell is Margaret?'

'She came over with her dad, Fergus. He's not so well, poor wee soul. But she said you gave him a lotion to rub in and it's working wonders for him. She said it had nearly stopped him complaining, which is a bit of a feat in itself, knowing Fergus.'

I waited until the little family had gone, speeding off out of their gateway with Freya waving me farewell by means of a waggled Tigger, before I opened the envelope.

It was a card. The sort of thing my mother always insisted on having in the house 'just in case', with a noncommittal bouquet of flowers on the front. Useful for anything from late birthday greetings to news of deceased husbands, she always said.

This one was a thank-you card. Margaret, in carefully formal handwriting, reiterating what she had told Innis, and thanking me in enthusiastic terms for helping her father and giving him comfort.

I closed my fist so tightly that the card crumpled between my fingers. It was almond oil! I wanted to shout. Almond oil and a few herbs that I'd got from the local shops! No secret healing ingredients and *definitely* no witchcraft!

From behind me, Cushie honked impatiently. Innis had caught me about to feed the geese, and I still had the bucket at my feet.

'All right, all right.'

The goose paddled her feet, and the goslings waddled around her, pecking idly at tufts of grass.

'I still haven't decided whether or not to give Magnus roast goose for dinner, you know.'

Cushie ignored me. She knew, and I knew, that this was a vain threat. There was a boeuf bourguignon bubbling away in the oven and a shop-bought pavlova defrosting in the cupboard. She honked again, and I began to spread goose pellets on the nearest flagstone, with one eye on the lake in case the local inhabitants heard what was going on and came to take advantage.

Although, I thought, carrying the empty bucket back indoors, good luck to them if they tried it. Cushie was a one-goose army, and even the previously cute goslings were now learning to get beak-happy. I rubbed, ruefully, at my arm, where my lack of immediate doling out of food had earned me a pecking, and went back to the kitchen, where the smell of casserole was perfuming the air.

I propped up Margaret's card on the tiny shelf between the stove and the kettle, and looked at it again, feeling a tiny glow of unearned pride. I mean, obviously I hadn't really done anything. Some oil and a few herbs were hardly going to improve the lot of a man clearly dying, but... *but*. Fergus felt better. Maybe it was just the massage, rubbing the oil in twice a day was perhaps more physical touch than he'd had in a while, poor soul, and maybe that was all he'd needed.

I thought then about the way I'd felt, held against Magnus amid the shrugging stones; the warmth and comfort of another body so close, and I had a moment of echoing loneliness. The gulf between my contactless York life, with its paperwork and duty, and the world here, where it seemed that everyone was fond of everyone else and shoulder-slapping, hand-shaking and bear hugs were the order of the day.

How long had it been since I'd had proper, affectionate, physical contact with another person? Hugging and kissing and the general day-to-day demonstrative loving that made one feel included in the human race, rather than a note-taker on the sidelines, armed with spreadsheets and calculations and the voice of stringent warning? Inserting myself into my parents' lives to make me feel wanted and needed, when, as was becoming obvious, they were perfectly capable of having a wonderful time without me.

The sun was right at the back of the house now, gently slanting through the kitchen window rather than bouncing in off the surface of the loch, making the tiny room seem bright and appealing. The open pages of Jennet's *Book of Shadows* looked artistic. I flipped through, drawings spinning as though alive; hares and leaves, seals and orcas twisting and leaping, and the doodles that reminded me of that silver around Magnus' neck.

Magnus. He'd be here soon. I pushed the bucket into a cupboard and hastened to tidy around, tucking Jennet's book away under the mattress of my bed, putting a display of freshly picked grasses and other, unidentified but attractive, plants in a jug on the table. The place looked lovely and I felt a momentary pang at the memory of the papers I'd signed in Donal's office that morning, but only a momentary one. Then I put on the new dress that I'd bought in Kizzie's shop, picked up a magazine and sat on the sofa from where I could be surprised to see Magnus, having, of course, *completely* forgotten that I'd invited him over.

17

The sun had fallen from its arch, heading down toward the flat horizon where I knew the coastline of Scotland lay. Beyond that was York and home. I tried not to think about it, but flipped the magazine, which told me how teal and magenta were the new 'in' colours, and tried to sell me wallpaper with designs unappealingly like bare wall plaster.

A car pulled up over at the house. I'd got the door propped open again, so I heard the rattle of the engine as it stopped, and then a very long pause before the 'chunk' of the door opening and closing. What was taking Magnus so long? I laid the magazine down and went to the door, trying for a wistful 'prairie woman awaits her man' pose with one hand on the door jamb and the breeze in my hair, with my skirts blowing about my knees.

It wasn't Magnus. It was Kizzie. She was knocking at the door to the house, leaning against the door as she did so, with one hand on her bump.

'They've gone on the ferry!' I called over.

Kizzie slumped, both hands on her belly now. 'I need Innis,' she said. 'I think something's happening.'

'Well, she's not here.'

I'd advanced across the bog now, and stopped, halfway between the house and the cottage. Kizzie looked pale, her skin was almost transparent and her hair hung down around her face, uncombed.

'Are you all right?' I asked.

Kizzie took a deep breath. 'I don't know,' she said, and burst into tears, slumping even further now until she was sitting on the doorstep, fragility and pregnancy mingling to make her look like a very ethereal garden gnome. 'It *hurts*,' she said ruefully, amid the tears.

'Don't you think you should see your doctor?' I came closer, slowly.

'I haven't really got one.'

'Aren't you seeing someone about the baby? A midwife or a health visitor or someone?' I asked, my voice rising to a tone of desperation.

'Oh, no. I want a natural birth.' Kizzie breathed heavily again.

'Seeing a doctor won't make it not a... oh, look, come into the cottage. You can't stay down there.' I was about to quote my mother's favourite saying, 'you'll get piles', but I was rather afraid, given the heftiness of the pregnancy bump, that that ship may well have sailed.

I helped her to her feet, slowly. Kizzie grimaced and blew out as though she was attempting to persuade a dandelion clock to tell us it was one o'clock. 'I saw the doctor right at the beginning,' she said. 'To make sure it was a baby and not just me being silly or something. And Alison, the health visitor, she lives next door and she's been very kind. But...' She trailed off into a low groan.

'When is the baby due?' I didn't like the look of this at all.

'I'm not sure. About now, I think.'

'About now,' I repeated. I helped her through the bog. Was she in labour? Where was the nearest hospital? I thought there might be one in Kirkwall, or was it Stromness? Should I put her in my car and drive her there?

Kizzie leaned against the wall. 'The food smells nice,' she observed. 'Why isn't Innis here? I thought she'd help me.'

'Look, sit down.'

I tried to make room for her on the sofa, moving cushions and piling them up at the back, but Kizzie seemed too restless to sit. She paced around for a moment then grabbed the back of the sofa and leaned forward over it. 'Ow. This hurts. Why does it hurt?' Wide, innocent eyes looked at me, she was scared, but I was terrified.

'I think you might be in labour, Kizzie. Your baby is coming.'

She shook her head. 'Oh, no it can't come today. I have a painting to finish.'

'I don't think you get much choice in the matter. Look, we need to get you to hospital.'

At the sound of the word, Kizzie went rigid. She half-crawled away from me, inching herself along the back of the sofa, hand over hand as though climbing a rope. 'No. I can't go to hospital.' She sounded panicked. 'Don't make me go to hospital—?'

'Brid,' I supplied.

'—Brid. *Please* don't. Say you won't, you won't, will you?' And now she was crying again and I was looking down the wrong end of being a birth partner to someone who only seemed to have a vague grasp of how the damn thing was going to get out of there.

'Kizzie.' I tried to sound gentle. 'Things can go wrong. You *need* to be in hospital for the birth.'

I tried to pat her back, gently, but she grabbed hold of my arm and started wailing, a high-pitched sound that was halfway between a scream and a groan, whilst at the same time squeezing my wrist so hard that my fingers started to tingle.

'I won't! I won't!'

'Ow, can you just...'

'I *won't!*'

'All right, all right, calm down.'

She was crying, groaning and wailing, I was trying to extricate my blueing fingers from her grasp whilst supporting her weight so she didn't collapse down onto the floor in her desire to make me understand that she didn't want to go to hospital and into this mixture of despair, pain and terror walked Magnus.

He was casually dressed in an open-necked shirt and chinos, russet-brown hair newly cut and a light dusting of stubble adorning his cheeks. He was also carrying a bottle of wine.

'Ah,' he said. 'Hello.'

'We,' I said, gritting my teeth against the grinding of the bones in my wrist as Kizzie hung onto it, 'have something of a problem.'

'Oh, aye,' he said, with a farmer's calm in the face of dreadful circumstances. 'Hey, Kiz, what're you doing here?'

'I came for Innis, but she's not here.'

'Aye, she's away to Scotland to see her granny.' He was keeping his voice level and soothing, but then he had more experience of talking to Kizzie than I did. 'So, the baby's coming, is it?'

'Looks like it.' I tried to inch Kizzie away from me but her muscles seemed to have set with me in her grasp. 'And we need a...' I gave him a wide-eyed stare and mouthed, '*hospital,*' so Kizzie wouldn't hear me and panic again.

Magnus pulled a face. 'Just you stop there a wee minute, Kiz,' he said. 'Get comfortable – or as comfortable as you can. I want a word with Brid.'

To my relief, Kizzie let go of me and slumped down onto the sofa, crouching forward over her bump but not speaking. She was blowing again, as though she were trying to extinguish the birthday candles on an octogenarian's cake, one by one, and rocking slightly.

'Magnus?' He took me by an elbow and hustled me into the kitchen, where Cushie had been eyeing up the oven. 'She has to get to a doctor, at least.'

'She won't.' He upset his obviously carefully done hair by running his hands through it. 'Kizzie – well, she's had bad experiences with the medical profession.'

'But she's having a *baby*!'

'That had not escaped my attention.' He flashed a quick grin. 'Look, Kizzie's not... she's not like you and me. She looks like an innocent wee girl, but she's had a life that we can only imagine. Contrary to what you might think, though, she knows her own mind and you'll not get her within feet of a hospital if she can do anything to prevent it.'

From the room came the sound of another rising wail-groan.

'Do you know how to deliver a baby?' I asked tersely. 'Because that baby's coming out, and very soon by the sounds of it.'

'Well.' He rolled up his sleeves. 'I can deliver a calf. And this will be smaller, and the mother can talk, so it can only be easier. How about you?'

'Of course I can't! I'm a sodding *accountant*! I don't even watch *Call the Midwife*!'

We stood and looked at one another, while Cushie huffed herself back into the larder, where the goslings were faffling about, pecking up spilled feed by the sounds of it. 'Then I think you are about to experience what is known as "a very steep learning curve".' Magnus patted my shoulder. 'Besides. You're the witch. That counts for a lot.'

'I really don't think placebos and positive thinking are going to help Kizzie right now,' I said, my voice tight. 'We're a little bit past raspberry tea and a massage.'

'Then you'll have to channel your inner Jennet.' He opened the kitchen door again and we went out, to find that Kizzie was on the floor. She had her top half on the sofa, lower half kneeling so that she was resting her weight on her arms, and she was making a long, drawn out 'uuuuuuuuuhhhhhhh' sound.

'I think we'd better wash our hands,' Magnus sounded slightly nervous, 'because things are happening.'

We duly washed our hands, hoping that the imminent baby wouldn't be offended by its birth attendants smelling of Fairy Liquid, and rushed to Kizzie's side.

'You're going to have to take off your knickers,' Magnus said.

'I can't move,' she whimpered.

I took her head in my hands, looked her deep in the eye and said, 'Your baby is coming, Kizzie, and you can't push it out properly with your pants on,' with, I hoped, enough authority and witchiness for her to concentrate.

'Oh. Okay.' Without raising her top half, Kizzie managed to scoop off her knickers, and then went back to the slight rocking.

'Right, I can see the head,' Magnus said, slightly surprisingly, from the business end. 'You just keep pushing when you need to, Kizzie, slow and steady.'

Terrified eyes met mine. 'I don't think I can.'

Speaking slowly, with absolutely all the influence and psychic power I could muster, which wasn't a lot, I said, 'Yes. Yes, you can. You're going to have this baby and you are going to be the best damn mother in the world to it. You're going to give this child everything you never had, and it is going to grow up to be happy and healthy and amazing, but you *have to push, now*.'

'I don't want to. I mean, can't I just go home and...'

'No.' I sounded as though I did this sort of thing every day now, and even managed to reassure *myself* with my certainty. 'You breathe and you push, Kizzie.'

Another contraction overtook her and she grabbed my arm,

squeezing it to the bone. It seemed churlish to complain that it hurt, when she was clearly in quite a lot more pain.

'Steady now,' Magnus said. 'Here we go.'

'You've got this,' I whispered, not sure who to.

Kizzie dropped her head and pushed. And, guided by Magnus, with the skill and expertise of one who had delivered more calves and lambs than he'd had hot dinners, the baby slid into the world, blue and steaming.

'Right.' Magnus handed the child to its mother, who managed to raise herself to turn and fall back onto my sofa amid the cushions, while more blood and goo issued forth. 'Okay, we've got the placenta.' He looked at me now. 'We may need some newspaper and some scissors. Oh, and towels.' A brief glance at the gore-fest that was my new furniture. '*Lots* of towels.'

All the brown packing paper that had hidden Jennet's book came in very useful. I didn't have many towels, but we used all the bedding – except the lovely hand-stitched quilt, I drew the line at that, and most of my spare clothing. In the end, Kizzie lay back holding her infant, which was swaddled in my jumper, its little face, now a more normal colour, scrunched up and crying. Kizzie was covered with my blankets, lying on my Pokémon towel, and still managing to look unearthly and serene.

'You've got a little girl,' I said, trying to stuff the stained packing paper into a rubbish bag. 'What are you going to call her?'

Kizzie was staring at her baby as though she couldn't believe it was real. 'It's a baby,' she whispered. She had lifted her top and put the baby to suck as though she'd been a mother forever, and I reassured myself that she may not have seen any doctors, but she had clearly read books about motherhood, and had a vague idea of what to do now.

'Aye. I'd have run screaming if it had been a horse.' Magnus brought through a bowl of hot water and we began mopping and washing. 'So. D'you have a name for her?'

Kizzie stroked the top of her daughter's head. 'I've always liked Emily,' she said, and then raised her eyes to mine. 'But what did you say your name was, again?'

Ridiculously proud, I said, 'It's Brid.'

'Oh.' A pause. 'I think I'll call her Emily.' Another pause. 'But maybe Brid as a middle name. Or Octavia, I like that too.'

'As soon as you think you can stand, I'll drive you home, Kiz.' Magnus gave the floor another quick wipe. 'I'll give the health visitor a ring so she can come over and take a look at you both too, if that's all right.'

Kizzie continued to stare down at her daughter's head as though she still couldn't quite believe her. 'Oh, yes,' she said. 'Alison. I like her.'

'And she can give you advice and everything,' I said, relieved to the nth degree that we weren't going to be without some form of official medical back-up.

'Then shall I come back?' Magnus threw me a quick glance. 'For dinner? Or has it passed its best by some margin now?'

'It's boeuf bourguignon, it doesn't really have a "best".' I tied the neck of the rubbish bag and handed it to Magnus. 'It will sit, all docile, until we decide to eat, although it may get a bit crusty if you take too long. I'll just drink the wine while I wait.'

'You told me I was going to be a good mother.' Kizzie looked up at me now. 'And I want you to be right. Can you do a spell for Emily, for her future? Like a fairy godmother?'

'No. Can I?' I hadn't looked away from Magnus yet, he was smiling. 'What kind of spell?'

'Wishing her health and a long and happy life, that sort of thing. You are the witch, aren't you? I know you are, because I felt the magic when you were telling me to push. It was like I couldn't *not* push, like something had taken me over and was making me have my baby, and that was you, wasn't it?'

'That was biology, sweetheart.' I sat on the sofa arm, next to where her baby suckled, quiet and content, the sleeve of my jumper waggling as the tiny arms moved, as yet beyond their owner's control. 'But if it makes you happy, I'll do a spell for Emily.'

The endorphins of relief were flooding through me now. Everything had ended well and, apart from some near-terminal staining on my sofa cushions, it was all right. The sheer backwash of satisfaction at a happy ending made me generous. Who cared if Kizzie thought I was a witch? Who cared if *everyone* thought I was a witch?

I put my hand in the air over the baby's head and moved my fingers as though drawing in the space. 'You're going to be everything you ever want to be,' I muttered, loudly enough for Kizzie to hear, but quietly enough to sound slightly mystical. Then, mindful of one of Jennet's often written phrases about 'the power of three', I repeated it another couple of times.

Kizzie sighed happily and leaned back. 'I think I might be able to get to the car now,' she said. 'Please will you take me home, Magnus?'

We got her on her feet, largely swaddled still in the Pokémon towel – poor old Charmander was never going to be the same again – and with blankets around her and the baby, we supported her out to Magnus' Jeep and helped her into the cab.

'I haven't got a baby seat!' Kizzie said, suddenly alarmed. 'What do we do with Emily?'

'Look, this is an emergency.' Magnus tucked the blankets around her again. 'I'll drive really slowly and carefully, and you know this road, Kiz, we'll likely not meet another car until Kirkwall junction.'

'What if you go off the road into a ditch?'

I found her preoccupation with safety reassuring. Kizzie might be vague-minded, but she was going to care for her baby with everything she had.

'I promise I won't, all right?' Magnus winked at me, jumped into the driver's seat, and the pair of them were gone, taking all my blankets and my only big towel with them.

18

Once the adrenaline of dealing with the birth had drained away, I felt weak and shaky. Every alternative whirled around in my head; *what if the baby had got stuck? What if it hadn't been breathing? What if Kizzie hadn't known what to do? What if... what if...* It was exhausting.

I tried to make myself tea, but my hands were trembling and a lot of the water slopped over the worktop, which I couldn't then mop up because all my towels were currently sitting in a blood-stained pile by the door. Magnus had taken the rubbish bag full of paper and 'other stuff', just in case the health visitor needed to see the placenta, apparently. I had no idea what she would do with it, or why she'd want to see it, maybe there was some kind of competition? But at least the disposal would be her problem rather than mine.

I drank the tea and realised that I was also cold with shock, and all my jumpers were adorning Kizzie and the infant, so I put my coat on. I couldn't sit on the sofa – which I didn't even dare contemplate at the moment – but I needed something to calm me, something regular, ordinary and routine. Something that would make the last hour or so fade in my memory, if that was ever going to happen. So I sat on the floor and opened my laptop.

Emails felt like a strange concept out here. As the simmer dim began to fade down towards proper darkness, making outdoors look as though a solar eclipse was taking place, I sat and flicked through my inbox, neglected for the past few days in favour of – what? Hanging around with Magnus, talking to Innis, feeding Cushie and the goslings and signing the cottage up for sale.

It came as a shock almost equal to that of the precipitate birth that I'd not logged in for a while. That I'd not checked my work emails with the almost clockwork regularity that I normally did when on holiday, study leave or even at weekends; opening my emails like a nervous tic every ten minutes in case someone needed me. I shook my head at the number of unread mails in my inbox – 147. I'd been lax. I'd taken my eye off the ball, and that feeling of duty, of having a job to do, pushed the cold, weak feeling into second place, so I began checking through to sort through the incoming, while the room filled with the smell of rapidly desiccating beef.

Advertising. Delete. Sale on at John Lewis. Delete. Can't-be-missed opportunity for networking. Delete. One email from my mother, keep that. Delete, delete, delete. One email from work and a sense of relief, keep that to open. Delete, delete. Another email from work, and curiosity pushed me to open that one immediately, it had arrived yesterday.

A bulk email, lots of blind copies, very much 'to whom it may concern'. Office rationalisation, ongoing immediately. 'Due to ongoing cost issues, streamlining, leaner, cost cutting, strategic', the usual buzz words. But nothing personal, nothing to make me fear that my position was particularly in jeopardy, just the usual seasonal attempts to make us all work harder and the redundancy of the casual and temporary workers.

Then the email from my mother. Chatty, full of her usual mala-propisms and in-depth analyses of superficial things. It sounded as though she and my father were getting a lot out of the MS group; they'd made new friends, were socialising like a pair of It Girls, had found new resources for help and physical assistance, and she ended with some cheery lines about hoping I was getting on all right, no need to hurry back on their account, everything was fine in Yorkshire.

The email left me feeling empty, for some reason. Reiterating her phone call, that they weren't missing me even a little. Back in York I'd become so used to making the phone calls – even if many of them had gone unanswered due to my mother's tendency to put the phone down and forget about it – and the daily visits that her cheerful re-ignition of a social life that had largely stagnated after my father's diagnosis made me feel a bit brushed off. Their lives had been my life, and now I could stay in Orkney for all they cared. A curious sensation of uselessness crept over me and I had to give myself a stern talking to. I was still in shock, of course I was. I was still feeling the withdrawal of the adrenaline that had stopped me running screaming from the birth of a baby on my living room floor. I was *vulnerable*, that was it. Not something I was used to, and it was giving rise to this impression that I'd been deserted.

I opened the other email from work. Sent before the Round Robin, it was asking when I was due back in the office, how much holiday I had still owing to me and whether I could take on any work while I was away. A final sentence hoped I wasn't overstaying my 'time in lieu' and would be back within the next week.

It had a vaguely threatening tone, which was a bit rich since I'd not had any holiday at all the previous year, only some study leave, and two days off sick when Annie had generously given me the norovirus she'd inherited from another student. But at least the hinted-at repercussions if I stayed out of the office for too long made me feel wanted. Missed. *Necessary.*

I think I must have dozed off, because I was snapped into sitting upright by a hand on my shoulder. It was Magnus.

'Look, it's really late,' he said in an undertone which was unnecessary because there wasn't anyone else for miles. 'Why don't you just go to bed and we'll try again another night?'

Blurrily I blinked to bring him into focus. 'I can't. All my bedding went with Kizzie.' I elbowed myself into a sitting position, the laptop sliding from my knee onto the floor beside me. 'I didn't really think that through.'

He hesitated. 'Turn the oven off,' he said. 'You can come back to my place for tonight, I've got a spare bed.'

I was too sleepy to argue. I clambered to my feet, inelegantly, and turned the stove off, leaving the sad remains of the boeuf bourguignon to quietly cool into something that resembled a scale model of the Alps, done in brown. Then I picked up my bag and followed Magnus back out to his vehicle.

'You must be sick of driving up and down by now,' I said, as the cool night air revived me a touch. 'Was Kizzie all right?'

'I waited with her until Alison came over, then I left her being examined. She seems to be fine, and the baby is good and healthy. Alison said that she was the sturdiest newborn she'd ever set eyes on.' He side-eyed me as we drove out over the cattle grid onto the road. 'Kizzie said it was because you were her fairy godmother.'

'Did she now?'

'Mmmm.' His lips twitched. 'It's probably worse that Alison just nodded and agreed with her.'

'I'm not sure you are allowed to disagree with new mothers, though. Kizzie did really well, she must have been terrified. And you...' I trailed off, looking out through the window at the acres of blackness that were Mainland once the night had come in. Distant lights, like irregular sequins, showed farmsteads and houses fringing the darker black of lochs and the tyres swished through the leavings of a recent rain shower.

'You kept your head well,' Magnus said eventually. 'And you helped Kizzie keep hers.'

'You did the hard work.'

'I think Kizzie did that. I just had to steer and catch.' He looked thoughtful. 'Human babies aren't very streamlined, are they? Calves and lambs come with their noses down on their legs, head-first like little missiles. Babies are all lumps and bumps, like trying to get a load of corks out of bottles all at once.'

'At least you knew what you were doing.' I was cold now, even with my coat still on. And tired. And hungry. 'Are there any chip shops still open?'

'I'll make you a sandwich.' He pulled the car down the hill towards Kirkwall. There was no other traffic to be seen in either direction; it felt a little as though we were the only people moving through this temporary darkness. The lights of the little town spangled the hillside as we drove down a back street and pulled in behind the row of shops. 'Come on.'

It felt entirely natural that Magnus should take my hand to help me down from the cab and then keep hold of it as we went in through a small door and up a flight of narrow stairs to his flat. 'You're freezing,' he said, rubbing at my fingers.

'I think I'm still in shock. Plus only half awake, and cheated out of my dinner. None of these things are designed to make you feel alert and happy.'

The whole flat smelled of Magnus. That citrusy fresh smell that I'd noticed on him before filled the main room, which the front door opened straight into. A small wood-burning stove sat in one corner with an enormous squashy sofa opposite, as though he spent his evenings watching conflagrations, and there were sheep-skin rugs dotted around the pale wood floor. 'It's like a Viking's *Ideal Home* magazine spread,' I said.

'It's small, but it's mine.' Magnus went through an archway and I could see a little fitted kitchen beyond. 'Bathroom is through the first door, if you want to have a shower, and I'll make you that sandwich while you get cleaned up. You can take my bed, the sofa pulls out and I'm used to sleeping on it.'

I paused, halfway to the bathroom. 'I can sleep on the pull-out. Honestly.'

'Och, you're all right, I changed the sheets just this morning, you'll no die of some awful disease.'

'That's not what I meant. I don't want to put you out of your own bed.'

Magnus popped back under the archway. 'I know. And it's fine. You look dead on your feet, get that shower and then into bed. You can wear one of my T-shirts.'

I showered, for the first time since I'd arrived in Orkney, luxuriating in the feel of hot water that I didn't have to splash all over myself, the fact that my bum wasn't squeezed into a little metal tub, and some shower wash that Magnus kept in a cubby hole in the wall in the neat and gleaming room.

Then, feeling as though I'd walked into an American TV series, I came out to find that he'd put a clean white T-shirt just outside the door, so I popped back in, hung up the towel I'd been wearing and put it on. It was, in the approved fashion, long and I wondered what I would have done if his T-shirt hadn't fitted, or had stopped somewhere up my midriff, and why that possibility never occurred to TV script writers. But I was half asleep already and probably wouldn't have noticed, and, in fact, hardly registered Magnus leading me through another door, pointing me towards an enormous bed all made up with pure white bedding, and saying, 'I'll see you in the morning.'

I went out like a light almost before I hit the mattress.

* * *

I woke up, not knowing where I was.

The arched, beamed ceiling close above my head made me wonder if I'd fallen asleep in an oddly comfortable church, but then the smell of clean linen, the feel of a comfortable mattress and the fact that I was wearing a T-shirt that had ridden up in the night over my ribs came in, along with memory.

This was Magnus' flat. I was in a bed I could fully stretch out in, not my little cupboard. The furniture, well, bedside table and a chair over by the window, were carved wood. There were no carrier bags of stuff lying around, no discarded clothes draped over the chair, only a couple of books very neatly angled next to a stylish lamp beside the bed. The room looked like a magazine shoot.

Then I smelled breakfast cooking and nearly levitated up at a speed that would have knocked me out against the ceiling beams had I gone high enough.

'Ah. I thought food might get you.'

Magnus was in the little kitchen, tea towel tucked around his waist, frying something. I was so hungry that I didn't care what it was – it could have been blubber and tripe, I was almost hooking it out of the pan with my fingertips.

'Well, we never got our dinner last night, did we?' I sat down where he pointed, at a small bench and tiny table set in the corner of the kitchen. 'It was going to be boeuf bourguignon too.'

'I'm sure it would have been lovely,' Magnus said gallantly, putting a plate in front of me and loading it with bacon, sausage and egg. 'But I thought something a little more down to earth might suit this morning.'

'I don't imagine it's lovely any more,' I said sadly around toast. 'Kizzie rather put paid to that.'

'Ah, yes.' Magnus sat beside me, pan still in hand. 'You were amazing, Brid. Honestly.'

I hid the hot rise of pleasure at his compliment behind my toast.

'You'd have every right to have sent her on her way, y'know.' Magnus slid the rest of the contents of the pan onto his own plate. 'Especially knowing that she and I had history.'

I stared at him, arrested as I was in the act of putting bacon in my mouth. 'Do you really think that crossed my mind at the time? "Oh, this is Magnus' ex-girlfriend, I am absolutely not going to help her when she's so clearly in pain and crisis"?'

He shrugged, and picked up his fork.

'And don't flatter yourself, sunshine. You and I are... are...' More confusion, covered this time by egg dripping down the borrowed T-shirt and my hasty attempts to rectify the situation.

'And you are the witch.'

'Oh, yes, and that, obviously.'

He was grinning at me, using his toast to sandwich some bacon, and I realised with a start that this was the first man who had ever cooked for me. The first man ever to give up his bed for me without making some lecherous remark or attempt to climb in alongside me. The first man, in short, to ever treat me like a real person, rather than a woman who existed simply to fill a 'woman-shaped hole' in his life.

I grinned back. 'But I'm really not, you do know that?'

Eyebrows raised, he paused, chewing. 'You knew what to say to Kizzie. You've been helping people, aye?'

'I've been reading Jennet's book. It's not witchcraft, it's just listening to people. They really just want reassurance that they've been heard; that someone is listening to them and taking them seriously. That's what Jennet says, anyway.'

'Does she, now?' The eyebrow was still crooked.

'Yes. Although I have to say that taking advice from a woman who's been dead for half a century is very nearly as bonkers as thinking I'm a witch, so there's that.'

Magnus really was very attractive. Even with a mouth full of toast and bacon, he was attractive. The high sun sneaking in through the little casement caught in his hair, netting it with gold and red, while barely-there pinpricks of auburn stubble glowed on his cheeks and chin. Eyes of green hazel were regarding me steadily.

'We can't,' I whispered. 'I'm going back.'

'But that's for then.' He was whispering too now, as though we didn't want our intent to seep out to the sparrows listening on the guttering outside. 'What about *now*, Brid? What about throwing all that good sense and duty out for the *now*?'

It turned out to be easier than I thought to disregard the fact that I was leaving soon, that this couldn't be a 'thing', that it would never be more than a temporary good time. We were kissing over the plates of half-eaten egg and the toast crumbs, me with my elbow in the bacon fat and Magnus with both hands balled into my T-shirt holding me steady. We kissed under the kitchen archway, out across the sleekly stark living room, feet catching in the sheep-skin rugs, and then on into the pale bedroom beyond.

The sun was already lying in the bed, warming the sheets, we did no more than assist its heat, tangling together into the smooth linen in an urgency of limbs and mouths as though we couldn't get enough of one another. It ought to have felt slightly awkward, this first time, but we fitted together so well, so instinctively, that I lost my usual self-consciousness about being tall and angular and went with the movement and friction and followed Magnus into sighing and mumbling satisfaction.

Afterwards we lay, me with my head on his chest, as our breathing caught up with us. His silver necklace rose and fell gratifyingly quickly at his throat and I had my hands splayed along his ribcage, feeling his heart calming back down to a more normal speed.

'Wow,' he said.

'It was a bit, wasn't it?'

'I do have to say, in my defence, that it usually goes on a wee bit longer than that.' He laughed and my head bounced until the light sprinkle of golden hair on his chest tickled my ear. 'But it's been a while, so, y'know.' He moved to sit up, grasping for the edge of the duvet.

'Where are you going?' I asked, sounding a little panicked and yet also resigned. Men leaping out of bed and going on with their day after sex wasn't exactly an unknown experience in my life, but I'd been enjoying this quiet moment of feeling close.

'Och, woman, I'm not going anywhere. I'm going to fetch the rest of the toast back here. I don't know about you, but missing dinner last night means I'm bloody starving and that's a good breakfast out there going begging.'

I couldn't help it, I laughed. And I was still laughing when he came back with plates heaped high with well-buttered toast and two mugs of coffee steaming fragrantly into the beams of light latticing their way along the wall.

'I don't think anyone's ever made me breakfast in bed before.' I took a plate and mug and humped myself back against the pillows.

'Aye, well, I'm still trying to make a good impression. Give it a few months and I'll be nudging you out with an elbow to go and make me a cup of tea, when the frost is on the inside of the windows.'

There was a moment's silence. 'I won't be here in a few months, Magnus,' I said, gently.

He kissed my shoulder. 'I was forgetting there for a moment,' he said softly. 'It feels like you've always been here and you always will be.'

And there was nothing I could really say to that. Nothing I *wanted* to say.

19

Magnus offered to drive me back to the cottage, but had to open the shop first, so I went for a wander round Kirkwall while he did so.

The air had a morning stillness to it, the trees that fringed the Bishop's Palace were gaining a few reluctant leaves, and the rooks were stomping sulkily about in the grounds, deprived of their usual updraughts. The sun was shining with a hint of warmth, shops were opening and I was greeted by raised hands and 'good mornings', and I was perfectly content to wait for Magnus to lay out the silver displays.

'Hi there!' It was a jaunty greeting and I turned around from my perusal of some lovely leather handbags in a window, to see a vaguely familiar man standing behind me. My brain whirled and shrieked at me as I tried to place him, and then the sculpted facial hair triggered my memory.

'It's Kerr, isn't it?'

Kerr, the estate agent that I'd met at the bar. Thin and handsome and just a teensy bit too aware of it for my liking.

'It is, aye. How're you doing? Fancy a coffee? I'm just away to open my place and fire up the machine.' He waved a hand at the small side street.

I checked the time. Magnus had said he'd be about an hour and I still had three-quarters of that time to wait. I didn't want to weaken and buy any more soft furnishings, so I followed Kerr down to the narrow door in the little white building, and inside.

'I'm just waiting for Magnus,' I explained, so that Kerr didn't think I'd been hanging about waiting to catch a glimpse of him. He looked the type to think just that.

'Oh, aye.'

'So I can't be long.'

'No.' Kerr took off his jacket, hung it up and switched on a coffee machine that was all malevolent blue lights and flashing displays. 'I just wanted a quiet word, and I don't think out in the street was the best place,' he said, sorting through a handful of envelopes that had been left on his desk, but in the kind of absent-minded way that made me think he was trying to think what to say.

'A word about what?'

He put the envelopes down and began busying himself with the coffee machine, almost nervously. 'You've put the cottage on with Donal then, have you?'

'Well, yes.'

The machine spurted steam and chuntered to itself. Kerr still looked nervous. 'He's not put it out, though, anywhere? I've not seen it go up for sale.'

'No. He said he's already got someone who wants to buy it. I just want...' I tailed off. I *had* been going to reiterate my need to sell quickly and head back to York, but breakfast and what came after slightly got in the way. 'I need a quick sale,' I finished.

'Look, this is probably nothing. Just stupid tattle and stuff, but I thought you ought to know.' Kerr spoke quickly, shaking the coffee spout until drops of fragrant liquid fell into two cups. 'Donal is saying that you are the witch.'

I stared at him. 'Kerr, *everyone* is saying that I'm the witch.'

'But it had to come from somewhere first. And I think it was Donal. Before you even came over, he was saying that the witch was coming back for her cottage.'

I stared even more. But I still took the coffee he handed me. After all the effort it had evidently cost the machine, it would have been mean to refuse. 'But how would... oh.' Donal was friendly with Innis, wasn't he? She, presumably, had told him I was coming to clear out Jennet's place and put it up for sale. 'Surely he doesn't believe in all that nonsense, though?' I thought of Donal, so urbane that he was almost friction-free. The idea of him believing that I was a witch was ridiculous.

'Well, no. I'd think not. But anyway. It was what he was saying. And you say he's already got a buyer for you?' Kerr looked at me over his coffee. 'That's good. What are they offering?'

I wavered over telling him, but what did I have to lose? What was I afraid of, that he'd march round to Donal's office and arm-wrestle him for the place? So I told Kerr the figure that Donal had told me.

He pulled a face. 'Seems on the low side.'

'It's basically one room, though. No access.'

'But there's sewerage and electricity to the site. And you'd only need to negotiate for an access strip down the side of Torstein's land, you can't get a car over the bog anyhow, and that wee stone path won't make a driveway. I'd have thought...'

I wondered if Kerr wanted me to take the cottage away from Donal and give it to him to sell. He would, no doubt, promise me a higher price. But, for one thing, I didn't know if I could legally take it back, I'd signed papers to give Donal the right to sell, and for another, Kerr could promise anything. Whether he could deliver or not was something else.

'I just want a really quick sale and to go back to York,' I finished.

Kerr nodded. 'Of course. Low price for a quick sale, that's reasonable.'

I narrowed my eyes. 'Why? How much do *you* think it's worth?'

He shrugged. 'I've not seen inside.'

'Ballpark figure then.'

I got a grin now. 'Are you trying to obtain my professional expertise without paying for it, now?'

'Look, you started all this! I was happily window shopping until you lured me in here with offers of coffee and then dire warnings about – actually, I've got no idea what you think you're warning me about.'

'Nothing. I just wanted to let you know that if everyone thinks you're the witch, it probably started with Donal.' Kerr drank some more coffee. 'It just felt like telling you was the right thing to do.'

'And not because of some Mafia-esque estate agency wars that I know nothing about?'

He snorted. 'This is Kirkwall, not Chicago. The worst we're going to do is steal the odd For Sale board from one another, not issue dire warnings and poach customers.' He drained his mug. 'Well, not often, anyway.'

But what he'd said made things make sense. People pitching up at my door wanting help, wanting the witch. If Donal had told them that I actually *was* a witch – yes. I could imagine it now, he'd have had his tongue in his cheek and a half smile on his face as he did so, not thinking for a second that anyone would actually believe it – and here I was now, handing out herbal tea and hand cream and trying to pretend I knew what I was talking about. What a bastard.

'In that case,' I swallowed down the last of the bitter, and not very hot, coffee, 'it's just as well if I leave as soon as possible, really, isn't it? Before people *really* start to think I've got magical powers!' I laughed, slightly disconcerted when Kerr didn't laugh along with me.

'May be a wee bit late for that,' he muttered.

'This is all just so ridiculous.' I put my cup down firmly on the edge of his desk. 'There's no such thing as witches. Magic is imaginary, and anything I've done has all been psychological trickery. People just want someone to listen to them and care, that's all it is.' As I parroted Jennet's words from the *Book of Shadows*, I heard them echo in my ears with a kind of hollowness, as though I was reciting into the cave of my chest made by my heart dropping out. *Someone to listen. Someone to care.* Which was what I'd found here, just maybe, in Magnus.

But I had to go.

'I'd better get back,' I said through my inner turmoil. 'Thanks for the heads-up, Kerr. I'm sure Donal thought it was just a joke and he never meant for people to take him seriously.'

'Aye.' Kerr fidgeted, flipping the edges of some pieces of paper. 'Aye. That'll be it, for sure.'

'He wasn't to know that I'd get them pitching up and wanting treatment, after all. You've got perfectly good doctors and a hospital here, after all.'

But, I thought as I left, the little door pinging its bell shrill in the early morning air, those people I'd treated hadn't been doctor or hospital cases, had they? They'd wanted comfort, reassurance, not medicine. Was there a holistic treatment centre anywhere that I could point them towards? Acupuncture, hypnosis, floatation tanks, that kind of thing? I should look into it. And hand out cards.

Magnus was laying out the last of the velvet-lined trays in the window when I got back to his shop. Dark blue, they made the silver glint and wink against their textured surface and I was briefly reminded of the sea, deep and dark with the flicker of silver waves breaking the surface. That twist of blackness of the orca moving within the depths, hunting along the fathomless channels...

'No shopping?' Magnus enquired cheerily as I went in. 'I thought you were going to get some replacement cushions?'

'I, um, I got distracted.' I didn't want to tell him what Kerr had said about Donal. It was something of nothing, it couldn't be undone, and I didn't want to cause any kind of personal rifts between people who had to live here so closely that they almost jostled. What did it matter, after all? A few jokey remarks about the witch coming back to the cottage? It was hardly ruining my life, was it?

'So, shall I run you back now? I need to come back to do some work, I'm afraid, but we could meet up this evening?'

There was an almost unbearable hopefulness in his voice. As though he really, really wanted to make sure that I wasn't going to shake off this morning as a one-off, and I realised that I wanted him around.

'I still owe you a dinner,' I said and his grin was my reward. 'I think I've got enough stuff left over to knock up another stew, but it might not be as grand as the ruined one.'

'Och, it's just food,' Magnus said with a casualness that belied the way he'd tucked into his breakfast. 'And I'm coming for the company, after all.' Then, appearing to think about what he'd just said, 'But no expectations. Obviously. I want you to know that, Brid. No strings, no "Oh, can I just stay over?" I'm not that type of man.'

No, I thought, as we walked back to his van, parked around the back of the little row of shops, you aren't, are you? I glanced quickly up at the windows of the flat above, where the sun had moved from the bedroom and was warming the rooftops now, ornamented with basking gulls hunched along the ridge like Roman antefix. I shook my head. Too many school trips, that's what that was. There was nothing Roman about Orkney, this place was Viking through and through, wild and windswept and they wouldn't have known a toga from a trumpet.

'Are you all right?' Magnus asked quietly, as he started the engine. 'It was all a wee bit spontaneous back there, I hope I didn't... I mean, we didn't discuss anything...'

'It's fine, honestly.' I knew what he was asking. 'I've been on the pill since I was seventeen, although lately I've been beginning to think it was a waste of medication.'

'Oh. Oh, good.'

'And I think Kizzie yesterday has put me off breeding for life.' I paused. 'On other people's sofas, certainly.'

'Yes, a spot more "planning" about the family planning, that's what she could do with.' Magnus seemed to pause for thought for a moment. 'She's a lovely wee artist, though, our Kizzie.'

I was reassured, although I hadn't even thought I needed to be. He spoke about his ex now as though she were a slightly troublesome younger sister, rather than 'the one that got away'.

We drove through the brittle light past acres of grassland, flat to the edges of the lochs as though ironed in place; past beckoning fingers of stone curling into the sky and past brooding howes, which blistered the ground like agricultural acne. Water on all sides reflected the light, the air threw itself joyfully over our heads, happily celebrating the lack of rain clouds and the millennia of settlement anchored the islands firmly into the sea. It was wild and treeless and the horizon was so far away that it bent with the curve of the planet.

Magnus dropped me at the house and turned the van around to head back, with a raised hand of farewell. I looked at the blank windows of the empty house and almost wished that Innis was here so that I could pop in and ask her what she'd said to Donal to make him think that I'd enjoy being painted as the local witch. But

I had to settle for stomping heavily and irritatedly past, splashing mud up the Wendy house and an assortment of piled trikes on my way down to the cottage.

Cushie side-eyed me, waddling past as I opened the door as though she'd been trapped in overnight, and with the goslings prancing their high-pitched, voice-breaking teenage honks behind her she stalked into the day, pausing only to dollop a sizeable helping of goose poo on the step to register her displeasure.

'Love you too,' I muttered to her feathery back, winding through the cotton grass and rushes to the edge of the loch. Then I stared at the room, the stained rug, the pile of soaked cushions, where our brief attempts to clean up last night had done little more than smear blood around. Thank goodness Donal had already taken the photographs, because now the place wouldn't appeal to anyone who didn't have a career in serial murdering lined up.

'Oh, bugger,' I said, and went to fill the bucket with bleach water, even though there was already so much bleach in here that the floor smelled like a swimming pool and the cushions were beginning to disintegrate.

20

That evening, Magnus turned up with company.

'Hey.' He tapped quietly at the door, waking me from the light doze I had fallen into, curled up in a slightly chilly fashion, in the bed-cupboard. 'I hope you don't mind. I brought Kizzie back to pick up her car.'

'I brought your things back.' Kizzie's voice, still as enthusiastic as ever, came at his shoulder. 'Your blankets and stuff. It's all right, they're clean, I put them through the machine.'

'Are you all right to drive?' I blearily stared at the pair of them. Well, the three of them, Emily was there too, a pale doll-face peering at me from a car seat. Now she was clean, I could see the fair wispy hair high on her forehead and the determined expression already on her little face.

'I think so. I feel fine. More than fine – and it's all thanks to you.'

Oh no, I thought, sleepily rubbing my hands over my eyes to try to pull myself out of the surreality, but then realising that all my life was pretty surreal at the moment. Not more 'perfectly normal things being attributed to witchcraft' nonsense. 'I didn't...' I began.

'You and Magnus, anyway,' Kizzie went on. 'Delivering Emily and helping me through the birth.'

Well, she was right there, I supposed. I rubbed my face again.

'I can follow Kizzie back to hers, if you think it's safer.' Magnus loomed into view now. I had to get out of this cupboard.

'Can... can *you* follow me, Brid?' Kizzie juggled Emily's chair again. 'Only I've got something for you, back at my house.'

Which was how, instead of waving her a cheery goodbye and tucking into dinner with Magnus, I found myself following Kizzie's slow and steady progress back to Kirkwall, and a tiny row of houses perched up on the cliffs above the town.

I muttered to myself that I'd worn a groove between the cottage and Kirkwall, and was ushered into Kizzie's lovely little home; an ancient fisherman's house with boarded floors and paintings on every wall, plus a really modern kitchen and heating system. Kizzie might behave as though she didn't know what day it was, but she kept a beautiful home and I felt even more inadequate at my one room, and now-stained-and-never-to-be-used-again sofa.

Kizzie swung the car seat onto the table and stared at the face of her newborn daughter. 'She's asleep,' she said, proudly.

I was irritated by my own lack of sleep and wanted to go home. 'She's hardly likely to be dancing the tarantella, is she?' I asked, somewhat waspishly. Then I softened. 'She's beautiful, Kizzie,' I said, softly. 'Really beautiful.'

I had never really considered babies before. There's a distinct lack of infant around accountancy and I'd not felt the pull of motherhood in any way. Watching Kizzie tenderly fold a corner of soft blanket over Emily's pearl-like fists, I wondered why. Then I remembered Innis' struggles with the multiple toddlers and knew *exactly* why.

I gave myself a stern talking to. Witchcraft was one thing. I could head back to York and ignore that. Motherhood was something else entirely and I needed to take some deep breaths and remember that I didn't have anywhere of my own to live.

'She is, isn't she?' Kizzie replied, complacently. Then, 'Here. I wanted to give you this. I painted it for Donal, because he asked me to, but I think you should have it to say thank you for yesterday. I can always do him another one. I didn't want to bring it over to your cottage, just in case you didn't like it but didn't want to say so.'

She pulled a picture off an easel, which had been propped near the window. It was a painting of Jennet's cottage from the other side of the loch, so the water was big and mirror-grey in the foreground and the cottage a small, ivy-covered building behind it.

The detail was amazing. I half-expected the figure of Jennet to come bustling around the wall, shaking a broom handle at the artist daring to spy on her from across the loch. The dance of the ivy in the breeze was frozen in motion and the water gleamed in pinnacles and troughs of glaring silver and deep black.

I stared down into the painting. Inside me, a curious burning sensation took hold, the feeling of looking into... into *something*. Comfort and annoyance and worry and peace, all warring inside me in an emotional storm that settled into one word. *Home.*

'Wow, thanks.' I couldn't stop looking at it. 'That's amazing.' The words were breathed, not said.

Kizzie bustled with pride. 'Thank you. It's one of my best.'

Her previous words percolated down through my brain and I lowered the picture to look at her properly. 'You painted this for *Donal*?' Her downcast eyes and the glance she briefly flicked at her daughter told me everything I needed to know. 'Donal is Emily's dad?' Now the baby's hairline made sense. 'Does he know? No, forget that, I mean, just, *how*?'

The thought of the amphibian Donal with the fragile Kizzie was too unbelievable to get my head around. I stared at Emily as though I expected her to suddenly start snatching flies out of the air and eating them.

'He's quite nice, really.' Kizzie began fiddling with piles of sleep-suits, stacked on the table next to the baby seat. 'We went to North Cornwall last summer; I've got a foster sister who lives down there and she invited me, so we spent a week. Donal was doing research,' she added, proudly, although what he could have been researching, apart from basking in the sun and regrowing limbs, I didn't know. 'We were together for a little while, but he's so busy. Oh, he's paying for Emily, it's all right. I... when I grew up, I... well, I won't let her be without a father.'

Now she was looking at me directly. Her blue gaze was unusually straightforward, held no guile or guilt. 'You're going to be a cracking mum, Kizzie,' I said, genuinely. 'You really are.'

Then I left her to get on with baby things, and took myself and my picture back to the cottage, where Magnus was trying to find somewhere to sit that wasn't the sofa. He had perched on one of the chairs by the table, and was being stared at by Cushie with an intensity which made it look as though he were afraid to move.

'Er,' he said as soon as I came through the door. 'D'you think you could call your goose off? It's a wee bit unnerving.'

'Cushie,' I said, although I had no idea why the goose would listen to me, 'go away. You're being a nuisance. Here, go outside, the babies are out on the water.' I flapped the leading edge of the door in invitation, sending a cool blast of air that rippled the rug. 'Go on.'

Cushie switched her vitriolic attention from Magnus to me. With a set to her beak that told me I would regret this later, she stalked out of the open door, pausing only to give me a vicious peck on the leg as she went. I slammed the door on her tail feathers.

'That bird has *got* to go,' I said, rubbing my shin.

'Aye, well, I expect Donal will send the bailiffs in, once you're gone.' Magnus slumped down over the table as though his muscles had all relaxed now the goose was out of the house. 'Or whoever buys the place. There's no word out on the street, by the way, about who's put in the offer.'

'"On the street"?' I wandered into the kitchen. Today's much more homely beef stew smelled glorious. 'There aren't any streets. It's all fields and water. And stones.'

'Och, you know what I mean.' Magnus followed me in and there was a brief moment of thrillingly being pressed against one another as he tried to fit past me into the corner of the kitchen. 'How did it go with Kizzie then?'

I showed him the picture, at which he pulled an impressed face, and then I told him what Kizzie had told me, about Donal being Emily's father and their trip to Cornwall, because otherwise her painting a picture of my place for Donal just sounded weird. Knowing they had been – or still were, it was hard to tell with Kizzie – involved to the extent of conceiving a child made it make more sense.

'Aye, we wondered.' Magnus leaned against the corner. There was a suspicious sound of MDF buckling under stress. 'They did knock about together at one time when he came over.'

'I think they knocked more than that,' I said tartly. Then, 'Are you sure you're truly over each other, Magnus?'

He angled his head. 'Sure. It was a mistake in the first place, we were two strangers in a strange land, drawn together.'

'Not *that* strange a land. Only Glasgow,' I reminded him, still sounding slightly sharp.

'It's no Orkney, though. And a wee far cry from Exeter, from where our Kizzie hails.' Magnus' voice softened. 'We were adrift, Brid. We found each other, we admired each other and we were out of our depth. Well, Kizzie was looking for something, and I was – dislocated, shall we say? It happened, and I'm not sorry because it brought her over here, where she seems to have found a kind of peace, a place, if that makes sense. And now she's got her baby, so it's all worked out for Kizzie. And I...'

He stopped abruptly, and took the half a step that meant, in my tiny kitchen, he was right beside me. 'I've found something that means a lot too,' he whispered, taking my face in his hands and looking deep into my eyes.

'Don't, Magnus,' I whispered back. 'Don't make me feel guilty for this.'

He smiled. 'Now, why would you feel guilty?' A hand brushed across my hair.

'Because you know I can't stay. That we can't be – well, anything to one another, other than whatever *this* is.' I waved to indicate that *this* may well be a small, mostly plywood and damp, kitchenette.

'Oh, aye. But *this*,' he moved in closer, until all I could see were his eyes, not so much hazel now in the dim lighting, but dark, darker than the water beyond us, '*this* is fine for now.'

Then he kissed me. It wasn't a kiss that dragged lust up by its boots, dusted it off and set it loose. It was a kiss that enveloped, wrapped me in a softness that cushioned me against the inevitable parting.

'All right?' He moved back, still looking into my eyes.

'Oh, *bugger*.' I looped my arms behind his neck, closed the distance again and returned the kiss, but I let desire have its head on this one. Less of the soft promise and more of the dark heat and red flashes; lust rode in with all flags flying, and the ending was inevitable, even though the standing-up-against-the-cooker part was something of a surprise.

We were breathless and laughing, faces hidden in one another's shoulders as we held each other, our legs shaking. Most of my weight was still being borne by the oven door and I was immensely glad that the beef stew was in the slow cooker, otherwise I would have had some incredibly difficult-to-explain burns.

Despite the laughter, part of me wanted to cry, and I suspected that the tears weren't far beneath the giggles of surprised delight. Gradually, slowly, I was realising that Orkney held the things I lacked in York – a man who seemed to like me, and a home, even though it was only one step up from a feed shed. I kept my face hidden down on Magnus' neck until I was sure that the tears weren't about to surface, feeling his hot skin against my forehead and the barbs of his almost invisible golden stubble catching in my hair.

All right, so my parents might not need me as much as I'd thought they did, and I didn't feel bad about leaving them to it, knowing they'd found themselves a support group, something my father had resisted up until now. He'd not wanted to admit, I suspected, that vulnerability that *needed* a support group, and his present remission probably made him feel as though it were a nice addition to life rather than the necessity it could be.

My mother would join any group that would have her, and a tiny piece of me felt relief that she had someone else to tell now about Marks and Spencer sandwich prices and the entire plot of whatever TV drama was currently engaging her attention.

And perhaps – the thought was creeping up on me like the kind of shame that strikes in the night – maybe they had *never* needed me as much as I'd thought in the first place? All those evenings I'd sat in with them, watching TV and listening to them sporadically discuss their day... Had I been using them to keep me from having to go out and find a life?

Had she sent me up here to get rid of me?

My face felt incredibly warm now and I was glad I could use the very satisfactory sex as an excuse. A horrified realisation was beginning to dawn, as though the spectacles of past belief had been removed and I could see it all with a new clarity. I'd been stopping my parents from living their lives. I'd been treating them as though they were a pair of elderly recluses, when they were only in their mid-fifties. A sudden rush of blood to my cheeks made my ears sweat as I thought about all those nights in front of the TV. Had they been pining to get out and go to places? Had they been staying in because of *me*?

But there was still work. I gave myself a mental shake. I still had a duty to the office, to my clients and my coworkers. I had a *place*, a livelihood to earn and people who depended on me. Orkney, with its bright waters and perpetual skies, had a distinct lack of racing stables and horse-owners keen to lose as much tax as possible between the feed costs and premises rental.

Tomorrow, I'd do it. Tomorrow I'd get the paperwork signed and the cottage would be on sale. I'd apologise to my parents and learn to leave them alone. I could use the evenings to catch up on work, after all. I *had* to go back to York.

Orkney had much to recommend it, *but it wasn't enough*.

* * *

We ate the stew and I drank most of the wine that Magnus had brought over the day before. He had half a glass. 'I'm driving,' he said.

'You could stay.' I drained another glass.

'I *could*, but I don't want to make it a necessity.' Magnus took another small sip. 'Besides, I'm not sure about your bed, and I certainly can't have the sofa.'

We both looked at the sofa, and then away, with joint shudders. The frame was all right, but it was going to need completely new upholstery. What was left looked as though it had been the victim of a particularly savage slasher attack; the bloodstains had proved impossible to get out and the bleach I'd used to try to remove them had eaten the cushions to shreds of fabric.

'The bed is fine.' I looked at it, newly made up with the clean sheets and blankets. With the possibility of the addition of Magnus, it now seemed inviting and cosy. 'As long as you leave the doors open.'

'Oh, aye.'

'And I've decided to go over to Donal's agency tomorrow. To talk about the paperwork that needs doing.' I didn't know why I said this, although it was true; why I felt I had to torture myself with the inevitable ending of this relationship, just when we could have been pretending it would go on forever.

'I promise not to make you late.' Magnus looked very solemn. 'Is there any pudding?'

We ate the sadly collapsed pavlova. I'd had to put it in the cool of the larder, and, to avoid Cushie's close attention, I'd chopped it up and put it in a plastic box. It now had the slipped and layered effect of a landslide, and tasted slightly of Tupperware.

Then we went to bed.

21

Magnus left the next morning to open the shop. We were both a little bit bleary-eyed as a result of a night in the cupboard-bed, squeezed so tightly together that the inevitable had happened several times, and I was sleeplessly irritable and emotionally overloaded by the time he went.

I decided not to head straight to Donal's office. The tears that had threatened the evening before were still not far away and I didn't want to suffer a sudden emotional outburst, not in front of Donal and his shiny suit and suspiciously wide smile. I had the feeling that he'd take advantage of any sign of weakness, and I couldn't get my head around the idea of him with Kizzie and didn't want my disbelief to manifest in any way. Anyway, it wasn't really Donal, it was the situation that made me feel so fragile and I needed to lose that feeling before I got down to financial business. Accountancy had taught me that emotion had no place when you were discussing money. I needed to be cool, I needed to be as unruffled as the currently mirror-like surface of the loch, weighted smooth beneath skies heavy with sunshine.

So instead of driving straight to Kirkwall, I headed up to the coast, away from the route that took me down to that imposing circle on the pinch point of land. Up to what felt like a corner, where what Magnus had told me was a 'broch' stood like a ruined circular barn amid a tangle of half-walls and ridged grass, looking out over a rocky shore to another island.

I got out and wandered for a while, taking advantage of the lack of wind, which was only temporary, I was sure, to read the information boards dotted around the site like the yellow flowers that decorated the rise and fall of the grassland. It was too early even for the most dedicated of sightseers, and the place was left to me, some birds and the odd rabbit, which made it feel even more out of its time; this site would once have been an imposing building, surrounded by its own village. Now it was all quiet amidst the gentle swilling of low waves against the stony shore. Across the water, the small island stood impassive, as though it guarded the scenery at a respectful distance.

Suddenly the water broke. In the middle of the channel, a black shape curved into the air, splitting the wavelets into foam, and was gone in a shimmer of darkness. Another orca. Or possibly the same one as I'd seen before, I knew nothing about the habits of the killer whale, whether they were solitary travellers or hung around in packs, despite my mother's best attempts to interest me in nature documentaries. I didn't know if these sleek hunters were common around the Orkneys or whether this was a rare sighting. I kept my eyes on the silver strip of water, but there was nothing else to see. The orca had dropped by and gone, leaving me again with that sense of shimmering darkness in the green depths.

I took another look around. Timeless water edging around the fallen history. A building whose constructors must have believed was going to stand forever, now tumbled into a meaningless stone-strewn field. A defended site, meant to loom imposing on the coast-line, that now had rabbits bouncing around in its foundations and which bore the fragility of tiny flowers amid its double-skinned walls. A place of calm, where once all would have been activity and noise.

I turned and walked back to my car.

Kirkwall was opening for business by the time I arrived. The uneven roofline of the main shopping street was decorated with rooks cawing into the blue sky, feathers ruffled by the rising breeze, and the occasional early shopper browsed about among the windows. I walked past Magnus' shop, carefully not glancing in to see if I could catch his eye, and on down the hill to Donal's agency, where the glass was reflecting the light, whitening out the properties for sale adverts.

He'd obviously not been in long himself, because he was slithering about, writing something in pencil on a piece of paper on his desk with his coat still on.

'Ah. Good morning, Brid.' The smile switched on, expansive and as shiny as his suit. 'What can I do for you?' He folded the paper over very firmly, as though it contained national secrets.

I wanted to snap, 'That's Ms Harcus to you,' but didn't. I needed him. I needed him to facilitate the swift sale of the cottage, even though the thought made my heart dive towards my stomach. 'I thought I'd pop in and sort out the paperwork for the cottage sale,' I said, trying to sound blasé. 'As I was coming into town anyway.' I eyed him. 'I'm on my way over to visit Kizzie. You know she's had the baby?' I added this in a spirit of mischief, a quick flash of showing him that I knew things too.

'Oh, yes.' He looked away now, his fingers toying with the folded paper on the desk, swivelling it around 180 degrees and bending the corners. 'Yes. I did know. I'm, er, I'm popping over this afternoon.' His head came up. 'I've bought an elephant,' he said proudly.

'An...?'

'Elephant. Blue, fluffy sort of thing. Makes a squeaky noise.'

'Oh. For the baby,' I said, with some relief. 'That sounds lovely. But, if I were you, I'd add in a couple of packs of nappies.'

We exchanged a look which told him, very clearly, that I knew exactly what his relationship was to Kizzie's child, and that he should step up and take his responsibilities seriously. His fingers stopped bending and folding the paper, and he tapped at it with nails that were very clean and slightly too long.

'Oh. Oh, yes, of course. I will. Thank you.' Donal looked away again, and I smiled to myself. Then he glanced back up and the greased-smooth smile was back in place. 'So. Paperwork, you say? I'll just nip out and sort out what we've got to do next. Your file is in the back room.'

As his computer was very much in *this* room, I suspected he just wanted to get away from me for a minute, so I nodded and sat down, uninvited, on the slouchy leather chair in front of the desk. As he vanished through the half-glazed door, I saw a brief, blurry image of him resting his forehead against the wall beyond before he moved out of my sight.

Lazy morning sunlight wormed its way between the posters on the window and lay on the piece of paper Donal had been playing with. The page was still folded, but I thought I could make out the indentations of the pencilled words, as though he'd been pressing really hard when he wrote. It was upside down and reversed, but years of accountancy had taught me to read very, very fast and in all formats, because it was amazing what incriminating evidence clients would keep around littering their desks.

I could swear that the writing said *Midness Cottage*.

With a furtive glance at the doorway Donal had gone through, hoping that he was still gathering his strength and excuses, I grabbed the paper and unfolded it.

It looked as though Donal had been working out the wording for a brochure.

Midness Cottage ~~*Witchcraft Museum*~~ *Museum of Witchcraft*
   This cottage has traditionally been the home of the local witch for ... (check number of years) and now provides a ~~*home location*~~ *home for items of witchcraft paraphernalia from all across the islands.*
   A perfect place to visit to learn more about the customs and superstitions of Orkney. Entry ~~*£7.50*~~ *£10.*
   Use Kizzie's painting as the cover, add pictures of relevant items.
   Get some relevant items (witch chair? Ducking stool?)
   Get leaflet onto ships (Ailsa @ US cruise line)

There were some doodles and a phone number, which indicated that he'd been working on this whilst chatting on the phone, perhaps keeping the paper close to hand when he wasn't basking on a rock somewhere.

I stared again at the words. Museum of Witchcraft? But Midness Cottage was *my house*... And then, with the feeling of combination lock numbers sliding into place and opening a door, I put it all together.

Kizzie had taken him to North Cornwall. I'd take almost any bets that they'd visited Boscastle and the Witchcraft Museum there, and that it had put the idea into Donal's head of buying Jennet's cottage, with all its history, and turning it into an Orkney equivalent. He'd advertise it on the cruise ships, it was just the sort of homespun, traditional attraction with a hint of mystery that would appeal to the tourists in their thousands.

Donal had told everyone I was a witch before I arrived. No doubt I was supposed to be terrified off by their approaches, either that or my inability to treat even the most minor of ailments would bring about community disillusion. Or maybe even just the gossip about me would have been enough. God only knew what else he may have said about me. Perhaps my gangling height and obvious solitary nature had disproved any other rumours.

And... and... I had to restrain myself from screwing up the paper and throwing it against the door with force, he'd obviously had his eye on my cottage from the moment he'd had the museum idea. He must have been wetting himself with glee when he realised that it was on land owned by someone he already had acquaintance with, no wonder he'd been popping round to see Innis all the time! It wasn't to chat about old times, it was to make sure nobody else was interested in buying, and probably to make a few disparaging remarks about how awful it would be to have people tramping past their house to get to it.

Only they wouldn't, would they? I remembered Fergus and Margaret, her worry about launching the boat from Donal's land – *he'd bought the other side of the loch*. Was probably planning boat trips across to the 'museum', which he would have bought at a knock-down price because of my desperation to sell and my desire to get away from everyone wanting me to use my 'craft' to help them...

I glared at the door to the back room so hard that it was a wonder I didn't drill through the glass. When the door opened to reveal Donal with a sheaf of paperwork in his hand, I had to avert my eyes for fear that he'd see that I knew.

'Well, here it is!' he trilled. 'You just need to...'

He leaned over the desk as I stood up, so I nearly headbutted him. What did I do? Tell him I knew what he was up to? Tell *everyone else* what he was up to? But he hadn't broken any laws, and he was still Emily's father and Kizzie's – well, whatever he was to

Kizzie. Innis would find out and be horrified that she'd inadvertently assisted this.

So I bit my tongue. 'Actually, Donal,' I said, carefully measuring the words so that they didn't fall out wrapped around 'you are a mercenary snake'. 'I'm having second thoughts at the moment about selling. I might just hold on to the cottage, you see. We could use it as a family bolthole for holidays.'

His face was a frozen mask of frantic brain activity desperately trying not to show itself. 'Well,' he said faintly, 'that's, er, entirely up to you, of course, although I would like to warn you...' He seemed to be groping for words. 'That house prices are beginning to fall – cost of living crisis starting to bite and people deciding not to downsize or buy extra property, that sort of thing.' His voice strengthened as his story ironed itself out. 'So the price you've been offered is for a quick sale and probably won't be repeated should you try to sell at a later date.'

I waved airily, as though money was the last thing on my mind. 'It is what it is,' I said meaninglessly, channelling my mother. 'I'll be in touch if I decide to put the place on the market with you in future.'

Then, with my hands balled into fists so tightly that I could feel my knuckles creaking, I stalked out and let the bell ting my leaving. I walked back up the road to the front of St Magnus, which stared impassively over the town, its red sandstone strangely bloodlike in the early sun.

I waited until nobody was around, and then roared my indignation and anger at the blameless pigeons pecking blankly around the churchyard. 'Fuckity fuck!'

A middle-aged couple rounded the bulk of the building and looked at me. 'It's just the wee witch,' said the man, adjusting his shopping bag on his arm.

'Oh, aye,' said the woman, and they walked on by, unruffled, as though the local witch screaming at an ecclesiastical establishment was the *least* weird thing about a Saturday on Mainland.

I watched them go, and once they were at a safe distance, I continued my self-abasement. 'I can't sell it now! Even if I put it up for sale with Kerr, Donal will just buy it from him instead. But if I *don't* sell, then there's no money for anywhere in York! And what do I do with it, Innis can't look after it – I wonder if Magnus might…?'

I shook my head. What exactly was my objection to Donal turning the cottage into a museum anyway? It would be another attraction for Orkney, another draw for travellers – the intrepid tourists who came out of season, dressed like mountaineers and polar explorers, and culture-seizing cruisers who'd pile into Jennet's cottage exclaiming about how tiny it was, how 'cute' and 'adorable'. They'd all run their hands over Jennet's things, all claim to feel the mysticism and magic, wondering at the – no doubt mostly fake – stories that Donal would spin around the place. They would pay a fortune to squeeze into my living room, mutter about myth and tradition, and then head back to Kirkwall for shopping and restaurants. So what would be so bad about another museum, amid all the rest of the history?

It's my cottage. Jennet's cottage. It was a little house on the edge of the water where a lonely woman had eked out a living using wisdom, folklore and a lot of common sense. 'Witchcraft' wasn't something you caged and made people pay money to come and see. It was something ordinary and everyday and I was *buggered* if I'd let some slimeball turn it into a historic display to get money from tourists.

But then, I *had* to sell. Maybe I could get Kerr to ask a ridiculous amount of money for the cottage? Like, half a million pounds, or something? Would Donal pay that much or would I just be left with a festering ruin while everyone talked about greedy south-erners with ideas above their station?

'You look like you're thinking.' Magnus tapped me on the shoulder. 'There's no need to strain yourself, aye.'

'I can't sell the cottage,' I blurted, then bit my tongue. Magnus had to live here. I didn't want to slander Donal's name with him, not when they all had to rub along together – any feuds here would assume epic proportions and probably pass down two or three generations, and I couldn't bear the thought of Kizzie and Emily getting dragged into the inheritance of hatred. 'I just can't.'

'Oh?' There was a flash of hope in his eyes. 'Any reason? Are you having a rethink about leaving?'

There was a hand on my arm now, warm and grounding. I couldn't let him carry that hope any further.

'No, not that. I'm only... it's just... I think Donal may want to buy the place and I can't let him,' I finished.

'Well, no.' Magnus let his hand fall away from me, as though embarrassed, and tucked it into his pocket. 'I can see that. It would, possibly, be a fate worse than death to sell to that slimy wee shite, but what are you going to do?' He looked up at the impassive face of his namesake cathedral as it glowed like a marzipan figure on an enormous cake. 'We could, maybe, think of a long-distance relationship?' His voice was hopeful again. 'You could come up the odd weekend, stay at the cottage and we could – well.'

'But how long would we be happy with that, Magnus?' I asked quietly. 'Being in a relationship means having someone there to support you, to be on your side and to make you cups of tea in bed. That's a bit tricky when there's the best part of five hundred miles between you.'

I turned away from him and looked off across the little town of Kirkwall; at the fingers of streets stretching away from the church, at the rook-haunted trees around the Bishop's Palace and over toward the hills that cushioned the place from the everlasting history in those beckoning stones and the curved roofs of ancient burial places.

'Besides,' I said quietly, 'you wouldn't leave here, would you? To come to me?'

I looked at him, hoping to see a dawning recognition that relocation worked both ways. That he could move to York, open a little jewellery shop and together we could—

'Maybe the odd weekend.' At least he sounded as though he'd thought about it, but there was regret dripping from every word. 'But I couldn't move. Not with Innis about to have another baby, they need the help on the farm, y'see. And you've said, everything down there costs about a million pounds. I have the shop and a workshop and a storage space and the flat here. I couldn't have that, down south.'

Without meaning to, I moved towards him and we hugged; a deep, tight hug as though we were holding on to these last moments as hard as we could. 'It's a bit shit, isn't it?' I said.

'Aye, well, we can't say we didn't know what we were getting into.' He gave a deep sigh. 'So. What are you doing with your day today?'

'I'm going to head back to try to find an agency that might let the cottage out as a holiday place, and deal with the upkeep and everything, I think. I can't expect Innis to do it any more – who used to look after it before Innis?'

'Aunts and great-aunts and so on. Keeping it nice for when the witch came back.' Magnus smiled a rueful smile. 'They're all gone now. Probably all whirlwinds under the ground, at the thought of the cottage being out of the family.' He gave me a final squeeze and then let go, stepping back out of the shadow of the church. 'But times move on. It can't be helped.'

I left him heading back to the shop, while I went to my car. As I drove back across Mainland, with the blue skies winking alluringly from behind occasional cloud and the water stretching satin skirts below the cliffs, I cursed again.

It wasn't *fair*! A good job, a home and a partner, that's all I wanted. Now I found myself in the middle of that game where you can get two of the three in one place, but always one element unreachable. In York, I had my job. A proper job, clients, a job I knew I could do. I had a home, of sorts, with Annie and Steve in the little rented house by the river. But Magnus – Magnus would always be five hundred miles away, under this huge sky, being whipped by the weather and stood on by cows, making his beautiful jewellery and meeting someone else.

So, here was Magnus, and a home, if you could call one room and a bucket home. Goose-haunted and now liberally coated in Kizzie's blood, but I could change both those things with a new rug and a plank over the broken window. I could live there. And have Magnus. But no job. And work *needed* me still, even if my parents didn't, all those emails telling me to get a move on and finish whatever I was doing up here proved it. If I stayed here, I'd run out of money very quickly, and what was there that I could do? Work in a shop in Kirkwall? Try to find an accountancy business that needed someone? But stepping back from my career, going back to little bits of bookkeeping here and there and making coffee for someone who took the most interesting work – could I do that? Could I *afford* that?

Back at the cottage, I dragged all the ruined upholstery off the sofa and threw it outside. Cushie strolled over for a look and a peck, then settled down on the least ruined cushion like an imperious ruler on her throne, and watched the goslings tiptoeing into the waters of the loch. She could keep the cushions. Maybe she'd nest in those, rather than in the larder? I went back in and stared at the now-skeletal sofa, perched upon its stained rug, then dragged that outside as well.

I was going to have to spend *more* money to replace them. There was no way the cottage would work as a holiday let if everyone had to sit on the plain wooden chairs with the uncomfortably upright backs, unless I only let to BDSM groups. And the bed, the bed was only any good for single people, Magnus and I had proved that last night... My thoughts ran up against memory; last night, Magnus and I tangled together in the narrow bed within the wall, like a pair of explicit ornaments. Laughing and sighing and whispering confidences and – no. I had to stop this.

I opened the doors to the bed and tweaked the covers tidy with a savage hand. I'd let the place out, Magnus and I could try to keep something going between us, there were Zoom calls and emails and phones, maybe those would be enough? The distance was such that I couldn't even commit to every weekend, I'd need to take extra days because of the travelling. Maybe once a month? *Would* that be enough?

My hand stilled, pulling the embroidered blanket tight over the bed and remembering last night. Our closeness, breathing one another in within the dark confines of the cupboard, doors closed against the world. Magnus had his whole life here. If I came and went, how long before he needed more than I could give?

Oh, bugger!

I slammed my fist on the mattress and went to turn on my laptop. Order was what I needed, the comfort of setting figures into columns and having them add up. Knowing my clients, knowing their strengths and weaknesses and their tendencies to forget whole tranches of expenses or to put earnings into their back pockets, that was what kept me sane. That was what I lived for. York was where I belonged, where my home and my job and my family were, and Magnus would become a sweet memory for the darkest nights.

Work had emailed me, I noted with a quiet pride. Then I opened the email and jumped up, the laptop clattering to the floor with a heavy plastic sound as I got to my feet and stared at the screen.

Ms Harcus

As you may be aware, we are streamlining the business model at the agency in order to implement essential cost-cutting measures. Your client list is extensive and your work impeccable, but I'm afraid that we must insist on your return to the office by Monday at the latest, or your post will go into redundancy.

Your work is already being handled by other members of the team in your current absence, so it is believed that removing your post would cause the least upheaval to our end users.

We would be grateful if you could let us know of your intention to return by the stated date.

Best wishes

Management Team

I didn't know whether to be sick, cry or start laughing. Here I was, weighing up pros and cons for returning, and they were forcing my hand. Or *something* was.

'No, Jennet,' I said aloud to the dust swirling, caught in the beams of light sneaking in through the tiny windows. 'No. It has to be a decision, not a *fait accompli*, that's not how it works.'

Silence. I didn't even know why I was talking to a dead woman who hadn't left so much as a trace of a ghost about the place. All she was now was a memory and a reputation, and I didn't have to honour either.

I composed a hasty email, telling the management that I would, of course, be returning immediately, and booking myself and the car onto the first ferry to Scotland that had space. It was on Sunday morning, and I'd be hard pressed to drive all the way down to be back in the office by Monday, but, hell, I'd do it if I had to drive through the night to get there.

I looked around the cottage. Yes. Probably for the best. No time to dwell, no time to get further involved with Magnus. This had all been a pleasant interlude, but now it was time to get real. Go back, pick up my life where I'd left off...

...sharing a house, shopping with Mum. Working in an office with people who made jokes about my height.

But then, what was the alternative? Scratching a living on Orkney? Just because there was a *man* here?

My mind roiled over the memories of tumbled rocks, fallen history. The sleek dark bodies of orca circling in the deep waters. Over on the table, Jennet's book rustled its pages in the draught from the door and the sun lay like a solid thing across the floor. Cushie honked, solitary and long, from outside.

Then the honking became a hissing, and there were voices.

'It's only a goose! Go on!'

'But it's pecking me!'

'We need help! Go get the witch!'

'These cushions here are covered in *blood*...'

A pause. 'Look, you're hurt. We need to clean that cut.'

'*Blood*... All right! Ow! Ow! Get away, ye wee besom!'

And then a face appeared through the gap. Nervous and pale, a young woman. 'Please, can you help us?'

I followed her out. Up by the house, a car sat with its bonnet in the hedge and the driver's door open. A young man was just behind her, now sitting on the path in the bog, blood on his forehead and a dazed look in his eye.

'The car came off the road,' the girl said, breathless. 'Kenny banged his head.' She sounded close to tears. 'I don't know what to do.'

Between us, we got Kenny into the cottage. I sat him on a chair and looked at his head, the wound wasn't deep but it was bleeding an impressive amount and I wasn't sure that the cottage could take much more blood, so I cleaned him up and talked down the girl, whose name was Anya. She was panicking, although whether about the car or Kenny it was hard to tell.

I treated Kenny much as Magnus had treated me when I'd banged my head on the kitchen cupboard. Looking at pupils to check for distortion, feeling over his head for any mysterious dips or fractures, but it really did just seem to have been a crack on the forehead and a little bit of blood. Kenny was soon coming back from the shock and resting his elbows on the table while he occasionally put a hand to his forehead to check whether it was still bleeding.

'So, how did you go off the road?' I looked at them both. They'd been on their way to Stromness, apparently, down to see Anya's parents, nothing that would indicate careless driving and these roads didn't really lend themselves to recklessness.

'I don't know.' Kenny passed another hand over his eyes. 'It sounds stupid.'

'Go on,' Anya urged him. 'This is the witch, remember? She'll believe you.'

'No, I mean *really* stupid. I'm no a bad driver.' He turned pleading eyes on me. 'I passed my test last year, and I'm careful. I need the car for work, not chasing round the lanes like Lewis Hamilton.'

I made circular 'get to the point' movements with one hand.

'Aye, well, we were coming along yon road, just chatting, and Anya said something about the witch's cottage being down here by the loch. And then.' Kenny stopped and looked at his girlfriend, as though for confirmation, or permission.

'Something ran across the road,' she supplied. 'A hare.'

'Aye, and it's bad luck to hit a hare,' Kenny broke in now that the worst was out there. 'We all know that. So I was slowing down and trying to get out of the way and...' He stopped again.

'And it *looked at us*,' Anya said, words heavy with portent.

I waited, but nothing more seemed to be forthcoming. 'It looked at you?' I raised my eyebrows. 'With its eyes? Like I'm looking at you now?'

Now they talked over themselves and each other, trying to explain.

'Not like an animal...'

'It's hard to explain...'

'It just sat in the road, watching...'

'Eyes, almost like a person...'

'Like it was waiting for us to do something...'

'I was watching the hare so I steered into the hedge,' Kenny finished. 'And cracked my head against the window.'

We all looked in the same direction, out of the open door and up towards the road where the car had two wheels off the road in the narrow hedgeline.

Kenny's forehead was still bleeding. The cut really wasn't that deep but right up by the scalp, so blood kept trickling down his face in a 'horror movie' kind of way. 'I can't go to see Anya's parents like this.' He touched the cut and moved his hand away to check his fingers. There was still a smear of blood. 'They'll think I'm no fit to be her boyfriend.' He frowned, which made the blood situation worse.

I remembered a page in Jennet's book about bleeding, where she'd recommended cobwebs. I got up and flipped through until I found the reference.

If a cut's not deep but more of a slice, and you're sure it won't need stitches, to stop the bleeding, pack with clean cobwebs.
  But: always thank the spiders, and ask their permission first.

Well, it was worth a try to stop the annoying trickle that was obviously worrying Kenny. And cobwebs were one of the things that this cottage did well. I went into the larder, where I surprised two of the goslings poking themselves back in through the broken window, and scooped a handful of the least dusty cobwebs which looped between the unused shelves like forgotten tinsel.

'Sorry, spiders, may I take these, thank you,' I muttered, feeling stupid as I said it. I really *was* getting way too involved in Orkney life; in Jennet's witchcraft – it was a good job I was leaving. The sticky webs swung between my fingers, but the spiders didn't reply, which was just as well because if I'd heard one squeaky voice issuing from behind the shelving with a 'that's all right', I would have packed the car there and then and spent the night at the ferry embarkation point.

'Here.' I rolled the webs into a small package and pressed it to Kenny's cut forehead. 'Hopefully this should help.'

His fingers encountered the wodge of soft stickiness and retreated. 'Urgh, what *is* this?'

'Witch's secret. Hold it there a minute.' I had no idea how long it would take to work, but wanted to distract him. 'Did you see where the hare went? You didn't hit it, did you?'

'No.' Anya took over the conversation now, Kenny was too busy clasping the soggy package to his forehead with an expression of acute disgust. 'No. It just disappeared after we hit the hedge. Must have run off across yon field there, down towards the loch.'

'At least that's one less corpse to clear up,' I muttered, having worried that a dead hare might be in the middle of the road causing an obstruction, but both Kenny and Anya clearly heard me, because they began looking around the room and the pile of bloodied upholstery outside clearly played on their minds.

'We just needed somewhere to sit,' Anya said, a little too hastily for my liking. 'Just to make sure Kenny wasn't badly hurt.'

'I feel fine now.' He was getting to his feet, one finger still pressing the cobweb bundle to the cut. 'Brilliant. Well, yes, thank you very much.'

'There's no damage, I don't think,' Anya said. 'We were just a bit panicked and Kenny's head was bleeding and the first thing we thought was to come and see you.'

'Being as we were right outside your cottage.' Kenny was already halfway out of the door, and obviously trying not to look at the bloodstained cushion pile, on top of which Cushie was sitting complacently, dabbling her beak at the piping round the edges.

'Thank you for helping us.' Anya made an odd move, somewhere between a nod and a curtsey.

'But the car...?' I waved a hand and they both looked up towards the road, as though they expected to see the car floating out of the hedge.

'Och, we can push it out, it's no stuck. T'was just my head, y'see.' Kenny seized Anya's hand and the pair of them almost ran over the surface of the bog, back to the road.

'Well, that was odd,' I said to the goose.

22

I packed my things, slowly. The cowardly part of me wanted to run away, maybe stay overnight in Stromness to be on the eleven o'clock morning ferry without running the risk of seeing Magnus. Just to go, pretend none of this ever happened. Deal with all the paperwork regarding renting out the cottage from York and never set foot on these windswept, howling islands again.

Then I thought of Magnus. His lanky shape decked out in milking overalls, with the sun bringing out the gold in his hair and the green in his eyes. The silver swinging at his neck, echoing the drawing in Jennet's notebook – the notebook that I'd tucked inside my rolled-up pyjamas to take home as a souvenir of this crazy time, this crazy place.

I couldn't leave without seeing him again.

Which was just as well, because he turned up that afternoon, van rattling into its place beside the house. I'd had half an ear out for car noises because Innis had messaged me to let me know she'd be calling in to pick up her key once the ferry rolled in, and to warn me that Freya was tired, grouchy and wailing about leaving her great-granny behind, so I might want to leave the key somewhere rather than risk a 400-decibel tantrum.

I'd left the key under a brick and messaged back accordingly, but wanted to make sure that it wasn't intercepted by any roaming gangs of burglars.

So, when I heard vehicular sounds I poked my head out of the door, to see Magnus, and had to fight a dual urge to nail the door shut and pretend already to have left, or to tear across the bog and fling myself at him in a sobbing, wailing heap that Freya could have taken lessons from. In the end, I did neither. I sat at the table and waited.

'Hey, there,' Magnus greeted me cheerfully, whilst trying to avoid Cushie. Then, coming through the door, 'Oh.'

I looked at what he saw. Cottage tidied. Kizzie's pictures taken down and packed. Sofa carcass replaced, but cushions and rug rolled up in a heap together around the back, where I hoped that wind, weather and the geese would dispose of them. Floor swept, interior bare.

'It's very... tidy,' he said, carefully.

I took a deep breath. 'I'm leaving, Magnus,' I said, with only the slightest tremble to my voice. 'Work will fire me if I'm not back by Monday, and I've already been here longer than I really meant to.'

He gave me a steady look, eyelids hanging heavy over eyes dark in the muted indoor light. 'You've made up your mind, then.'

'It's a good job. Good jobs aren't ten a penny, talking of which, I have to make money.'

He was standing an arm's length away from me, hands deep in his pockets. I wished he'd either hug me or walk out, this stasis was tearing at my heart. 'When do you sail?'

'Tomorrow, on the eleven o'clock ferry.'

Magnus took a deep breath. 'Right. Then we'd better make the most of our time, no? Come on.'

An arm came out and scooped me against him. But instead of holding me in for a kiss, he carried on moving, taking me with him. 'Where are we going?'

'You'll need to say goodbye. And have some food, aye.'

I'd been anticipating a long, slow love-making and leave-taking, fraught with tears and promises of eternal fidelity, so this brisk motion took the wind from my sails. 'What?'

'Come on.'

He didn't say anything else and we crossed the green squelch of the marsh, now so familiar that I knew where to put my feet even if I didn't use the stepping stones. Little thrusts of bog cotton waved a farewell in the breeze, like tiny banners, and the harsh grass hissed at me as though I were a pantomime villain.

It was late afternoon and the light was diamond-bright, as though the island wanted to show itself off to best advantage now I was leaving; high sun and mild winds made the sea glitter a million facets and the lochs were smooth mirrors of dark water as we passed.

'Where are we going?'

Now Magnus looked at me. His air was jaunty enough, but his eyes were still heavy and there was a pull at the corners of his mouth as though the whole situation had its own gravity. 'You ought to say goodbye to the stones.'

'Why? Will they follow me home and throw themselves through my window if I don't?'

He didn't smile. He just raised his eyebrows.

All the stones were where we'd left them, with no signs of vituperative uprising. The improved light made them less forbidding, grey rather than black, but still mysterious and unknowable, tilted on their ancient horizon between the waters. Almost tame. I walked through the circle, touching each stone and feeling the weathered surfaces, slightly warm.

'Are you sure?' It was practically the first thing Magnus had said, and the words seemed to burst out of him. 'Do you really have to go back?'

I sighed. What I *wanted* to say was, 'No, of course I don't. I want to stay here, with you.' But I only wanted to say it for a second. How many people had I seen who'd ruined their lives for a man? Or found themselves in a life they'd never anticipated, never planned for?

Images of my mother, driving my father about and pushing his wheelchair when he couldn't walk, crept into my mind. She'd always said she didn't mind, that she'd married for better or worse; that my father was still just James, whether pottering in the garden or being helped around the countryside. But did she *really*? Had his diagnosis shrunk her world?

Then I looked at Magnus, and understood. I wouldn't have cared if he'd been in a wheelchair. I'd happily have helped him through any physical or mental frailty. Hell, I would even have offered to milk the cows for him, should it have been necessary, and I barely knew which end the milk came out of, let alone how you went about actually getting it out.

But.

'I've got to,' I said, trying to avoid those eyes. 'I owe it to people. I took that job, took on those clients, with the promise that I would do my very best for them. It's duty, Magnus.'

Now I met his gaze. Steady, calm and almost unemotional, he was watching me. 'And you don't think being the witch is a duty?' he asked, softly. 'Helping people here?'

I touched his arm. 'It's not real, Magnus,' I replied, equally softly. 'It's expectation and trickery, that's all. With a big side-order of coincidence.' I took a deep breath. 'Plus, it won't pay the bills.'

'You could find a job.'

'I've got a job.'

For some reason, whether the stillness of the air or the weight of its warmth or something to do with the stone circle surrounding us, my words sounded flat. Hollow. I half-expected a mist to swirl up from the ground and make everything otherworldly, but it didn't. The sun continued to shine, the birds continued to fling themselves skyward above our heads.

'It's a *good* job.' There was nothing else I could say. No words that would sum up the half pride, half self-satisfaction I felt about having a title. Being able to show my erstwhile schoolmates that, tall, awkward, not pretty as I was, I'd *achieved* something. All those giggly overheard conversations about how I was probably going to transition to male, because who would ever take me seriously as a woman? How I'd have to take jobs where I could crouch or only ever sit down, so that people could actually see me, and not just the snow on the top of my head. I'd *shown* them. Or, at least, I would have done if they hadn't all moved away. But I posted regularly online, so they knew.

Brid Harcus was a success, despite what everyone had said.

It shouldn't matter what they thought of me. But it did.

And I couldn't step away from that.

'You've made up your mind, then.'

How could I express it to him? That York was a known quantity. House, job, routine. It all fitted with my approach to life, knowing what was going on. Out here, where it seemed the weather could change with every air current, I didn't even know if I should be putting on a T-shirt or an anorak every morning.

'I think so, yes,' I said, gently.

He sighed, just once, very deeply. 'All right. Well then, we'd better make the most of this, hadn't we? Let's go and eat.'

He took me to a restaurant somewhere overlooking the sea,

where we ate fish so fresh that it seemed to have leaped straight from the water into the pan, and I drank too much wine to deaden the awfulness of what was coming. Then we went back to the cottage.

'I'll take you to the ferry,' Magnus said. 'In the morning.'

'Don't you have to open the shop?'

We both stared out across the field at the lights in the house, where Thor and Innis were clearly now home and wrestling Freya. 'I may never see you again,' Magnus said quietly. 'The least I can do is to see you off properly.'

Then we went to bed.

It was sweet, tearful and full of promises that I suspected we both knew we wouldn't be able to keep. I lay awake, listening to his breath and smelling that citrusy scent, feeling the winding of his limbs around mine and wondering how I would feel when this was just a memory. When I was back in the office, amid the clack of keyboards and the heat of the photocopier, would this feel like a particularly realistic dream? When I visited clients on their farms and in their barns full of hay and horses, would I remember the smell of hot stone and lapping water and smile?

Would I ever come back? *Could* I ever come back?

We were both awake as the simmer dim muted itself through the grey and back into dawn and the light, filtered over the loch, came through the windows. Everything inside me felt heavy, as though my stomach were lead and my heart had somehow become attached to the table.

I opened the back door and Cushie waddled in and pecked at my feet, proprietorially.

'What shall I do about her?' I asked Magnus, who was putting on the kettle.

'Och, you can't take her with you, now. She'll have to stay. As long as she doesn't go far from the cottage, she'll be fine.'

I looked at him. 'Why wouldn't she be fine otherwise?'

A sad look, through the steam. 'The greylags, they're a menace. September to January is open season.' Then, apparently noting my frown, 'The farmers shoot them.'

Cushie honked, then hissed her way past me towards the feed sack. Unthinking, I threw out a couple of handfuls of pellets and felt her feathers comb past my legs as she dashed back outside again, calling the goslings away from whatever they'd been up to. Five hard beaks made 'pok pok' noises against the stone as they gobbled down the food.

'Stay here, Cushie,' I whispered. 'You and the babies.' An orange eye rolled malevolently in my direction.

Magnus and I drank tea. I stared out over the loch, which had been my backdrop for such a short time and yet now seemed to be the only scenery I could imagine. Breakfasts in the little house in York, with the crowding of other houses being my only view, seemed a million miles away. Another universe.

'Right.' I picked up my bag. 'We should go.'

'Should we?' For the first time in daylight, Magnus broke. In the dark of the night, the emotion hadn't seemed real, almost as though we'd been indulging ourselves. Now, in the glare of the sun, it all felt suddenly awful. He held me close, the silver fern leaf at his throat catching and tangling against my skin, as his voice caught and tangled in my hair. 'Brid, please. We need our witch.'

'But that's not me,' I whispered.

We stood for an irrationally long time. I cried into his jumper and he cried against the top of my head. From beyond us, at the house, the sounds of Freya starting the day, and the delivery of Innis' other charges, began to break through our emotional turmoil and we straightened away, with covert nose-blowing and eye-wiping.

'Shall we go then, aye?' Magnus said at last. 'Let's not prolong the agony.'

Innis popped out of the front door as I was getting into my car. 'You're away then?' she asked, idly standing a fallen toddler back upright.

'Yes. I don't know when I'll be back,' I replied, trying not to replace 'when' with 'if' as hard as I could.

'Oh, aye.' She smiled, and then hugged me, surprising me. 'It's not always as easy to leave as you think.' Magnus closed his van door, very firmly. Innis looked from me to him, then back again. 'Not as easy as that,' she said again, softly.

'Well, good luck with the baby, and everything,' I said, feeling inadequate.

Innis just nodded and turned to go back inside, where there was a small riot breaking out over paper.

Magnus and I drove to the ferry port. I pulled my car into the line for embarkation, he parked his van on the roadside and came to lean in through my window. The ferry had docked and disgorged the early passengers and the furious activity of the men on the dockside led me to believe we'd be boarding soon. I tried to memorise every last centimetre of this little place, Stromness, with the snaggle-built houses along the waterfront and the slow climb of the road up and away.

I'd never come back. I knew that. This was too painful.

'Oh!' Someone was waving to me from a bench. It was Margaret and Fergus, he had a rug over his lower limbs and a flask of something in his hand, which steamed gently as he thrust it at Margaret for her to pour.

'Come to see you off,' Magnus said, sounding a bit throaty.

'Making sure I'm really going, I suspect.' I tried to sound matter of fact. I glanced around, just in case there were other people here, trying to make me feel guilty about leaving, but, apart from orange-suited workmen doing things to the boat, the dock was quiet and almost deserted.

Margaret poured Fergus another steaming cup and the first cars in the line drove up the ramp, guided into place by another orange boiler suit. I started my engine.

'Well. Goodbye, then,' I said, the words feeling too solid to say. 'Thank you.' This came out as a whisper.

Magnus leaned in again further and kissed me. His silver necklace swung, catching the light in points, splintering the sunlight. 'It can't end like this,' he whispered back, sounding fierce. 'It just *can't.*'

I inched the car forward, and he came with it. One more car in front of me now, and the boom of the previous car driving over the metal ramp to board. 'It has to,' I whispered back.

Then a cry went up. Margaret was standing up, pointing at the water. The ferrymen stopped the boarding and walked to the rails, everyone was looking now. Even Magnus had straightened away from me, shielding his eyes against the light with one hand.

I looked too, but the reflection on my windscreen meant I couldn't see anything other than my own face, looking blotchy and sullen. 'What is it?'

'Orca.' The word echoed round the little port. 'But so *close...*'

And suddenly, there it was. The big black fin heralding the rest of the beast, which crested the waves and hung for a moment, formed from water and light. White patches merging into silken darkness, so close that we could see an eye, bright against the water.

'We'll have to pause boarding,' a uniformed man said. 'Until it's cleared the harbour.'

The orca swam in, until it was almost lying against the ferry.

Blew once, water spraying. I got out of the car and joined the people who had gone to stand by the rails; we lined the little port as the passengers were lining the deck of the ferry, all of us watching and marvelling at the huge beast that sat like a stationary depth charge, alongside the boat, as though bent on preventing me leaving.

I looked down and across. A white marking ran along the orca's head, almost like a grin, and I found that I was smiling back. There was something about this whole scene, the power and wildness of a creature built for the sea against the feeble human imitation of the ferry, and the little dark eye almost hidden amid the silken black. For a moment, just one moment, with the excited voices chattering along behind me and the click of cameras, I looked deep into the eye of the whale.

And my life swung.

As though the idea had been sitting there all this time, I saw the farm gate, now bearing an additional sign next to the Midness name. 'Brid Harcus, accountant.' I saw Cushie and her brood ushering clients inside, and the main room of the cottage set up with a desk, computers and books.

The kitchen, with herbs drying and oils in jars ranged along the worktop.

The vision was so strong and hit me so suddenly that I gasped and took a step back, and as I did so, the orca flipped itself lazily around, curved once above the waves, and dived. I could see the silhouette under the water, swimming away from the land, back out to sea, now nothing but a change in water colour and a casual tail flap.

I got back in my car and pulled away from the embarkation line. I didn't wait for Magnus, I didn't even look at him, I just drove. Back up the hill, between the little stone-walled fields, along the grey line of horizon where the road met the sky. Past the stone circles and the grass mounds of ancient burials. Past the settlements so old that they had no names, and past the curved fallen walls of the brochs, studding the coastline as though nailing the island in position.

Back to Midness. To my cottage, still ivy-covered and sunken into the landscape.

Innis was outside, wrangling toddlers who had a large sandpit out on the grass and were largely using it to stamp in. She saw my car drive up, but didn't approach me, although it would have been tricky anyway as she had a child stapled down each side. She just raised her head and looked behind me at Magnus, following in his van. I was sure I saw her nod, just once.

Then I was parked and running. Down over the grass, skipping over the bog and flinging open the door, to surprise Cushie, who had settled herself in the living room, and who hissed herself to her feet at my sudden arrival.

I caught at the doorframe, feeling the warmth of the wood beneath my hand. Of course. *Of course.* Start my own accountancy practice. Build up clients. Not sell the cottage and run the risk of Donal buying it, but stay here, watch Emily grow up, serve raspberry tea and herb-infused oil, simplify tax for local farmers. Help Magnus with milking – once he'd shown me what to do. It was as easy as that.

Magnus was not far behind.

'So,' he said, and he was trying not to laugh. 'You're staying then, aye?'

My head was too full of ideas to speak. I just waved an arm at the inside of the cottage. Cushie pecked at me.

'Aye,' Magnus said again, but quietly now and with less laughter. 'I didn't think Jennet would let you go so easily.'

We hugged. This time there was no bitterness of parting, but instead a long, sweet hug of potential. He kissed me and I kissed him and it was all a confusion of relief mingled with a slight tinge of guilt.

'I ought to email the office,' I said. 'And let them know I'm not coming.' I disentangled myself from Magnus. 'I'm going to need a new sofa. And a rug. But a bigger one this time.'

Redundant. The word shot into my brain. Let them. Let them make me redundant. The full significance followed, surfing on a lacy tide of pound signs. They'd have to pay me redundancy. That should be enough for me to live on, with the savings I had left, until I set up the business.

'I need to let my parents know.' I looked at Magnus. 'And it wasn't Jennet. It was the orca, in a weird, complicated way, that made me decide to stay.'

He grinned and dashed hair away from his face with one hand. Blond stubble gleamed in the sun. 'Och, you didn't know, Jennet had the orca as her familiar. Is it not in yon book, somewhere?' He looked around as though I might have left Jennet's notebook in the cottage, despite my intention never to return.

All the uplift I'd been feeling, as though my heart had been filled with helium, drained away and a sensation akin to dread pulled its way in through the back of my head. 'No,' I said faintly. 'No, I'm fairly sure she didn't mention that.' Then I thought of the sketches, of the hare. Of the orca. She'd told me, without telling me.

'She did nothing but blether on about it in the letters she left for the family,' he went on, cheerfully. 'But she was completely gyte, apparently, by the end.'

I frowned and his smile broadened.

'Mad. Bonkers. Senile. Well, no, not senile, she knew what was what, but she was given to ranting, so the family stories say.'

'She chased Fergus with a clothes prop,' I said, weakly.

'Aye, sounds about right. But she was the witch, so.'

I thought of the orcas I'd seen. Or maybe it had all been the same one, haunting me with brief appearances, making me think of the hidden darkness amid the history of this archipelago.

'Jennet, you absolute cow,' I muttered, into the complacent falling dust.

23

I spent that night with Magnus, in his flat. 'We're needing a proper night's sleep,' he said, presenting me with the packet of chips he'd dashed out to buy. 'After last night. In a proper bed. And then tomorrow you can see what you need to do about setting up your own accountancy – you'll likely get plenty of business out here.'

'I'm going to need a new computer,' I said. I'd changed my clothes, to the sturdy jumper and trousers I'd bought from Kizzie. 'And I ought to buy Kizzie something for the baby, now it looks as though I'm going to be around to watch Emily Brid grow up.'

Magnus nodded. 'And you can have a proper shower. Maybe we can look into getting permission for an extension on the cottage? For a wee bathroom?' He pushed my bag towards me with his foot. 'You'll be able to get your towel back.'

'I've missed Charmander,' I said, unzipping the bag and getting my pyjamas out. I didn't, for one second, think I'd be wearing them for long, we had a lot of ground to cover now, Magnus and I, but for sitting and eating chips, post-shower, I didn't feel nudity was appropriate.

As I pulled the clothes out of the bag, Jennet's notebook fell from the folds and sprawled onto the polished boards of the floor. Magnus picked it up and handed it to me.

'You really got all your witching from this?'

I stroked the black, fragmented cover and little flakes of leather peeled away under my fingers. 'Yes. It's full of Jennet's wisdom.'

'Can I look?'

I hesitated. Jennet had hidden the book in the cottage, presumably for the next witch. For *me*. But then, it wasn't witchcraft, was it? This was just a notebook of herbs, practical advice and some pretty drawings. It didn't say FOR YOUR EYES ONLY in big letters on the opening page, there were no dire warnings about showing it to anyone else.

I handed him the book. Then I went to unpack some more of my clothes. Magnus had a washing machine, and I was going to make hard use of it.

Magnus had gone very quiet. I looked up from sorting dirty laundry. 'What?'

'You're the witch.' His voice sounded strange, slightly thick, and his accent had slithered from the Glasgow-mitigated vowels I was used to into the soft burr of the pure Orcadian.

'Well, no, not really,' I said. 'We've had this conversation.'

His gaze was very steady now, deep and holding an element of something that wasn't fear, but more like a kind of respect. 'Here,' he said, handing me the book. 'Look.'

I took it. It felt warm again, alive. 'At what?'

He just nodded at the cover. 'It's a good job I love you,' he said. 'Otherwise I'd be pretty scared right now.'

I smiled at his words, a soft detonation of delight inside my chest made me raise my eyebrows. 'Ditto, Magnus,' I said, quietly, 'but what the hell are you on about?'

'Open it.'

I opened the book. Flicked one corner so the pages flew, raising a draught that sent my hair rioting.

'Now look at it.'

I slowed the flicking, allowing the book to drop open. Then I picked it up, dampened a finger, turned the page. Turned another. Then back to the front, to those first pages, where I'd seen the drawing of the design that had gone to make Magnus' necklace.

Every page in the book was blank.

ABOUT THE AUTHOR

Jane Lovering is the bestselling and award-winning romantic comedy writer who won the RNA Contemporary Romantic Novel Award in 2023 with *A Cottage Full of Secrets*. She lives in Yorkshire and has a cat and a bonkers terrier, as well as five children who have now left home.

Sign up to Jane Lovering's mailing list here for news, competitions and updates on future books.

Visit Jane's website: www.janelovering.co.uk

Follow Jane on social media:

facebook.com/Jane-Lovering-Author-106404969412833

x.com/janelovering

bookbub.com/authors/jane-lovering

ALSO BY JANE LOVERING

The Country Escape

Home on a Yorkshire Farm

A Midwinter Match

A Cottage Full of Secrets

The Forgotten House on the Moor

There's No Place Like Home

The Recipe for Happiness

The Island Cottage

LOVE NOTES

LOVE IN EVERY CHAPTER

WHERE ALL YOUR ROMANCE
DREAMS COME TRUE!

THE HOME OF BESTSELLING
ROMANCE AND WOMEN'S
FICTION

 WARNING:
MAY CONTAIN SPICE

SIGN UP TO OUR
NEWSLETTER

https://bit.ly/Lovenotesnews

Boldwœd

Boldwood Books is an award-winning fiction publishing company seeking out the best stories from around the world.

Find out more at www.boldwoodbooks.com

Join our reader community for brilliant books, competitions and offers!

Follow us
@BoldwoodBooks
@TheBoldBookClub

Sign up to our weekly deals newsletter

https://bit.ly/BoldwoodBNewsletter

Printed in Great Britain
by Amazon

36264490R00139